SWEETFREAK

SWEETFREAK

Sophie McKenzie

SIMON & SCHUSTER

LONDON   NEW YORK   TORONTO   SYDNEY   NEW DELHI

First published in Great Britain in 2017 by Simon & Schuster UK Ltd
A CBS COMPANY

1 3 5 7 9 10 8 6 4 2

Simon & Schuster UK Ltd
1st Floor
222 Gray's Inn Road
London WC1X 8HB

www.simonandschuster.co.uk
www.simonandschuster.com.au
www.simonandschuster.co.in

Simon & Schuster Australia, Sydney
Simon & Schuster India, New Delhi

A CIP catalogue record for this book
is available from the British Library.

PB ISBN 978-1-4711-2223-1
eBook ISBN 978-1-4711-2224-8

Typeset in Times by M Rules
Printed and bound by CPI Group (UK) Ltd, Croydon, CR0 4YY

For Luke and Caitlin

*With thanks to Lou Kuenzler,
Moira Young, Julie Mackenzie,
Gaby Halberstam and
Melanie Edge.*

SweetFreak 13m ago

Can't wait til you're dead, Princess. Can't wait til I kill you.

FALL

1

Friendship matters.

Right?

Being loyal. Being honest. Being there. It's what really counts.

That's what I thought, anyway. That's why I was prepared to sneak out of my room that night to meet Amelia. My bestie who was in a state. Again.

Well, maybe I liked the fun of getting something past Mum too. She thought I was already fast asleep up here. Which, clearly, I was never going to be. It wasn't even ten thirty, for goodness sake. But that's my mum for you . . . she doesn't really get me at all. Nobody does, apart from Amelia.

Which brings me back to my late evening creep across the landing . . .

*

I close my laptop and check Amelia's message one last time.

rly need c u, pls com now, usual plce 🙏🙏 😔 😔 😔

She must really be upset. With a sigh I turn off my phone – just in case I get any alerts – and leave my bedroom. I take wide strides, careful to avoid the place where the floor creaks. The TV's on downstairs, but otherwise the house is silent. My little brother, Jamie, has an eight-thirty bedtime, which means that Mum makes us all keep it down after that. I'm more worried about Poppy – that's my older sister – catching me sneaking out of the house. She'd love to get me in trouble. She's in a massive mood with me at the moment because her stupid boyfriend George broke up with her and she blames me. It's so unfair. All I did was send Amelia a video of Poppy making out with a guy on the beach when we were on holiday. I was just having a bit of fun with the video. I certainly didn't mean to stir things up with Poppy's boyfriend. It was a private message and I made it clear the whole thing wasn't really Poppy's fault. I even put angel wings on Poppy's back and devil horns on the Spanish boy's head, just to show that *she* was the victim – seduced by a six pack with big brown smiling eyes.

The trouble was Poppy's boyfriend George is my best friend Amelia's brother. He's also – clearly – suspicious and nosy, because he deliberately went and snuck a look at Amelia's phone. He saw the video and then he dumped Poppy.

2

It really wasn't my fault. Or poor Amelia's. I mean, I feel bad that Poppy's all broken hearted over George, but if he's so untrusting that he thinks it's OK to snoop about on someone else's phone, then I reckon Poppy's better off without him.

I just wish she saw it like that.

George broke up with her the day after we got back from holiday. That was three weeks ago and my sister is still furious with me.

I stand outside her door, holding my breath, braced for Poppy to wrench her door open and start shouting. But all I can hear are sobs.

Is she crying? Guilt flushes through me. I'd give anything to make her feel better. Though if I'm honest I don't think it was true love with Poppy and George. I mean, I get she's upset about him finishing with her, but they'd been together nearly a year and if Poppy was as loved up over him as all that, surely she wouldn't have let that Spanish boy eat her face off?

I hurry into the bathroom at the end of the corridor. The window is hitched up a tiny bit, like it always is unless the air outside is literally freezing. I ease it fully open and scramble outside, hooking my feet around the drainpipe then letting myself carefully down on to the shed roof that's a metre or so below. Beneath me our cat, Rumple, is trotting across the patio, a dead bird in his mouth. Poor Mum'll go mad when he takes it into the kitchen. She gets really upset about Rumple's murderous tendencies and, like my sister, she can't stand the sight of blood. Still, Rumple's latest prey is a lucky break for me ... if Mum's preoccupied, she'll be less likely to check I'm in bed.

It's been a warm day, considering it's almost the end of September, but the night air is cool. I zip up my new jacket – a black satin bomber with flowery embroidery on the back – and inch across the shed, over the fence and on to the top of next door's kitchen extension. They had it put in last year. Mum was all nicey-nicey when they apologised for the noise and disruption, though she complained about it all the time in private. She'd have complained a lot more if she'd realised the flat roof gives me a perfect run over to the wall that borders the street at the end of our road. I'm there in seconds, easing myself down to the pavement. I race across the road and around the corner onto King Street.

In a couple of minutes I'm clambering over the railings into the park and heading for the kids' play area. Mum used to bring me and Poppy here when we were little. More recently I've brought Jamie, though now he prefers the nearby wood. The row of swings clinks in the breeze. Across the park I can just make out the edge of Bow Wood: dark and gloomy beyond the street lamps. Amelia isn't here yet. I lean against the spider-web climber with a sigh, wondering what's held her up.

I take advantage of the silence to run through the lines from my first scene in *The Sound of Music*. I was given the main part, Maria, after the auditions last week. Which, if I'm honest, is the most exciting thing that's happened to me all year. Not that I can let on how I feel, of course, it would be seriously uncool to show any of my friends that I'm over the moon to be involved with a school musical. Plus they'd all think I was full of myself if I started gushing about having the lead. It's not like I think I'm massively talented. That is, I guess I've always been able to sing and I don't have any trouble learning lines. Whatever, I spent most of Year Seven doing song and dance routines in front of my bedroom mirror, imagining I was a global star. Which is kind of embarrassing to admit to now. Anyway, we've only had one rehearsal for *The Sound of Music* so far – the whole cast doing group songs and it was fun. Amelia isn't in the show. She says the idea of standing up in front of everyone and performing terrifies her, though she might get involved with the set designs.

Where is she?

I suddenly remember that I switched off my phone when I crept out of the house. I turn it back on and, straightaway, it pings with an alert. Is that her? I check the screen, half expecting it to be a text from Mum, furious that I'm not at home and all set to ground me for a month. She caught me sneaking out a few months ago and I promised I wouldn't ever do it again. But it's a message from Amelia.

5

Carey, where r u? 🐱 🐱 🐱 🐱

I roll my eyes. Amelia's message clearly said we should meet at the 'usual place' which, all summer, has been the park.

Irritated, I message back:

im at swings, u? 🐺 🐺 🐺 🐺

we sed rec 😔

😔 we sed swings

Nothing back from Amelia. I stand up, tugging my jacket around my chest. Is she seriously annoyed? I'm sure I'm right about the meeting place. But maybe Amelia's too upset to think straight. She's been getting these mean private messages on NatterSnap from someone calling themselves SweetFreak all week.

If you're under ten or over sixteen you probably haven't heard of NatterSnap. It's an awesome app that lets you animate and manipulate images then share them. There are lots of apps like it, but NatterSnap is probably the most popular right now. And definitely the most realistic. Unlike, say, with SnapChat, the posts don't disappear unless you delete them. For instance, the last SweetFreak message

Amelia got showed a huge (real) pig with her face perfectly superimposed on it rootling around in mud, then falling onto a house which collapsed under the weight, sending neon letters sparking into the air that said: *Amelia woz here*. Which is crazy. Because she's not even remotely overweight. The opposite, in fact, though she always says she thinks she's fat.

I told Amelia to ignore the message. When she hesitated I took her phone and deleted it myself. People can be really mean on social media but you can't let nasty stuff like that get to you. I know that sounds brutal, but it's the only way to cope. I wish Amelia wouldn't let it get to her.

Another message beeps, bringing me back to the park and the chilly night air:

Please hurry, I rly need 2 c u

My irritation vanishes. Poor Amelia, she must be feeling terrible. It's all very well me saying she should just ignore SweetFreak's mean messages but it's horrible not knowing who they come from. Like, it's got to be someone who knows her, right? But who would hate Amelia so much that they'd go to all that trouble?

I send a message back to her:

On my way x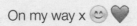

7

Hoping that will have made Amelia smile, I set off across the park. I speed past the edge of the wood, shivering as I glance into the shadows of the trees, then on, down a couple of deserted backstreets. As I turn the corner by the Duck and Dragon pub I pass a pair of teenagers: a boy about my age and a girl with pink hair who looks about eighteen. The girl is wearing DMs with rainbow laces while the boy has mismatching trainers – one grey Adidas, the other yellow Nike with a green swoosh.

I scurry on, wondering whether that's some sort of random style choice or because he can't afford new trainers.

Another couple of streets and I'm almost at the rec. It's closer to Amelia's house, just as the park is closer to mine. Though in my opinion the park wins hands down as a place to meet. Technically the rec itself is an old club building that was used a million years ago when Mum was a teenager, for something called the Cornmouth Youth Club. Needless to say nobody goes there any more, I think old people play bingo in it or something. There's a bus shelter outside – also unused, the last bus came through there about the same time Mum was going to the youth club.

When Amelia and I say to meet at the rec, it's this bus shelter we mean.

She's there as I approach, bending over her phone, her long straight blonde hair falling over her eyes. She never ties it back, whereas I'm always shoving my curls into hairbands.

'Hey!' I call out.

Amelia looks up. Her big blue eyes glisten in the lamplight. She looks really unhappy.

I run up. 'I thought the "usual place" was the park,' I say, panting for breath.

'It *was* in the summer,' Amelia sniffs. 'But now we're back at school we meet *here*.' She says it with a tinge of petulance, as if this is something I should have automatically known. A flicker of irritation passes through me, then a tear trickles down Amelia's face and I remember why I'm here.

'What's happened?' I ask. 'Is it SweetFreak? Have they sent another message?'

Amelia shakes her head. 'It's Taylor. He *still* hasn't called me. In fact . . .' Amelia says, choking back sobs. 'In fact he's just unfriended mc on *everything*.'

'Oh.' I sigh inwardly. Is that really what's upset her so much? I don't get it. I mean, she and Taylor only went on a few dates together. Nothing serious – just like my sister and George – and yet Amelia's totally obsessing about him. I hate seeing her like this.

'I was wondering about the messages I've been getting from . . . from SweetFreak.' Amelia's lips tremble. 'Do you think Taylor might have sent them?'

I wrinkle my nose. It seems unlikely that Taylor, who as far as I can see has basically lost all interest in Amelia, would

start sending her nasty messages out of the blue. But I'm pretty certain Amelia would probably rather he paid her any attention than none at all. Anyway, she's miserable enough about the guy ignoring her without me going on about it too.

'I don't know,' I say, trying to work out what to say that won't upset her any further. 'It doesn't seem like his style.'

I'm not sure if this is true, of course. I've met Taylor several times, but I don't know him properly.

Amelia is still sniffing, clearly trying not to cry again. I feel so bad for her.

'Are you OK?' I ask.

'Not really.' Another tear wobbles down Amelia's cheek.

I give her a hug and we sit down on the rusty old bus shelter seat.

Amelia's fingers stray to her silver necklace and the little heart-shaped pendant that hangs from it. 'I still can't get my head around it. Taylor seemed so *happy*.' She sighs. 'The last time I saw him he took me to the Haunted Hut outside the industrial estate. He'd got hold of a key to it somehow, a weird one with a skull painted on the end, and it was really spooky. I was all freaked and Taylor was really nice and we made out and it was *so* romantic and he gave me this necklace and then ...'

'... and then the very next day he just stopped calling.' I sigh. Amelia has already told me this story several times. 'I know, but, see, you can't think like that. It's boys. There's no way of understanding them. They're crazy.'

'He mentioned he'd met a girl hoping to be a model.' Amelia's face crumples again. 'So of course he wouldn't still want to go out with me after that. I'm so fat and ugly.'

'No you're not.'

'I am. You've never had a boyfriend so you don't understand.'

'Of course I—'

'No. It's obvious. He was just putting up with me until someone better came along.'

I press my lips together to stop myself pointing out that I'm certain Amelia's reading way too much into it. Anyway, Taylor is clearly an idiot if he doesn't want to be with her so why is she getting so upset?

What is it with her and Poppy that they're so hung up on stupid relationships?

Why can't they get excited about something else? Like, I'm not saying I'm so super-sorted or anything, but I've got the lead in the school show, I'm on track with my grades and while I wouldn't say I was the most popular person in my year, I don't have any beef with anyone. I'm certainly not hung up on a guy I only dated a few times, like Amelia is. Or heartbroken because I messed up like my sister.

I sit back, letting her go over the last meeting between her and Taylor yet again: how he was all handsome with his dark wavy hair and leather jacket and how maybe if she'd kissed better or worn a sexier dress he might have stayed interested. I'm itching to tell her to get over him, that he's a loser. Good-looking certainly and, by all accounts, popular. But a loser nevertheless.

'He's crazy if he doesn't want you,' I settle for saying.

Amelia gives a little cough. 'I was actually wondering if I could ... that is, I know Jamie is friends with Taylor's little brother, so maybe you could organise for them to get together and I could come with you?'

My mouth gapes. 'You seriously want to go to his house on the pretext of my kid brother having a playdate?' I hesitate. 'Oh, you must feel really awful.' That's what I say, but what I'm actually thinking is that it's a bit selfish of Amelia to be asking. No way am I using Jamie as some sort of chess piece to manoeuvre her in through the front door. My seven-year-old brother annoys me half the time, with his mischievous grin and his constant pestering, but I love him to death. And I refuse to use him just because Amelia's desperate to get back with a stupid boy who isn't worth her time or her tears.

I meet Amelia's soft, trembling gaze, my irritation mounting. She's my best friend and I love her, but she really can be a bit of a princess. Lately, I feel like all we ever do is talk about her. Not that I'd say that to her face.

I'm just trying to work out how to reject her Jamie plan without losing my temper, when Amelia herself gives a groan.

'Don't worry. I'm sorry, it was a stupid idea. Anyway, there's no knowing if Taylor would even be in, though I suppose once I'm in his house I could always try and sneak into his room . . .' She glances at me, then, seeing the look on my face, corrects herself. 'Sorry, it's fine. I'm fine.' She checks her phone. 'It's late. I'd better get home. Thanks for coming out.'

Is that it? I've risked being grounded for a month, just so Amelia can go on about Taylor?

I take a deep breath, struggling with my irritation. I can't let her see. It's not fair on her. And anyway, we're best friends. Amelia's awesome. She's always been there for me, like the time we went on a school trip to the London Dungeon and I got sick and Amelia stayed with me for two whole hours while everyone else was running about having fun. She's a great friend. And I need to be a good friend to her now. What is it Mum's always saying? Something about everyone being entitled to their own reality and that it's important to try and respect other people's points of view, even if you disagree with them.

Right now, for Amelia, her reality is that she's devastated *and* she's had to put up with those mean NatterSnap messages all week, so I say nothing, just hug her goodbye then run home through the empty streets.

A quarter of an hour later I'm hauling myself over our neighbour's wall and up onto their kitchen extension. I scramble across it, then hop over the fence to our back-garden shed and up to the bathroom which is, thankfully, unoccupied.

As I let myself in and pad across the landing I can hear Mum downstairs, on the phone to one of her friends. She's moaning about the dead bird Rumple dragged in. Suddenly feeling tired, I creep to my room, avoiding the creak in the same way that I did on the way out. There's no sound from Poppy. I slip out of my clothes and get into bed. I check my phone, yawning now. Nothing from Amelia, which hopefully means she's feeling better. I put the phone down on the little desk beside my bed. Its blue light illuminates my open laptop.

I stare at the laptop, frowning. I was sure I closed it before I went out. But I can't have done and neither can anybody else in the house. Jamie's been fast asleep for hours. And if Mum had come in here and discovered I wasn't in bed, there'd be hell to play. As for Poppy, the mood she's in right now, she'd definitely have grassed me up if *she'd* realised I'd gone out.

I'm asleep within seconds, forgetting all about my laptop. It's not until the end of the following day that I realise what has happened.

And my entire world comes crashing down.

2

'Carey!' Mum's voice in my ear startles me awake.

I open my eyes to see her looming over me. She's in her work suit and half made up, one eye complete with eyeliner and a smudge of pale grey eyeshadow, the other bare.

'Will you please get up?' She gives my shoulder an irritated shake.

I grunt and turn over, pulling the duvet over my face. Mum has already opened the curtains and bright sunlight glares in.

'*Please*, Carey. And I need you to walk Jamie to school. I've got an early meeting.'

'Why can't Poppy do it?' I grumble.

'She's not well,' Mum says. 'Tummy bug.'

'Yeah, right.'

'I have to go.' I'm still under the duvet but I can hear Mum's footsteps padding across the room. 'Come on,

Carey, you'll need to leave in twenty minutes if you're going to drop Jamie at breakfast club, and make sure you have something to eat.'

'That's loads of time,' I mutter. But Mum has already gone.

I lie still for a few minutes, then shove the duvet off me and get up with a groan. I throw on my uniform, then spend five minutes working product through my hair. Unlike anyone else in my family I've got wildly curly hair and it has to be tamed every morning. I'm just finishing when Jamie bursts in and leaps onto my bed, jumping up and down and waving a plastic sword.

Did I mention Jamie's obsessed with a video game called *Warriors of the Doom Wood?* There's a cartoon as well, even a boring movie which Mum and I took him to over the summer.

'I'll be Sir Tamwin Star, you can be Lady Pretzel-loser.' Jamie wields the sword, his cheeks dimpling as he smiles.

'Pretzel-loser?' I grin. 'Are you sure you've got that right?'

'Whatever.' Jamie spins around on the bed, flourishing his sword again. 'Get away from her, you fiend!' he shrieks in a mock posh lord accent.

'Aaagh!' I shrink away, playing along in imaginary peril.

A thump on the wall that divides my room from Poppy's. 'Be quiet!' comes her muffled yell. 'I'm not well.'

I roll my eyes. She might fool Mum but as far as I'm concerned there's nothing wrong with my sister – not

16

physically at least. Her so-called tummy upset is all about George dumping her. 'Come on, Jamie, let's go.'

With a roar my little brother jumps to the floor and races out the door. As I pick up my school bag my eye is caught again by the open laptop on my desk. I shut the lid, my mind flitting back to last night when I'd been certain that I'd closed it before I snuck out.

'Carey!' Jamie calls from downstairs. 'Come *on!*'

'All right! I'm coming!' I yell back and the laptop mystery flits from my mind as I hurry out of my room.

I can tell something's wrong the moment I walk into my form room. I spot Amelia straightaway. She's sitting on the table by the window, surrounded by girls. She's nodding as Rose, her shiny brown bob swinging as she speaks, says something in a low, serious voice. Rose is one of the most popular girls in our class. Not that I'm a big fan myself. Most people think she's lovely but to me she's one of those girls who make out they're your friend, but who you're never really sure of. She's in *The Sound of Music* with me, as Mother Superior. That's basically Maria's boss when she's a nun at the start of the story. I'm pretty sure Rose wanted to be Maria. She's been all gushy to my face about how good I am, but I sense she resents me getting the role. She clocks me as I hurry over and her back stiffens. All the girls she's with are speaking at once.

'Unbelievable.'

'Who the hell is SweetFreak anyway?'

'Gone too far.'

The only one not talking is Amelia. She meets my gaze, tears welling as she sees the concern on my face.

'Look.' She holds out her phone.

The girls turn, acknowledging me with nods and grimaces. I'm certain – though it sounds mean to say it – that they're only surrounding Amelia for the drama.

'It's really bad, Carey,' Rose says with a solemn sigh. 'Poor Amelia.'

I brace myself for another mean, mocking, manipulated NatterSnap image, like the three Amelia has already received this week. But this time the post on the screen is so shocking that my breath actually hitches in my throat. It's the same photo of Amelia as in the pig-face video, but in this film her eyes have been manipulated to look wide and terrified and a long, serrated knife is being drawn slowly along her throat. As the skin is slashed through, blood pours out. The post with the video says:

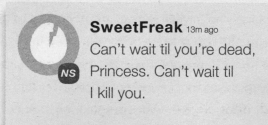

SweetFreak 13m ago
Can't wait til you're dead, Princess. Can't wait til I kill you.

18

The whole effect, like all NatterSnap stuff, is made worse by being so sickeningly realistic.

I shiver and hand back the phone. 'This is from SweetFreak again?' I ask.

Amelia nods. Her face is pale, her red-rimmed eyes as unhappy as I've ever seen them.

'I can't believe she'd go this far,' I say. It sounds hollow. Insufficient to the nastiness of the post. Because we're all used to snide, mean messages but this one is in a different league altogether.

The other girls start talking all at once again. Amelia gives me a puzzled look, then her face crumples and she holds out her arms for me to hug her. Which I do, obviously. Truth is I'm shaken. I've never seen anything as vicious as this before. 'Have you told anyone?' I say, my mouth close to Amelia's ear. I mean one of Amelia's super-busy parents. She lives with her mum and stepdad and sees her dad every other week. The three of them make Mum's working life look like a part-time hobby.

'I've told Mrs Marchington,' Rose interjects bossily. 'She should be—'

'Girls, stand back, please. Let me through.' The brisk tones of our form teacher echo over our heads.

Mrs Marchington is not a teacher you mess with, so we scatter. I step away from Amelia, but not too far. I am her best friend, after all. Mrs Marchington sweeps across the room. Amelia holds out her phone and the teacher takes it.

Her face betrays little emotion as she gazes at the screen, but there's a tightening around her lips and she blinks rapidly.

'Come with me, Amelia,' she orders.

Obediently, Amelia follows the teacher out of the room. The girls who were with Amelia when I arrived erupt into hushed, gossipy whispers again, most of which focus on the potential identity of SweetFreak. I would probably have joined in, but at that very moment, Heath Sixsmith strides in.

Heath is playing Captain von Trapp, the male lead in *The Sound of Music*. Lots of heads turn as he walks towards me – he is tall with dark blond hair and chiselled cheekbones and everyone thinks he is the best-looking boy in our year.

'Hi, Carey,' he says with a warm smile. He starts telling me about an extra rehearsal lined up for lunch break. I'm not really listening. Mostly I'm worrying about poor Amelia but, if I'm honest, I'm also enjoying the looks I'm getting from across the room. Rose is definitely jealous. Her dark eyes glint as she stares at us, then she catches me watching and flicks back her hair in self-consciously casual fashion. One of the girls in her group says something and Rose nods, suddenly looking very interested in what the girl is saying. Yeah, right. Normally Rose is only interested in the sound of her own voice. She has a little gang of girls who hang on her every word. They even copy her look – shaggy long bob, off-the-shoulder tops and big hoop earrings. Amelia and I call them the Rose Clones.

The memory of the many laughs we've had over this

brings poor Amelia to the front of my mind again. I wonder how she's getting on with Mrs Marchington.

'I don't mind how many rehearsals we have,' Heath is saying.

'Really?' I ask, tuning back into the conversation.

'Yeah, I want to be an actor when I leave school,' Heath says earnestly.

'Right.' I shoot a glance sideways. Rose and the Rose Clones are still watching us. Heath doesn't appear to have noticed. He's gazing down at me with a big smile on his face, now telling me about his cousin who is already at drama school. Does he fancy me? He's certainly in no hurry to leave, even though his own form room is on the other side of the school.

Though I'm not interested in him, the thought is kind of gratifying. Out of the corner of my eye I can see a couple of the Rose Clones throwing envious glances in my direction, though Rose herself is now staring at her phone. Heath carries on chatting to me about the play until Mrs Marchington strides back in and he scuttles off.

'Seats, please,' Mrs Marchington orders.

I put up my hand. *Where's Amelia?* I need to find out if she's all right.

'What's happened to Amelia, miss?' Rose asks without bothering to put her hand up.

'Sit down,' Mrs Marchington snaps, ignoring the question. She glances at me. 'You too, Carey. Hurry up, everyone.'

21

I lower my hand and take my seat. Poor Amelia. Most likely she's been taken to talk to the head. Which she will hate. Maybe it's for the best. Whoever SweetFreak is, they've really got it in for her. Not that our headteacher can do much about what happens online. There's no proof that the person behind the messages is even at school with us. Still, maybe it will make Amelia feel better to know that it's being taken seriously.

Amelia doesn't reappear all morning, not even for Art, which is her favourite class. She's known for her hand-drawn birthday cards – she's got a real talent for it and is doing a bigger version as part of her GCSE Art project. I know all the Art stuff is here, at school, and that Amelia has been working on it all hours, so if she's too upset to have taken it with her things must really be bad.

I call her at break, but it goes straight to voicemail so I send a NatterSnap message asking her to let me know how she is. I attach a gif of a kitten with huge blue eyes. Amelia loves kittens. I hope it cheers her up.

The lunchtime rehearsal for *The Sound of Music* helps take my mind off her.

'Isn't it mad I'm supposed to be the dad of the year sevens and eights playing the kids?' Heath says to me, grinning from ear to ear. 'I reckon I only got the part cos I'm tall.'

'Tall and talented,' I say with a smile.

Heath blushes and I look away, as if I'm a bit embarrassed

22

too for having praised him. I'm trying to pitch myself as slightly more than friendly, but without giving too much encouragement. I've got no intention of taking things further with him, but there's no harm in spinning things out for a bit, especially if it makes Rose jealous. I can't wait to tell Amelia what's going on, but she doesn't call back all afternoon, so I send another text on my way home.

When I get in, Poppy is in her PJs, casting her laptop onto the TV in the living room. Jamie is still at after-school club. Mum will collect him on her way back from work. I grab a cereal bar from the stash in the kitchen cupboard and wander into the living room. When Poppy sees me she turns away.

'What's your problem?' I demand, instantly irritated.

'You,' she snaps, turning the volume up.

I can't be bothered to argue with her. She seriously needs to get over herself. So I traipse up to my room. An hour and a half later Mum and Jamie bustle in and an hour after that I wander downstairs wondering what we're having for dinner. To my surprise Mum isn't in the kitchen. She's in the living room sitting next to Poppy on the sofa. Two police officers sit opposite. All of them have solemn faces, which turn in my direction as I walk in.

'Oh, Carey.' Mum stands up. She's trembling. 'I was just about to call you down.'

'What's happened?' I gasp. 'Is it Dad?'

Funny I should immediately think of him. Most of the

time I forget about my stupid father. He walked out on us five years ago and apart from the occasional message we never hear from him.

'No, love.' Mum bites her lip. 'Come and sit down.'

I take a seat on the other side of her from Poppy, feeling uncomfortable. The older police officer peers at me intently. He has a saggy, creased face and is dressed in a suit that looks at least a size too big on the shoulders. After a moment's awkward silence, he clears his throat.

'I'm DS Carter and this . . .' He points to the woman beside him. She's much younger, with short, jet black hair and sharp little eyes. 'This is DC Kapoor. We'd like to talk to you about a death threat against Amelia Wilson that appeared this morning on the social media platform NatterSnap.'

'Talk to *me?*' I stare at him. Wow, Amelia's parents must have gone ape over the message. I'm certain Amelia would hate having to talk about it, especially to police officers.

'The first thing to say is that we have a community initiative with local schools that prioritises early intervention to ensure zero tolerance on this kind of bullying and intimidation.' DS Carter sounds like he's learned that off by heart.

Beside him DC Kapoor rolls her eyes. 'All of which means our precious time is periodically taken up with young people who've decided to take private arguments too far and who need to realise there are consequences for such actions.'

'OK . . .' I hesitate. 'I can see why you'd want to follow up

24

that thing Amelia got sent.' The image of the knife slitting Amelia's face flashes into my head. I blink it away. 'But why do you want to talk to me? I don't know anything.'

There's a horrible pause. Mum makes a strange noise: a sort of strangled sob. Poppy puts her arm around her.

'I'm afraid there has to be a bit more to it than that,' DS Carter carries on. I frown. What does that mean?

'For goodness sake,' Poppy snaps. 'Even if you don't care about your best friend, how can you do this to Mum?'

'Do what?' Exasperation rises inside me. 'Why don't you just shut up, Poppy?'

'Why don't you—?'

'Let's just take a look at what we're talking about.' The unsmiling DC Kapoor hands Mum a tablet. It shows a screen grab of the SweetFreak death threat Amelia got this morning. Poppy and I peer over Mum's shoulders as she swipes the screen to video mode, then presses the play button. On screen Amelia's eyes widen in horror as the knife makes its slow, tearing way across her throat. Blood spurts out. I gag, bile rising into my mouth. It's just as horrific as it was the first time.

Mum turns away. 'Ugh,' she says. 'I can't bear to look at it.'

I glance up at the detective, fear rushing, like cold air, down my back. Do these police officers think *I* sent Amelia this death threat? 'I didn't have anything to do with this,' I

25

say, my stomach tightening. 'Amelia's my best friend.'

'As the sergeant said, there's a bit more to it than that.' DC Kapoor narrows her mean eyes. 'We've traced the sender,' she says. 'We know who sent the message.'

The tension in the room reaches an unbearable level. I can feel my cheeks burning. Stupidly I feel guilty, even though I've done nothing to be guilty for.

Mum is wringing her hands.

'I . . . I don't understand,' I stammer.

Poppy pushes the tablet across Mum towards me. 'You did this,' she growls. 'That's what they're saying, stupid.'

'No.' My head spins. I want to articulate the million reasons why it's impossible that I could have created and sent such a horrible message, but my brain is a scrambled mess.

DC Kapoor hasn't taken her eyes off me. 'The message was sent from an IP address located in this house. From a specific computer.'

My jaw drops.

'Your laptop,' Mum adds, lips trembling. 'They're saying this horrible things came from your laptop.'

'Which never leaves your bedroom,' Poppy adds.

'In other words,' DC Kapoor says. 'It looks very strongly as if the death threat came from you, Carey.'

3

I look around the room, at the four faces ranged against me. Both police officers are frowning: though DS Carter's expression registers concern while DC Kapoor is more suspicious.

'Er, you mentioned your dad earlier, Carey.' DS Carter turns to Mum. 'Is he likely to get home soon?'

Poppy snorts.

'No, he's not . . . um, we're not in touch any more,' Mum says. 'I wouldn't even know how to get hold of him.'

'I didn't do this,' I say, aware my burning cheeks must be a guilty shade of bright red.

'Of course you didn't,' Mum says. She turns to the older male officer. 'Of course she didn't, Carey's a good girl.' She hesitates. 'I hate to say it, but is it possible Amelia sent the messages to herself, as a way of gaining attention?'

'We've checked all Amelia's devices and her whereabouts

when the message was posted.' DS Carter pats his notebook, as if to confirm what he's saying. 'She's definitely not responsible.'

'Well it couldn't have been Carey,' Mum insists.

'It's not quite that simple,' DS Carter says apologetically. 'I understand from Amelia this is just the latest in a series of bullying messages from the same anonymous source.' He looks up, into my eyes. 'I also understand, Carey, that you insisted on her deleting those messages?'

'Yes, but that makes it sound . . .' I try to focus, my mind skittering over the times this past week that Amelia had showed me what SweetFreak had sent and how I'd kept telling her to ignore it. *Just delete it, put it out of your mind.* I'd even taken her phone and got rid of the pig-video post myself. 'I only told her to delete them because they were upsetting her.'

'I see.' The detective doesn't sound convinced. 'So there hasn't been any bad feeling between you and Amelia? No falling out over friends or schoolwork or boys?'

'Amelia is my best friend,' I insist, my voice rising. 'I would never do horrible stuff like this.' I can't believe the police are basically accusing me of sending the messages. I look down at the video of Amelia's face, paused as a drip of blood falls from the knife pressed against her neck.

'I wouldn't do this to *anyone*,' I say. My voice sounds flat, as if it's coming from across the room. I can't seem to focus.

'I know, sweetheart.' Mum puts her arm around my shoulder. I let her draw me into a hug. I can't remember the last time I wanted her arms around me, but right now I lean on her. At least she believes me.

I glance over at Poppy. Her face is a blank.

DC Kapoor purses her lip. She is definitely still suspicious. The thought that I'm in trouble with the police gnaws at me. I've known kids at school who've had run-ins with the cops for shoplifting and anti-social behaviour, but not me. Never me. This isn't who I am.

'This is a mistake.' I draw back from Mum. 'What's going to happen? Because I didn't do what you're saying.'

'We'd like to question you about this morning.' DS Carter flips open his notebook. 'Nothing formal, just a chat here with your mum over a cuppa.'

'Of course.' Mum gulps. 'Poppy, will you make us all a cup of tea?'

My sister looks, for a second, as if she's about to refuse indignantly, then she seems to think better of it. Nodding, she leaves the room.

I bite my lip. Perhaps a quick talk will resolve everything. Surely once I prove I was nowhere near my laptop when the death threat was sent this morning I'll be in the clear.

'So we have traced this morning's private message from SweetFreak to your laptop,' DC Kapoor says briskly. 'How do you explain that?'

'I can't,' I say. 'It ... it doesn't make any sense. I only use my laptop for homework and ...' I trail off, realising that telling the police I sometimes stream movies and TV shows illegally on the computer might not be my smartest move. 'I do almost everything else from my phone,' I trail off.

'Yes, we'd like to take your mobile as well as your laptop.'

'What?' It's another slap. 'Take them *away*?'

'To examine them.' She holds out her hand. 'May I see your phone please?'

I look at Mum. Can the police really do that?

'This is a potentially serious charge,' DC Kapoor says in a steely voice. The inference is clear: *you're lucky we're not arresting you.*

Feeling numb I pass the officer my mobile. She examines the call and text log. I know she won't see anything there. I've been deleting everything out of habit, since Mum caught me lying about a party a few months ago and has used the incident to justify random checks on my phone messages ever since. The officer then opens my NatterSnap app. I cringe as she pores over my feed, thinking of all the stupid stuff that's on there.

Last night's exchange with Amelia is deleted of course, but I can still remember her miserable insistence that we meet up. *I rly need c u* she'd messaged.

Suddenly all I want to do is talk to my best friend. She must be devastated, especially if she knows the police suspect I might have had anything to do with the SweetFreak messages. I'm sure she won't believe I'm capable of sending her anything so horrible, but I want to tell her myself as soon as possible.

'Um, could I please have my phone back?' I ask DC Kapoor. 'I just need it for a minute.'

'I'm afraid not,' she says curtly.

I sit back, shocked at her vehemence.

'It's not a good idea for you to contact Amelia right now,' DS Carter says more gently, clearly reading my thoughts.

What? No way. 'I *have* to speak to her, explain this is all a terrible misunderstanding. But—'

'We would really like to understand what prompted such strong feelings,' DS Carter interrupts. 'Did Amelia do something to upset you?'

'No.' I stare at him. 'I didn't send any messages. I'm not SweetFreak. Why won't you believe me?'

Mum squeezes my hand. 'The detectives are just doing their job, Carey.' She turns to DS Carter. 'I'm sure this *is* all a misunderstanding. You say Amelia received the death threat this morning, at school, but Carey never takes her laptop to school, they don't allow it. Or mobile phones in class.'

There's a derisive sniff from the doorway. Poppy has reappeared, a tray of mugs in her hands. 'Oh, Carey's good at doing things behind people's backs.'

31

'We were just coming to this morning,' DC Kapoor says. There's a hint of irritation in her voice. She clearly knows as well as I do that it's perfectly possible to sit with a device on silent under your desk. Some teachers would spot it; others not. Mum sits back.

DS Carter turns to me. 'I'd like to know what time you left the house this morning, Carey?'

'It would have been about eight fifteen, wouldn't it, love?' Mum asks. 'You took Jamie to school.'

'Please let Carey answer for herself,' DS Carter insists.

'Like Mum says, about eight fifteen,' I say pointedly. 'Which proves it couldn't have been me because I think Amelia got the message when she arrived at school, which wouldn't have been until around eight thirty.'

'She received the message at . . . at eight twenty-seven a.m.,' DS Carter says, consulting his notes again.

'Which was when I was dropping Jamie at his school,' I exclaim, relieved. They'll have to believe me now. 'Nowhere near my laptop.'

'Can you confirm exactly when your daughter left the house?' DC Kapoor asks Mum.

She shakes her head. 'Poppy?' Everyone looks at my sister.

'I was asleep, I wasn't well, remember?' Poppy sounds mildly injured, as if no one is bothered about her being ill.

'We can ask Jamie,' I point out. 'He's only seven but he tells the time really well and—'

'That's OK.' DS Carter sighs. 'We'll take a look at your laptop, then if need be, we can have another chat afterwards.' He puts down his notebook and nods at his colleague. 'Perhaps you'd take DC Kapoor here to Carey's room now?' he asks Mum.

Mum looks dazed, but leads the female officer out of the room. The two women murmur to each other as they cross the hall. I can't hear what they're saying but as they reach the stairs I hear the words 'charging' and 'warning'.

'What will happen next?' I ask DS Carter. He has a much nicer face than DC Kapoor, with deep-set dark eyes under the worry lines that crease his forehead.

He folds his arms. 'That depends,' he says.

I sit back. How can this be happening? I try to focus. Once they examine the laptop they'll surely see this is all a mistake. I had nothing to do with the death threat. It's insane to think I could.

Poppy sets down the tray. She says nothing, but emotion is radiating off her in waves. Is she upset for me? Does she believe I could have sent Amelia those messages? Surely she can't?

And then she meets my gaze and I'm shocked by the look of pure hatred on her face.

Which is when it strikes me: Poppy was at home when the SweetFreak death threat was sent. It would have been the simplest thing in the world for her to slip next door into

33

my room while I was out and use my computer. She could have easily sneaked a look at my password. I'm careful with it when I'm out of the house, but not at home.

Could my sister have done such a thing?

I know she blames me for George finding out about her holiday romance but would she really go that far to get back at me?

I look at her again and the venom in her expression answers the question for me. Poppy hates me *and* Amelia for ending her relationship with George.

The death threat is her revenge. I'm sure of it.

4

I say nothing to or about Poppy while the police are here.

Mum and DC Kapoor come back from my room with my laptop encased in a clear plastic bag. DS Carter explains that they'll need all our fingerprints 'in order to eliminate anyone who hasn't used the computer from the enquiry'. He raises his eyebrows at Mum, like he's saying *please agree, so I don't have to march you all down the station to do this.*

Mum nods, looking shell-shocked. Poppy mutters something about police harassment, but acquiesces without a fuss.

I'm last to be fingerprinted, after which Mum signs for my computer and phone and the two officers leave.

As soon as they've walked out I turn on Poppy.

'You did this, didn't you?' I demand.

Poppy stares at me, her pale blue eyes wide with shock.

'*Me?*' she says, with withering scorn.

35

'That's enough, Carey!' Mum says, her voice so loud and harsh it actually makes me jump. I can't remember the last time she raised her voice to me. She's usually laughing, Mum. Easy-going. That is, she worries a lot, and if she thinks we've taken risks over our safety she comes down hard, but basically she's pretty trusting. Poppy says she was stricter before Dad left five years ago, but maybe that's just coincidence.

'I didn't send Amelia that horrible message,' I protest.

Mum hesitates. 'I believe you,' she says.

Poppy makes a harrumphing noise.

'I think they've probably made a mistake about the laptop,' Mum goes on, ignoring her. 'And I understand that you're upset. But that's no reason to take it out on your sister.'

'Suppose it *was* my laptop?' I look at Mum and Poppy. The two of them are pretty alike. Jamie too. All of them have blue eyes and fine, fair hair. I'm the odd one out in my family with my darker skin and curls. Like Dad's. 'Poppy could have snuck into my room and sent the messages. She was here, in the house, when—'

'You are unbelievable.' Poppy storms over. She's taller than me by a good few centimetres and it takes all my self-control not to shrink away from her.

Don't get me wrong, for the past five years since Dad left home we've been close – well, until the last couple

36

of weeks. But I have deeply-rooted memories of when we were little kids, of her pinching and pushing me behind Mum's back.

'How dare you accuse me?' Poppy roars. 'You're the one who doesn't care who she hurts or whose relationship she breaks up. You're the evil, selfish—'

'Girls, stop it,' Mum snaps.

Poppy folds her arms. Her face is red with fury. 'See how you're upsetting Mum?' she says.

'I haven't done anything—' I catch my breath. This is surreal. A nightmare. I try to stop the tears that prick at my eyes. 'I would never do anything to upset Mum. Or Amelia.'

'Yeah, right.' Poppy points her finger, poking at my chest. 'You are such a hypocrite. Pretending to be Amelia's friend when you're really sending horrible messages to her. Pretending to be tucked up in bed when you're really sneaking out of the—'

'Girls, stop this,' Mum cries, but I hardly notice.

'I'm not the one pretending,' I snarl. 'You're making out like you're so perfect, but you didn't have any problem going with another guy behind George's back! And *you* used to sneak out of the house too.'

'No I didn't.'

'You did,' I shout, clenching my fists. 'I saw you.'

'Stop it!' Mum shrieks. But I'm too far gone to hear.

'I think *you* sent the messages to Amelia and made it look like I did them to get revenge,' I shout. 'You'd love to break up our friendship but I'm telling you you—'

'I would *never* do that. *Never.*' Bursting into tears, Poppy storms out of the room.

'Carey!' Mum says.

I look her in the eyes. 'I need to call Amelia.'

'I don't think that's a good idea, Carey. Didn't you hear the police?'

But I'm already out of the living room and scurrying into the kitchen where Mum's phone is charging in its usual place to the left of the toaster. I know she has Amelia's number stored, because I'm with her so often. I snatch the mobile up and race out of the house. I hurry around the corner, intent on hiding from view in case Mum decides to come after me. I duck behind the wall next to the three garages and scroll to Amelia's number.

My heart beats fast as the phone rings. I remind myself that there's no way Amelia will believe I am really behind SweetFreak. I've been the one comforting her; I'm her best friend. The call goes to voicemail. I leave a garbled message, all incoherent emotion.

The stupid police have been here doing fingerprints and taking my laptop and my mobile which is why I'm using Mum's. It's all beyond crazy ... obviously I didn't do this, I know you know I wouldn't but ... this is so awful, I can't

38

imagine how upset you must be feeling . . . please call me . . . you're my best friend . . .'

I sit, my head bowed over the phone, waiting for some response. A few minutes pass. Nothing. I try again. Leave another message. Then send a text. Then another. Then a third phone call.

It's dark now and I'm cold. I rushed out of the house without a jacket and the wind is fierce across my face.

For a few moments I contemplate going round to her house. I glance at Mum's phone. I'll get into terrible trouble if I don't go home now. And I've already left Amelia a million messages. There could be lots of reasons why she hasn't answered. Maybe the police are still studying her phone? Maybe she's with her parents? Maybe she just wants to be on her own?

Whatever, I know by now Amelia will have been told the death threat came from my laptop and, whichever way you look at it, that will come as a terrible shock. I should give her time to let the situation settle, time to reflect on the insanity of the idea that I could possibly hurt her. She'll probably call back later this evening. If not, she'll definitely be at school tomorrow. I just need to see her and reassure myself that she knows I am innocent.

And I need to tell her that I'm pretty certain Poppy is guilty.

I trudge home, Mum's phone held in my palm where I

will hear when it rings. I brace myself as I walk into the house. If Poppy starts having another go at me I swear I might totally lose it. But Poppy is nowhere to be seen. I walk into the kitchen to find Mum sitting in glum silence at the kitchen table, a cold cup of tea in front of her. At the sight of her misery a fresh wave of unhappiness washes over me.

'Oh, Mum.'

She looks up.

'I didn't do it.' My voice cracks.

'I know, my love.' She opens her arms and I collapse into them, finally giving way to the tears that feel like they might drown me.

5

I barely sleep all night. I'm still sure Poppy is behind the death threat and the other SweetFreak messages and I alternate between bewilderment that she could be so cruel to poor Amelia, fury that she has set me up and fear that no one other than Mum will believe I'm innocent.

My worst fear is that Amelia herself won't believe it. Why hasn't she replied to my call? Or responded to my texts? I told her the police had my mobile, but could she be calling it by mistake? And what has she said to everyone else? Has she told anyone else that the police traced the SweetFreak message to my laptop?

No, surely she wouldn't have said anything without talking to me first.

Would she?

In the end I fall into a fitful sleep, waking late and foggy-headed. Poppy has already left for school and Mum is rushing with Jamie. She says nothing about the accusations in front of my little brother, but while he is putting on his shoes, she whispers in my ear that she loves me and believes in me and that she's sure we'll get a call today from the police explaining it's all been a terrible mistake.

She knows that I haven't spoken to Amelia yet and gently warns me not to pester her when I see her at school.

'Remember this will have been a horrible experience for her,' Mum says. 'She won't want to think you could have done this, but there's bound to be doubt in her—'

'Why?' I flare up again. 'I wouldn't believe it of her.'

'Sssh.' Mum points through the door, to where Jamie is sitting on the bottom step of the stairs, his little tongue poking out as he carefully places the velcro strap across his left shoe. 'Just don't go blundering in, pushing Amelia to make you feel better. Honestly, sweetheart, give her time to think it through. I'm sure she'll realise you couldn't possibly have done such a terrible thing once the initial shock has settled down.'

I nod, but inside I'm unconvinced. Surely the sooner I can face Amelia the better? I need her to know I would never hurt her. I need to know she believes me.

I hurry to school, preoccupied all the way. I can't see Amelia in our form room which is still half empty when I arrive. I scuttle over to my normal seat, putting my bag on the chair next to me, where Amelia usually sits.

42

I wait for her to arrive, looking up every time there's movement by the door. But Amelia doesn't come. Gradually the class fills up. A few girls smile at me or say hello, but the vast majority avoid meeting my eyes, then huddle in corners, having whispered conversations that I'm certain, from the occasional glances in my direction, are all about me.

By the time Mrs Marchington strides in, the register tucked under her arm, it is obvious that at least three-quarters of the room know exactly what I've been accused of.

What does that mean? That Amelia has told people? I frown, unwilling to believe it. Who else could be gossiping?

Of course. The answer washes over me like ice-cold water: Poppy.

Up until this point I'd imagined my sister's aim was to upset Amelia and break up our friendship. But suppose Poppy wants me to suffer even more than that. She could be trying to spread rumours about me, hoping to turn the whole school against me.

Before we head to our first lesson Rose and one of her stupid Clones (her hair styled into a careful copy of Rose's long bob) wander over and stand in front of me. Rose speaks loudly, her mouth twisted into a superior sneer.

'Poor Amelia is so upset she can't get out of bed.'

My head jerks up.

The Rose Clone – a sullen-faced girl called Minnie – nods, an expression of exaggerated concern on her face.

43

'It's Not surprising,' Rose goes on, giving me a sideways glance. 'What an evil cow that SweetFreak is.'

I hesitate. This is typical Rose, making snide comments rather than a direct accusation. It makes it almost impossible to react ... if I say something in response I'm kind of admitting I know she's referring to me. Which feels like it would be an admission of guilt.

I look away, still unsure what to do. By the time I look back, Rose and Minnie have gone. The situation gets worse through the day. Rose posts one of the SweetFreak private messages on YouTube: the one with the pig with Amelia's face landing on a house that Amelia shared with a few of us the day she received it.

Rose says she's done it in order to show everyone how nasty SweetFreak is, but I think the real reason is to put herself right in the middle of the whole drama. Whatever her motive, everywhere I go I seem to see people in small groups watching the horrible thing then looking at me with appalled faces and whispering behind their hands.

I'd seriously rather they challenged me directly.

It's always a bit odd when Amelia is away from school – we spend so much time together and always partner up in our shared classes. But this is in another league. I don't think I've ever had a day feeling so isolated and miserable in my life, and that includes my first day at secondary school – which was awful up to the point halfway through

the morning when I met Amelia. We've been inseparable ever since.

As I leave school there's only one thing on my mind: I have to talk to Amelia right now. And if she won't answer my calls, I'm going round to her house. I'm aware, somewhere in the back of my mind, that this flies in the face Mum's warning about not pestering Amelia, but if Mum had seen what it was like for me at school she'd understand. I *have* to make sure Amelia knows I'm innocent. At this point she's the only person who can make the rumours that are swirling around me disappear.

I head straight for Amelia's house. I don't exactly know what I'm going to say, but I don't stop to worry about it. I stand on her doorstep and ring the bell. There's no answer at first. Which often happens. Amelia's house is twice the size of ours.

Her mum and stepdad are away from home on work almost all the time – the Wilsons have always had someone living in: when I first met Amelia she still had a nanny, but for the past few years there has just been a succession of au pairs.

I'm anticipating one of these opening the door right now, though I'm hoping it will be Amelia, so it's a shock when I come face to face with Amelia's mother. She's wearing leggings and a designer-looking smock top – she's about half Mum's size and wears twice as expensive clothes – and

45

there are dark rings under her eyes. Her mouth drops open as she sees me.

'You've got a nerve,' she snarls.

Her tone is so ferocious I actually take a step back along the slate path.

'I want to speak to Amelia,' I say. 'Is she in?'

Amelia's mum shakes her head. 'You've got no idea, do you? Amelia's devastated. I've been up with her all night. Her brother's upset. Her father's furious. I've had to take the day off.'

'Oh, poor you.' The sarcasm shoots out of me before I can stop myself. How typical of Mrs Wilson to be more worried about the impact of the death threat on herself than on her daughter. 'I understand Amelia's upset. But I didn't *do* anything. I want to talk to her, make sure she understands that, because—'

'Go away,' Amelia's mum spits.

I stand my ground but inside I'm quaking. Mostly from shock. I've only met Mrs Wilson a few times – she's normally at work when I'm over – and she's never been warm or friendly, but this is outright hostility.

'I need to see Amelia.' I sound more upset than I want to, almost close to tears. Mrs Wilson is unmoved. She's actually shutting the door on me, when Amelia herself appears in the background. She looks paler than ever, her eyes red-rimmed and puffy.

'Carey?' she says, her voice breaking. 'What are you doing here?'

I step forward, pushing the door back against Amelia's mum. 'I had to see you,' I gabble. 'I didn't do anything. You have to believe me. I'd never do—'

'Amelia, go to your room,' her mum snaps.

Amelia shrinks back.

'Wait.' I push my way into the hall. 'Please.' Tears prick at my eyes. I can't bear this: my best friend so upset. The enormity of the situation boils up inside me – our whole friendship is at stake. 'It wasn't me,' I plead. 'I think maybe it was my sister.'

Amelia's mother shakes her head. 'I'd like you to leave, please, Carey.'

'Come on,' I urge Amelia. 'You know why Poppy might have done it.' I meet her gaze, trying to convey, without spelling out, what Poppy's motivation might have been in front of Amelia's mum.

Amelia's lip trembles. It feels like she wants to believe me. If only her stupid mother would get out of the way, but she's hovering beside me, radiating anger.

'Please leave,' Mrs Wilson snaps again.

'Wait, Mum.' A tear trickles down Amelia's cheek as she faces me. 'I just don't know, Carey.'

'Know what?' I ask, bewildered.

'It's … well … yesterday, when I got to school and

showed you that horrible, horrible message ...' She shudders, looking down at the polished wood floor at her feet. 'When you saw it you ... you said "she" when we were talking about SweetFreak. How did you know it was a girl if it wasn't you?'

'I *didn't* know ... I just assumed because ... I don't know.' I stare at her, feeling desperate.

'And calling me Princess in the message.' Her voice drops so that her mother can't hear her. 'I *know* you've called me that behind my back.'

I shake my head. But it's true, of course, though how Amelia has found out I can't imagine. One of the girls at school, I'm guessing.

'Getting that last message was *so* awful because it was *you*,' she continues softly. 'I can't bear the thought that you were laughing at me behind my back the whole time.'

'I *wasn't*.' Tears bubble into my eyes. 'And *I* can't bear you thinking I would,' I say, my voice cracking with emotion.

There's a long pause. Amelia's lip trembles. I hold my breath, sensing I'm getting through to her. Her mum stands between us, arms folded, tense with repressed anger. She's clearly itching to resume her attempt to throw me out of the house.

'I didn't send those messages,' I plead. 'I'd *never* do anything like that.'

'Please go upstairs, Amelia,' her mother orders.

Amelia turns away obediently and walks towards the staircase.

'Wait,' I call out. 'Please.' My hands are clenched tight. '*Please*, Amelia. I wouldn't believe this if someone said it about you.'

Amelia stops at the foot of the stairs. She puts her hand on the bannister as if to steady herself. For a moment I think she's going to turn around, then her mum lets out an exasperated sigh and Amelia trudges up the stairs.

I watch, misery sinking inside me like a stone. Amelia's mum takes the front door, ready to shut it on me. She towers over me in her heels.

'Out.' Mrs Wilson speaks with an icy finality.

Tears blind me as I stumble along the path, away from the house.

6

I spend the whole of the next day in a state of numb misery. Amelia doesn't return to school and is still refusing to take or return my calls. I cling to the fact that I was starting to get through to her but it's hard. I still can't get my head around how quick she has been to believe I would be cruel to her.

She's not the only one.

The rumours about me are getting wilder and wilder. Everyone's seen the death threat video as well as the pig film now. Someone – not Rose this time but a guy in Amelia's brother's year – got hold of it and posted it on the main NatterSnap feed, tagging me, and it's been reposted and commented on more times than I can see on my own feed. As far as I can make out everyone who's seen it believes that I not only sent the death threat but am seriously intent on carrying it out. I catch snippets of conversations as I walk along corridors and, on several occasions, when I'm in the loos on the second floor – the school's most popular indoor hideaway.

'She actually has a knife . . .'

'I heard she's made one attempt on the other girl's life already . . . been stalking her out of school for months . . .'

'My friend told me that she's got a record, but her parents kept it from the school . . .'

And it's the same online, where two of the milder comments include:

'Apparently after she sent the death threat, she lay in wait but the other girl got away . . .'

'She stabbed her in a fight . . . the police would arrest her but there aren't any witnesses . . .'

It's all untrue, of course, every last bit of it, but nobody cares about that. Scandal is like money – a way of trading things, in this case: information.

The fact that Amelia is staying off school is fuelling the hysteria; in the absence of proper information it's not surprising wild rumours are circulating.

This is bad enough from the people who don't know me. But what really hurts is how many people in my form who I've known for three whole years are joining in. Amelia might be my bestie, but I've always been friendly with everyone. Why does nobody stand up for me? Tell the rest that there's no way I could threaten anyone? Is it that they think I'm guilty? Or are they just keeping their heads down, unwilling to swim against the tide and support me in the face of everyone else's hostility?

I almost wish someone would confront me directly. At least then I'd have something to react to. But instead it's all hushed whispers and awkward silences whenever I walk into the room.

I don't tell anyone what's going on. The teachers must know why Amelia isn't here and what I've been accused of. They don't speak to me directly about it, of course, but I catch plenty of sideways glances, as if they're suspicious of me too: unconvinced I'm definitely guilty, but open to the possibility.

Mum thinks I'm innocent and I cling to that. But I don't want to worry her about people being mean at school – she's already looking grey with stress. I know she isn't sleeping well. I'm not either. I wake several times a night, often with the image of the death threat picture seared into my mind's eye. I see the knife poised under Amelia's throat; the drip, drip, drip of the blood down her neck . . . the wild, terrified eyes . . .

Under other circumstances I would have turned to my big sister. But I'm still certain Poppy's behind the messages. The thought that she is capable of putting me through this hurts almost as much as Amelia believing I'm capable of doing the same thing to her. Anyway, even if I wanted to talk, Poppy is keeping her distance. In fact she hasn't spoken to me since the police officers came to the house.

At last it's Friday and, apart from a *The Sound of Music* rehearsal for the group songs, which I thoroughly enjoy, it's a huge relief to get home from school.

I dump my bag at the bottom of the stairs and head for the kitchen. As I reach the door I hear voices. I push the door open, my heart thudding. Mum is sitting at the table with the two police officers from before. She's murmuring something in a low, strained voice, tears in her eyes.

The older male officer, DS Carter, has his arm round Mum's shoulders and is awkwardly patting her back. The younger woman, DC Kapoor, stares daggers at me as I walk in.

'We'd like to take you to the station for questioning, Carey,' she says.

'What?' I feel winded. 'Why?'

'We need to conduct a more formal interview,' DS Carter explains.

'I don't understand.' I turn to Mum, bile rising in my throat. 'What's going on?'

There's an awkward silence. I stare at Mum. Surely she will save me from this? Both police officers look at her too. Mum wipes her face and stands up, pushing back her chair.

'Come on, Carey.' Mum's mouth gives a little wobble. She presses her lips together for a second, clearly trying not to cry. 'The sooner we go and clear this up, the sooner we can come home again.' She turns to DS Carter. 'I need to pick up my son from his friend's house by seven at the latest.'

My chest feels tight as we drive the ten minutes it takes to get to the police station. In spite of my repeated questions, no one properly explains why I'm being taken to the station. Mum sits next to me in the back of the car. She doesn't speak the whole way. And she doesn't look me in the eye. The two officers talk to each other in low voices but I can't hear what they're saying. The atmosphere is far more tense than it was when they came before. I shiver, even though it's warm and stuffy in the car. Up until now I've held onto the fact that once the police find my computer is clean, everything will go back to normal, but surely if that was the case then the officers would have smiled and apologised rather than bundling us into their car and taking us to the station? What have they found?

The station is bland and beige, with chipped paint along the window ledge. Mum and I are whisked past reception, down a long corridor and into an interview room. A table containing recording equipment is surrounded by four chairs. I gaze around the bare walls. There are no windows, but a small camera peers down at us from the corner above the table.

'This looks serious,' Mum says.

'Why are we here?' I ask for the hundredth time.

The officers tell us to sit and the recording equipment is

54

switched on and DC Kapoor is talking but she's speaking so quickly I can't follow what she's saying until she pauses and coughs and says:

'So we are now absolutely certain that the death threat sent to Amelia Wilson on NatterSnap came from your computer, Carey. And that the laptop definitely wasn't accessed remotely.'

Mum bites her lip.

'But I wasn't even at home when it was posted,' I protest.

'Actually you were.' DS Carter sits back. 'The message was programmed into the computer the night before the morning it was actually sent.'

'What?' Something inside me crumples. How is this happening? 'I don't understand.' My voice quavers. I look around at Mum. She's frowning.

'I don't understand either,' she says. 'You said you had "proof". How does that prove Carey—'

'Let me explain,' DS Carter says gently. 'We can't trace any of the earlier, deleted SweetFreak messages, but the last one – containing the death threat – was programmed at 10.33 p.m. on a delay function to self-post the following morning at 8.27 a.m.,' DS Carter explains.

'But Carey couldn't do that,' Mum says, bewildered. 'That sounds highly technical.'

'Actually it's very easy to do,' DC Kapoor says. She turns her mean eyes on me.

'But Carey went to bed at ten o'clock that night as usual, she'd have been asleep by ten thirty,' Mum protests.

DS Carter looks at me. 'Is that right, Carey?'

I think back to the night before everything went crazy. At 10.33p.m. I was running through the streets on my way to meet Amelia. Nowhere near my laptop. I look down at my lap. I know I have to tell the police – after all it proves my innocence. But it's hard to admit in front of Mum that I was sneaking out.

'Carey was in bed. Asleep.' Mum sounds emphatic, but I can hear the note of doubt creeping into her voice. 'Weren't you, Carey?'

I hesitate.

'Carey?' DS Carter coughs. 'It's important you tell us the whole truth.'

There's something in his voice that tells me the police already know I wasn't at home. Of course. They'll have talked to Amelia. She'll have told them. Plus they've got my phone. I might have deleted the messages between me and Amelia that night, but the police will still be able to see exactly where I was from my phone's location history. I take a deep breath.

'Actually Amelia was really upset about … stuff, so I was out meeting her, because she needed a friend.' I don't look Mum in the eye but I feel her stiffen next to me. I sit up straighter. 'But that means I wasn't even at home at 10.33. I sent Amelia messages when I was waiting to meet her. You can see on my phone where I was.'

'We've seen,' DC Kapoor says icily.

'You went out?' Mum's voice is hollow with shock. 'Through the bathroom window?' She glances at me, furious. I'm certain that if the police weren't here she'd already be ranting at me. I know she's remembering how I was caught before, a few months ago, and how I promised I wouldn't ever sneak out again. However, the inevitable row this will lead to is the last thing on my mind.

'I'm sorry, Mum,' I say.

Mum blinks rapidly, her emotions rampaging across her face. She's clearly torn between anger and hurt that I broke my promise and fear that perhaps I sent the messages to Amelia after all.

'So I left the house at about twenty past ten,' I persist. 'Can't you see from my phone records where I was?'

'We can only trace your phone when it was switched on,' DC Kapoor says. 'And it appears to have been turned off between 10.21 p.m. and 10.40 p.m..'

My heart sinks. Of course, I turned the mobile off as I left the house in case I got an alert, and didn't turn it on again until I was at the swings. 'I put it on when Amelia didn't show up so . . . so I could send her a text,' I say. 'I was waiting in the park. But it was the wrong place. Amelia was at the rec. So I *wasn't* at home at 10.33, it just took me longer to get to the rec than it should.'

DS Carter sighs. 'You're claiming you were in the park

at half past ten and that you stayed there for roughly ten minutes on your own, messaging Amelia at 10.41, then leaving to go to the bus shelter where you met her?'

'Yes.'

'Trouble is, Carey, that the park is on the way from your house to that bus shelter,' DS Carter says. He gives a grim smile. 'I know Cornmouth like the back of my hand, so I know it would have been perfectly possible for you to have programmed the message on your computer at 10.33, then race to the Old Cornmouth Rec bus shelter for 10.50, stopping briefly at the park on your way to message Amelia. We only have your word for it that you spent ten minutes in the park.'

'But . . . how would I know to go to all that trouble to hide my tracks?'

'In my experience teenagers are capable of a lot more than they let on,' DS Carter says with a frown.

I turn to Mum. 'I didn't do this, Mum. I *swear* I didn't.'

Mum nods, but what she's not saying is clear: *how can I believe you about one thing, if you've lied about another?*

DC Kapoor narrows her mean eyes. It's clear she doesn't believe me either.

My mind races about, trying to think what else I can say to convince them.

'I just remembered something.' My stomach gives an uneasy twist. It feels horribly disloyal to accuse my sister of

58

being SweetFreak, but what choice has she left me? 'When I got home after seeing Amelia I was sure someone had been in my room. My laptop was open though I'm sure I left it shut.'

'Carey!' Mum's voice sounds a warning note. 'Stop right there.'

'I think my sister, Poppy, must have come into my room while I was out,' I persist. 'I think *she* used my computer to make it look like *I* sent that horrible message.'

Mum glares at me.

'Right,' DS Carter says, clearly unconvinced. 'I'd say there might be easier ways to frame someone, wouldn't you?'

'It's also interesting that since we took away your phone and laptop the SweetFreak messages have stopped,' DC Kapoor says drily.

'And we haven't found any fingerprints other than yours on the keys,' DS Carter adds. 'Does your sister even have the password for your laptop? Does anyone?'

'No.' I shake my head. 'But Poppy could have seen it over my shoulder.'

'For goodness sake, Carey,' Mum mutters. She turns to DS Carter. 'What about street cameras? If Carey was running around the streets like you suggest, they'd have picked her up.'

'I'm afraid there isn't any local CCTV, apart from on the main roads. If Carey stuck to backstreets as we suspect, she

59

wouldn't have been seen,' DS Carter says. He sighs. 'Cutbacks.'

'I didn't do anything.' Panic rises wildly inside me. It's like I've been thrown out of an aeroplane without a parachute. I'm spinning, whirling through space, lost and confused. 'I didn't do this.'

Mum frowns, her face suffused with doubt.

'Did you have some reason to be angry with Amelia, Carey?' DS Carter asks.

'No, we're best friends.'

'Are you *sure* it wasn't Amelia herself?' Mum asks.

'Absolutely. She was nowhere near any electronic device other than her own phone, which we've examined thoroughly. She did not send herself a death threat.'

'But somebody sent it,' DC Kapoor adds. 'And all the evidence points to you, Carey.'

I shake my head. 'No,' I protest. 'No way.'

'Oh, Carey.' Mum's voice trembles. 'Is this something to do with Dad leaving? Now you're getting older without a father around I—'

'*No*,' I snap, now embarrassed on top of everything else. 'I'm *not* upset, I'm *fine*. And I didn't do anything. Please, I'm telling the truth.'

But as I look into Mum's eyes I see that she no longer believes me.

There's a tense silence, then DS Carter clears his throat. He explains that there is no public interest in pursuing a prosecution against me and, anyway, he's confident I do not pose a credible threat to Amelia, that I'm just acting out. 'So all we are doing for now is giving you a serious warning, though I would strongly urge you to take responsibility for your actions.' He turns to Mum. 'We can recommend a local counselling service. Sessions are subsidised as part of the local initiative on zero tolerance for bullying I told you about before.'

Mum nods. I stare at my lap.

'But make no mistake,' DC Kapoor chips in. 'Any further threats of this nature and we'll be forced to consider charging you under the Malicious Communications Act.'

Mum is tight-lipped and stern-faced as we leave the station. The sun shines in my face as I lean against the rough brick wall while we wait for a taxi. Neither of us speak. I'm still in a daze and Mum seems lost in her own thoughts.

'Carey?'

I turn.

Mum is frowning, clearly exasperated. 'Are you listening to me?'

'Yes. No, I . . . I didn't hear what you said.'

'I said that I have no idea *what* to say to you. I don't know who you are any more. I can't begin to think of a suitable punishment, though you're definitely not getting your phone back.'

'What? You can't be serious. Mum, I didn't *do* anything.'

'How could you, Carey?' Mum says. 'To Amelia of all

61

people? Your best friend. I brought you up better than this.'

'But I didn't.'

Mum shakes her head. 'This is the worst thing, that you persist in refusing to take responsibility for—'

'How many more times do I have to tell you it wasn't me?' All my pent-up rage bursts out of me. 'You believed me until that stupid police officer came out with all that rubbish about my laptop and fingerprints and delay functions.'

Mum shakes her head. 'If you'd just admit what you'd done—'

'I *didn't* do it!' I'm shouting now, tears stinging my eyes.

Mum looks away.

It's the last straw. At least when she believed me I felt less alone. Now I'm totally isolated. I clench my fists. Poppy is going to pay for this.

7

We pick Jamie up from his playdate on the way home. He chatters on about a game he and his friends played. Mum nods and makes out she's listening but I can tell she's still thinking about what an evil daughter I am.

As soon as we get home I leap out of the taxi and rush into the house, determined to force Poppy to confess what she's done. But my sister isn't in her bedroom, just the lingering scent of her flowery perfume and a scatter of clothes across the bed and the floor.

I hurry down to Mum.

'Where's Poppy?' I ask.

'At a friend's house for a sleepover.'

I demand to know which friend, but Mum won't tell me, pointedly asking me to make Jamie's tea because she has a headache and wants to lie down upstairs.

'Fine,' I snap, swallowing down the resentment that burns

inside me. I stomp around the kitchen, fetching some slices of cheese and ham from the fridge and plonking some bread and hummus and tomatoes on a plate. Jamie plays in the living room, jumping on and off the sofa. If Mum were here she would tell him off, but she's already upstairs.

I *have* to talk to Poppy. No way can I wait until she lopes home tomorrow. It's not fair: Friday night and she's off out with her friends while I'm stuck at home without anything to do and everybody thinking I'm a horrible cow. And what about Amelia? It's bad enough she's upset over the messages but I can't bear how much more she'll be hurting thinking I'm behind them. She needs to know the truth.

I'm certain Mum knows where Poppy is. She usually insists we tell her exactly where we are and what we're doing. I check the Poldark calendar on the wall.

P @ Louisa is scrawled under today's date.

Well that's something, at least: Louisa is one of Poppy's oldest friends and lives just a few streets away. As soon as Mum thinks I've gone to bed, I'm sneaking out and going over there.

My plan goes without a hitch. After he's had his tea, I play with Jamie until Mum reappears. She looks just as harassed as when she went upstairs, a deep line riven between her eyebrows, but her voice is calm when she calls me into the kitchen and asks me, yet again, to admit what I've done 'so we can begin the healing and the learning from all this'.

64

I protest my innocence again but Mum has clearly decided I'm guilty. Only concrete proof will convince her otherwise.

Mum comes to bed soon after I've gone upstairs myself, which delays my exit from the house. I wait while she potters about, then peek outside to check her light is off. I cross the landing to listen at her door. I can hear her soft, shallow breathing: regular and even. For months after Dad left I used to do this every night, terrified that if one parent could walk out on us with no notice or explanation then Mum might suddenly be taken away too.

With Mum upstairs and fast asleep, there's no need to clamber out the bathroom window. Instead I tiptoe downstairs and let myself out the front door. I race along the few streets to Louisa's house. My heart beats fast as I reach her road. I'm not at all sure I can remember exactly which house she lives at. I used to come here with Mum to pick up Poppy sometimes, but that was a long time ago when we were both much younger. As it turns out I needn't have worried. A huddle of teenagers stand in the road outside number twelve, talking and laughing. Three of them are puffing away on cigarettes, I recognise Sam, a good friend of Poppy's, immediately.

I go up to him. Normally I'd be quaking at the thought of talking to a sixth former in front of his mates, but right now I'm so intent on confronting my sister I don't even think about it.

'Hey, Sam?' I ask. 'Is Poppy inside?'

He makes a silly face. 'Wouldn't you like to know?' He laughs as if he's said something hilarious. He's clearly drunk. They all are.

I grit my teeth. 'What's going on? Party?'

'Louisa's parents are away for the weekend so, yeah, I guess.' He sniggers. 'D'you wanna drink?'

His friend nudges him. 'She's a kid, Sam.'

'Yeah, but she's got big hair,' Sam laughs.

I curl my lip. 'That doesn't even make sense,' I say, smoothing my curls self-consciously.

Now all of them start laughing.

'You lot are the kids.' I stomp inside, their raucous voices echoing in my ears. Inside the house, the whole open-plan downstairs area is heaving. Poppy isn't here. I spot Louisa in the corner. She's swaying to some music, clearly off her face. Mum thinks Poppy's such a goody-goody, I'm itching to call her up and let her know exactly what's going on over here. But of course I can't, having no phone and not being supposed to be here myself.

I head up the stairs in search of my sister. There's a couple eating each other's faces on the top step. I wriggle past, peering into the bathroom where two girls are perched on the edge of the bath, deep in conversation. As I walk along the landing I hear Poppy's voice coming from inside a room on the left. She's pleading with someone.

66

'But you have to believe me.' She sounds close to tears.

I push the door open to reveal my sister in the middle of what is clearly Louisa's parents' bedroom, complete with four-poster bed. George, Amelia's brother, stands in front of her, a pained look on his face.

He sees me before Poppy does.

'What are you doing here?' he says accusingly.

Poppy's head whips around. 'Carey!' she gasps.

'I can't be in the same room as *her*.' George stalks off.

Poppy rounds on me. 'See what you've done? I'd just got him up here to try and talk to him and you've ruined everything. *Again*.'

I square up to her, my fury mounting.

'You have to start telling the truth,' I snarl. 'You have to tell Mum and the police that it was you who sent those messages from my computer, because whatever I did to you, it doesn't justify what you've done to me. And to Amelia.'

Poppy stares at me. There's what looks like genuine bewilderment in her eyes. 'It wasn't me, Carey.'

For the first time I doubt what, up to now, seemed so certain. I know Poppy better than I know anyone. She might hate me, but as I look into her eyes it's hard to believe she would have gone so far to get her revenge.

'Well it wasn't me,' I say.

We stand, facing each other. There is definitely no hint of a lie in her expression, only a terrible sadness. Most of which, I'm guessing, is to do with the boy who's just walked out of the room.

'I know I upset you about George,' I go on. 'I'm really sorry. And I'm sorry he reacted like he did but ... but ...' I hesitate, a previously unspoken thought hovering on my tongue. 'I don't mean to upset you again but don't you think if he really loved you he'd have listened to you about that Spanish guy, trusted that you meant it when you said it was just a stupid one-off kiss, that it didn't mean anything, that you loved him?'

Poppy stares at me. I brace myself, waiting for her to yell that it's none of my business. But she doesn't look angry. And, unlike the guys downstairs, she doesn't seem drunk either. Just deeply unhappy.

'Mmmm,' Poppy mumbles.

'What?'

'I'm saying that maybe you're right about George.' Poppy heaves a bitter sigh. 'The fight we just had ... I realised what he's most upset about is how he looks to everyone else. He doesn't really care if I was with someone else or not. I ... I'm starting to think he doesn't really care about me at all.' Her lip trembles. 'It's hard, though, because I liked him. A lot.'

'He's an idiot,' I say. 'You're worth ten Georges.'

Poppy offers me a wan smile. 'Maybe I'm the idiot.' She grips my arm. 'Carey, I'm so sorry about what's happened with Amelia and the messages. I can see how upset you are.'

We look into each other's eyes. She seems genuinely concerned.

'So it really wasn't you?'

'No.' Poppy sighs.

I'm sure, suddenly, that she's telling the truth.

'And you're not still accusing *me* of doing it?' I ask.

'No,' she says again. 'And I hate the fact that it's got you into so much trouble and upset Mum so much.'

'And Amelia,' I point out.

'Yes.' She pauses. 'And Amelia. She might be a bit silly and careless. You both are. But you don't deserve what's happening now.'

I take a deep breath, relief that my sister believes me washing over me.

'For what it's worth,' I say, 'I'm truly sorry that I sent Amelia that stupid video of you with the Spanish boy.'

Downstairs the music thumps, the volume surging.

'So what are we going to do?' Poppy asks. 'If it wasn't you and it wasn't me, then who is SweetFreak?'

'I don't know,' I say. 'It's hopeless. I can say over and over that I didn't do it, but my laptop says I did. The police are convinced. Mum is too, now. There's all this evidence against me.'

Poppy makes a sympathetic face. 'I've been thinking ... maybe it's someone hacking your computer. That would explain the lack of fingerprints and—'

'The police already told us my laptop wasn't hacked. They say they're sure,' I explain.

Poppy shrugs. 'They don't know everything. Maybe somebody really good could make it look like it *wasn't* hacked. I can think of loads of people in my year who might know how to do that, especially some of the guys.'

I nod. She's right. But who on earth hates me – and Amelia – enough to go to those lengths?

'You should get home before Mum realises you've gone out,' Poppy says with a smile. 'She might just explode if you get into any more trouble.' I gulp, fresh emotion welling inside me. This conversation is the longest and nicest talk we've had in weeks.

'Thanks.' I squeeze her hand, then turn and hurry down the stairs and outside, where the night air is cold against my warm cheeks. George is leaning against the front garden fence.

'Here comes SweetFreak,' he growls as I pass.

I turn on him. 'It wasn't me,' I said. 'And you should give my sister a break.'

'Shut your face.' George swears, rearing fully upright so that he towers over me. I shrink back. 'You little cow. *My* sister is in bits because of you. And that death threat ...' He shakes his head. 'I'm telling you, it's *you* who deserves to die.'

We stare at each other for a second, then I race away along the street, a new thought unfurling in my mind:

70

Could George be SweetFreak?

The police were insistent that the death threat came from my laptop, which they also claim never left my room. But suppose Poppy is right and someone hacked into it without the police realising? Could George have done that? I remember Poppy telling me before that he was always messing around on social media, and really into online pranks. What if he's secretly an IT genius who planned the SweetFreak messages to get back at his sister and at me for humiliating him? I've never thought he was very nice, he used to be horrible to Amelia whenever I went to their house, always teasing and sneering – not in the light way my sister and I did it, but with a real edge. And the way he's behaved with Poppy proves that even more. So do the nasty comments he made to me just now.

By the time I get home and let myself gently in the front door I'm convinced: George is SweetFreak.

Now all I have to do is prove it.

71

8

The weekend turns out better than I was expecting, thanks to Poppy. Mum is still angry and upset, but at least my sister believes in me now.

I tell them about my suspicions about George. Unfortunately Mum thinks the idea he might have hacked into my laptop is ridiculously far-fetched: 'The police already ruled that out, Carey,' she points out with a weary shake of her head.

Poppy at least admits it's possible.

'George is certainly mean enough,' she says with a sigh. 'It was so cold, the way he shut me down. Wouldn't even listen to my side of the story. And he does know loads about programming and IT stuff. I'm just not sure he'd go to all those lengths to take revenge on you and Amelia.' Her voice wobbles. 'I mean it's *me* he's really angry with.'

I reach out impulsively and touch her arm. 'I'm so, so sorry,' I say.

'Oh, Rey Rey.' Poppy uses my baby name as she draws me close. I breathe in the familiar scent of her perfume – light and flowery. It's a huge relief we're not fighting any more. It helps, as does being around Jamie, who clearly doesn't have a clue what's going on. He can sense Mum is in a bit of a state and gives her lots of hugs over the weekend, but when we're alone together he's the same dreamy, affectionate little boy he's always been. I play with him a lot – mostly watching then re-enacting scenes from *Warriors of the Doom Wood* with him.

Well, what else am I going to do?

I've more or less given up phoning Amelia and none of my other friends call or text me. I keep scrolling through my social media apps to keep up with what's going on, but I'm not included in anything and I don't try to push my way back in. I'm still hopeful that I can explain to everyone on Monday morning my suspicions about George and that they'll realise then the proof against me isn't as cast-iron as they all seem to think it is.

It doesn't quite work out like that.

On Monday I walk into my form room, my heart thudding in my chest. Surely Amelia will be back today?

She isn't, though everyone else is there. They all stare as

I walk over to my usual seat. My palms feel clammy as I put my books on the desk.

Rose is two seats down, busy with her phone.

'Hi,' I say, not particularly because I want to talk to her, but in order to break the ice.

She doesn't reply and I'm fairly certain from the way her head tilts self-consciously as I speak, that she's deliberately ignoring me. Irritation rises inside me. This is so unfair. What gives Rose or any of the others the right to judge me like this?

'Hey.' I go over and plant myself right in front of her. She doesn't look up. 'Hey. I'm talking to you.'

Rose lifts her head. Her long, freckled nose wrinkles with disdain.

'Can you smell something?' she asks the group of girls at the window.

They watch her intently. I hold my breath. What is she doing? She gives an exaggerated sniff. '*I* smell something,' she says slowly. 'I smell . . . the Freak.'

Two of the girls by the window giggle. My face burns.

Rose sniffs again. 'Yes,' she says. 'Definitely the smell of the Freak.'

I turn and walk away. I'm itching to rail at her, but I'm afraid if I talk I'll cry. And I don't want Rose or any of them to see how much their stupid insults are getting to me.

The day goes from bad to worse. Nobody speaks to me

in any of my classes. Most people won't even look me in the face. There's a rehearsal for *The Sound of Music* at lunchtime and I look forward to it more than I could have imagined. This time it's just me and Heath – rather than a big group thing – and it's obvious straightaway that the accusations following me around have poured a bucket of cold water on his interest. He's offhand and distant, as if he'd rather be anywhere other than having to read through his lines with me. It's not like I was ever seriously interested, but his obvious U-turn still hurts.

The final straw is when I trudge home, more miserable than I'd have thought possible, and Mum greets me as I walk in with the words:

'I think you need to talk to someone, Carey. Get to the bottom of what's going on with you ... so I've found you a therapist and booked an appointment for tomorrow evening. Her name's Sonia Greening and she's got a very good reputation.'

Tuesday, six p.m., I'm ushered into Sonia's living room. She's a big woman, wearing a shapeless dress and red-framed glasses. The bangles on her arms clatter against each other as she eases herself into a chair with a beaming smile. Her living room is as cluttered as ours at home, though whereas our place is just messy, Sonia's surfaces are carefully covered with all sorts of ethnicky knick-knacks:

wooden carvings, postcards, multicoloured scarves and loads and loads of tiny, unlit candles.

I sit on the sofa opposite Sonia's chair, hands in my lap, feeling desperately uncomfortable. Sonia starts talking about this being a safe space and entirely private and about her listening to me. I don't know what to make of it. I've never been in a situation remotely like this before.

'So, Carey ...' Sonia gives me an encouraging smile. There's something fake about her. It's that thing adults do when they're trying too hard to be 'down with the kids'. 'Why don't we start with how you're feeling physically?'

I stare at her. 'What do you mean?'

'Any tightness or tension?'

There is: my stomach is tied into knots and it feels like there's a band across my chest and throat. But I don't want to talk about it with Sonia.

'I'm fine,' I say, shrinking back a little.

'OK.' She nods sympathetically. 'How did you feel when the police were talking to you?'

'Great,' I say sarcastically. 'Fantastic.'

Sonia nods again, but the smile is looking even faker than before. 'I'm here to help you, Carey.'

'Help me do what?'

'Help you process everything that's happening ... but you have to open up to me if I'm going to help.' She clears her throat. 'Let's start with how things are at school.'

'OK,' I say.

'I understand you have the main part in your school production this year?'

'Yes.'

'And you have regular attendance with good grades across all your subjects?'

'I guess.'

'What about friendships? Boyfriends? Social life?'

She's trying to draw me out and it makes me just want to clam up.

'Up until a few days ago I had lots of friends and my social life was just fine and I don't want a boyfriend.'

'You don't want a boyfriend?' Sonia pounces on this. 'Tell me ... what's your situation at home? Is Dad around?'

From the way she's asking it's obvious my mum has told her about Dad leaving.

'My dad left when I was ten. He gives us a bit of cash in Christmas cards sometimes and last summer he sent a photo of his new baby. I don't think about him much.'

I can see the cogs whirring in Sonia's brain. She's clearly thinking that I've got issues because I don't have a father.

'Is the baby a brother or sister for you?' she asks.

'I don't remember,' I say. This isn't true. Dad's baby is a little boy called Teddy with a mass of dark curly hair just like Dad's – and mine. I don't know why my stupid father sent the stupid picture. It made Poppy furious and when Jamie

77

saw it he asked if maybe Dad had gone away because of him, because he was hoping to find a better son. I'll never forget the look on his face. It was the most heartbreaking thing I've ever seen.

'Where does your dad live?' Sonia persists, oozing with phoney concern.

I shrug. 'Dunno.'

This isn't true either. Dad lives at seventy-seven Camber Avenue, Broadcombe, just along the coast. I memorised the address before Poppy destroyed the note and picture, swearing me and Jamie to secrecy. 'We mustn't tell Mum,' she'd insisted. 'She'd be so upset.'

I fantasised for a while about going to find him, but what would be the point? If Dad wanted to see us he'd come to Cornmouth himself.

'I don't care about my dad and his stupid new family,' I say.

'I see.' Sonia pauses. 'Let's get back to things at school. Tell me about your friend Amelia.'

I shrug. 'She's cool. We're best friends. At least we were . . .'

'What sort of things did you used to do together?'

'I dunno. Chatting, hanging out . . .' Sonia looks at me expectantly, clearly wanting more. I rack my brains for something to say. 'Er, a couple of weeks ago we recorded ourselves singing and put it on YouTube, like we were a girl band or something.' This isn't exactly what happened.

We did record ourselves but Amelia just mouthed along to the words, saying she couldn't sing in tune to save her life.

'And, even before the recent upset, had your friendship changed recently?'

'What do you mean?' I ask.

'Well, new friends on the scene? Perhaps even a boyfriend . . . ?' Sonia lets the word hang in the air.

'I guess,' I say, feeling uncomfortable. 'Amelia started dating a boy called Taylor Lockwood. She got a bit loved-up over him.'

'Ah. How did you feel about that? Did her relationship with Taylor upset you?' Sonia raises her eyebrows.

'Not really, I just thought it was stupid when he dumped her and she got so upset.'

'You thought she shouldn't have been upset?'

I meet Sonia's intent gaze and feel suddenly wary. What is she getting at?

'I didn't say that,' I explain. 'Of course she'd be upset, but they weren't together very long and Amelia kept going on about it . . .'

'Did that make you angry?'

A switch flicks inside me. All of Sonia's softly pressing questions and her beaming smile are basically attempts to get me to confess. She isn't really interested in what I have to say. She's already decided I'm guilty and just wants me to admit it.

This isn't a 'safe space'. It's a trap.

'I thought it was an overreaction,' I say carefully. 'I was trying to be supportive, a good friend.'

'But what were your emotions?' Sonia persists.

I press my lips together.

'It's important that we own our feelings, Carey,' Sonia goes on earnestly. 'It's part of taking responsibility for ourselves.'

Taking responsibility. That's the same phrase the police officer used. And Mum. There's no point talking to this woman. She's prejudiced against me. Everyone is. And the only way I'll ever change anything, is if I can prove I'm innocent, which means unmasking whoever is guilty.

Which I'm now certain is George.

I barely speak through the rest of the session. As soon as Sonia says our time is up I hurry downstairs. Mum is waiting in the car, Jamie in the back seat.

'How was it?' she asks.

I turn my face away. I can't believe Mum is siding against me. It feels like the world as I knew it has ended.

'Carey?'

'Fine,' I grunt.

Mum sighs and drives off. Jamie keeps her chatting through the journey home. As soon as she's parked by our house I leap out and hurry away.

'Come back!' Mum calls after me. 'You're grounded. Carey! Where are—?'

80

I turn the corner and her voice fades away. There's a strong wind blowing gusts into my face. A piece of grit stings my eye. I blink it away, clenching my jaw. Fifteen minutes later I arrive outside Amelia's front door. There's no sign anyone's home. It's only seven thirty so her mum and stepdad are bound to be at work – they rarely get back before eight. Nevertheless, I hesitate on the doorstep. Suppose George answers?

I press the bell. No one comes. I press it again.

After a long minute, the door opens. Amelia stands there, her hair tied off her face in a ponytail. I'm used to seeing her in make-up both in and out of school, but right now she's not wearing any and all I can think for a second is how small her eyes are. They're screwed up, peering at me suspiciously.

'You shouldn't be here,' she says.

'I didn't do it,' I say.

Amelia starts to close the door in my face.

'But I think I know who did.'

The door stops moving. Amelia meets my eye. She raises her eyebrows.

'I think it was George,' I explain. 'Your brother, George.'

Amelia's jaw drops.

'Seriously,' I continue. 'George is angry at both of us, because I sent you that video of Poppy and that Spanish guy. And he could have hacked my laptop, no matter what the police say. Because *someone* must have.'

81

Amelia stares at me. Her fingers stray to the chain around her neck. The little heart Taylor gave her is on the end. Amelia rubs her thumb over the back of the heart, where I know the initials 'A' and 'T' are scratched.

How can Amelia and I be so close that I know such an intimate detail – and yet so far apart.

'Also, the last time I saw George he threatened me,' I say, thinking of the party last Friday night. 'He said he wished I was dead. Please, Amelia, you have to help me prove it was him so that—'

'George couldn't have done it,' Amelia says, her voice like ice. 'He was with Mum when the police said your laptop was being used.'

'I'm telling you, he must have found a way to—'

'And if George was angry with you it's because he's seen how upset I am, and how upset Mum and Dad are, especially now I'm missing so much school.'

'So come back,' I urge. 'Show Geor— whoever sent the messages how strong you are, that whatever SweetFreak throws at you, you're not going to let it change you or your friendships or . . . or your life.'

Amelia curls her lip. I sense I've said the wrong thing, though I can't work out what. A mask descends over her face and, when she speaks, her voice is thin and pointed, like a knife.

'You know why else George is angry?' she asks. 'He's

angry because his sister's supposed best friend has turned out to be a horrible cow.'

'But——?'

'Listen to me, Carey.' Amelia takes a step forward, filling the doorway. Her cheeks have pink spots. 'First you said it was Poppy, now my brother. You need to stop blaming other people and admit you're SweetFreak and that you sent those messages. And you can definitely stop pretending to be my friend.'

'But I'm not . . . I didn't,' I protest. 'And I *am* your friend.'

'Really?' Amelia says, her voice tight and thin. 'Like you were my friend when you called me Princess behind my back? Or when you totally took over when we did that YouTube video of us singing? Or when you were practically rolling your eyes at how stupid I was to get upset over Taylor?'

I stare at her, mouth gaping. What is she talking about? I was patient over Taylor. And it's hardly my fault if Amelia gets oversensitive about stuff. 'That's not what hap—'

'And you need to remember this one, specific, important thing,' Amelia snarls. 'I never want to speak to you, ever again.'

I open my mouth to protest again but before I can utter a word my best friend slams the door in my face.

83

9

A long week at school passes. Whichever way I turn, people treat me like I've got some hideous contagious disease. Some are openly hostile, calling me out over sending the death threat, bitter contempt in their voices. Others – mostly the younger kids – scuttle past me at top speed, clearly afraid I might get it into my head to attack them.

Horrible though these reactions are, I prefer them both to the meaner, more subtle campaign against me which is led by Rose and which involves most of the girls in my form completely ignoring me. From the scraps of conversation I overhear it's obvious that Rose has been in touch with Amelia and has lost no time telling everyone how devastated she is. Not that I hear this directly … thanks to Rose I'm left out of every conversation – both at school and online. Worse even than this, is the way when

I *am* in earshot, I'm referred to in the third person by my new nickname.

'There goes the Freak,' and 'Ugh, the stink of the Freak,' and stuff like that.

I hate, hate, hate the way it's impossible to face them down over it.

It's not much better at home. Mum's initial anger has turned into a sort of subdued unhappiness. She speaks to me about basic stuff like homework or when it's my turn to take out the rubbish, but she doesn't chat with me like she used to. I can't remember the last time she pointed out a dress I might like on ASOS or yelled up the stairs for me to come and watch TV with her. And she has given up asking me to confess to being SweetFreak.

When the police at last return my laptop and mobile phone, Mum hides them, informing me they are locked away in a secret place away from the house where I won't be able to find them. I ask repeatedly when I'll get them back, but she just shrugs and says 'when I think you can be trusted', which clearly isn't likely to be any time soon.

I'm also officially grounded from all non-school related activities for the rest of term. Not that I have anywhere to go or anyone to see. I think Poppy has an idea of what I'm going through, but for some reason, when she asks how I'm doing, I feel too ashamed to tell her just how horrible everyone is being to me. I do ask her to keep her eyes open for any clues

85

that George is SweetFreak, though as the two of them are barely speaking I don't hold out much hope this will get me any closer to proving his guilt.

The following Tuesday I visit Sonia again. If anything, this session goes even worse than the first one. I clam up completely in the face of Sonia's increasingly earnest attempts to draw me out. She keeps banging on about the importance of growth through personal responsibility:

'Unless you find a way of coming to terms with the hurt you've caused, you're in danger of remaining stuck in the past, weighed down by your actions. I'm sure if we can talk about it, Carey, we can find a way to help you face up to what you've done and move on.'

'I didn't *do* anything,' I want to scream at her. But what's the point. She's convinced of my guilt.

Everyone is.

How is it possible that just a few weeks ago I was as happy and popular as I've ever been? At the start of the school term I'd even thought about having a big outing to Nando's for my birthday. I'd planned on inviting loads of people and asking Mum to go halves on it. But now my birthday is less than a fortnight away, Mum hasn't mentioned it and I can't think who I'd ask anyway.

Amelia still hasn't shown up at school. She's been absent for a fortnight now. All the teachers will say is that she's 'off sick'. I can't imagine her mum is thrilled about having to take so much time off – if that's what's happening. Mrs Wilson was on the phone to my mum within an hour of my visit to Amelia, insisting I keep away from her daughter.

Mum was furious I'd gone around there. 'Don't you realise how humiliating this is for me?' she said. 'Not to mention how awkward for poor Amelia. Stay away from their house, or I'll extend your being grounded to the whole of next year as well as the rest of this.'

Great.

I'm torn between fantasising about making up with Amelia and forcing a confession out of George – which falters as I remember Amelia's insistence he was at home when the SweetFreak death threat was programmed into my laptop. I feel worried for my best friend too, at how devastated she must be, and angry with Mum for not taking my side.

And, of course, I feel sorry for myself as well.

The Sound of Music is the only good thing in my life. I sit in my room most evenings, learning my lines and making sure I'm note perfect on all the songs.

It's now three weeks since Amelia was last at school – and just two days until my own birthday. As I head to an after-school music rehearsal on the third Thursday in October I remember when I counted forward last year, the idea that I would turn fifteen on a Saturday filled me with joy: I'd

have a party, I'd kiss a boy, I'd be surrounded by loads of brilliant friends.

I try not to think about how impossible any of those things now are as Mr Howard gets us to run through the scene in the nunnery where Maria arrives late. At least he's impressed that I know all my lines. Rose, as Mother Superior, is still reading from her script.

Mr Howard hurries off to fetch the backing track so we can work on a couple of songs. I brace myself for Rose or one of the other three girls in the rehearsal to start with their snidey 'Freak' comments but instead Rose speaks directly to me, with something approaching a smile on her face.

'I can't believe you've learned your part already,' she says, sitting down at the table on the stage.

'Yeah,' chorus Minnie and Molly, the Rose Clones who have parts as nuns. 'Amazing.' They sit down on either side of Rose.

I stare at them, feeling suspicious.

'I don't know how you remember it all,' adds Lauren, another girl from our form, as she drifts to a seat opposite. Her part involves just one line. 'I wouldn't be able to remember *half* of it, I just know I wouldn't.'

I gulp. Rose and the Rose Clones are one thing, but Lauren has always been nice to me, one of the few people who has carried on talking to me as normal. We've never been close friends or anything like that – she's a bit of a star athlete who even ran for the county last year, though I think she's given up the hardcore training this year – but Lauren's nice. If this is some kind of trick, it's hard to believe Lauren is involved.

'I ... I guess I haven't had much else to do except learn lines recently,' I say, then immediately regret it. The last thing I want is to look self-pitying in front of them. But Rose doesn't mock or sneer like I'm expecting. Instead she makes a sympathetic face.

'I know,' she says. 'It must be hard for you to have to deal with what's happened.'

My mouth actually falls open, I'm so shocked at how nice she's being.

A fraction later and the moment passes. Rose turns to the Clones and asks a question about homework while Lauren peers at her phone.

I gaze round at them. It's hard to put my finger on, but something has shifted. The atmosphere feels lighter, somehow, and there's a glimmer of an unfamiliar emotion in my chest. It takes a few seconds to work out what it is: hope.

10

After Rose being so unexpectedly nice at rehearsal I get home in a better mood than I've had for days. As I open the front door the sound of Mum wailing echoes out from the kitchen.

My heart sinks. What's happened now?

'It's just a bird,' I can hear Poppy saying. 'It's what cats do. Rumple can't help it.'

'I know, I know.' Mum sniffs. She often gets super-emotional when she's with Poppy, I've noticed, though she rarely cries in front of me and Jamie. 'It just feels like the last straw. I'm at the end of my tether with everything Carey's put us—'

I shut the front door with a bang, not wanting to hear Mum complain about me.

'Carey?' Mum calls. 'Is that you?'

I hurry into the kitchen. Ugh. No wonder Mum's freaking out. Rumple has outdone himself this time. His prey lies on the floor in front of the cat flap: a small pigeon in a pool of blood with a gaping wound at its neck. It's clearly dead, which is at least better than when Rumple brings birds in that are half alive and flap, helplessly, across the tiled floor.

Poppy and Mum are standing on either side of the kitchen table. Poppy is running her hands through her hair, while Mum grips the back of a chair, her knuckles white. Rumple chooses this moment to stalk into view. He pads over to Poppy and rubs his side around her legs.

'No,' she says. 'Bad Rumple.'

A tear leaks down Mum's face. I'm not sure whether she's crying for the bird or because of all the accumulated trauma of the past few weeks. A fresh wave of anger washes over me. It was one thing George wanting to get back at me, but hurting his sister and my mother is truly and unnecessarily cruel. Poor Mum.

Poppy bends down and absently strokes Rumple's back. Her face is white. She's always been a bit queasy around blood and that bird is pretty horrible to look at.

I force myself to do just that. It's only a dead bird, a greenish sheen down one, torn, wing and a stump in place of its left foot.

'We need to do something,' Mum says and I can hear the panic in her voice. 'Jamie's out with Blake but Blake's mum will be dropping him back any minute. That pigeon can't be in here when he gets home.'

91

'I'll deal with it,' I say.

Mum's jaw drops. So does Poppy's. Usually I run a mile from this sort of job, but today, after Rose's sympathy, I feel stronger. Like I want to help.

Aware Mum and Poppy are still gawping at me, I march over to the cupboard where we keep spare plastic bags. I select two sturdy orange carriers then use one to shield my hands as I tip the bird on to the other.

I carry the pigeon through the house and outside to the wheelie bin, like I've seen Mum do in the past. I stand there for a second, feeling that any life passing deserves a bit more ceremony than being dumped in a bit of orange plastic with *Sainsbury's* written on the front.

'Rest in peace,' I mutter. Just as I'm about to tip the bird into the bin there's a honk and I look up to see Jamie racing out of a shiny white sports car. His little friend Blake waves at him from the back seat while the woman behind the wheel calls out of the window. I hurriedly shove the bird in the bin so that Jamie won't see it.

'Hey, Carey!' Jamie rushes breathlessly past me, one hand raised in a wave to Blake.

'Bye, Jamie!' Blake's mum calls from the car. Mrs Lockwood is, of course, also Taylor's mother. Her blonde pixie cut shines brightly under the street lamps. I squint at her face, but it's too shadowy to see her expression. Has Mum told her what I'm accused of? No, I'm certain Mum won't have wanted to spread the news around. What about Taylor? Might he have said something? He probably knows about the SweetFreak messages, even though he goes to a different school from me and Amelia. Gossip like that tends to travel fast. That's if Amelia herself didn't get in touch. It's even possible that the police questioned him.

I remember the night before the death threat and how Amelia asked me, almost hopefully, if I thought Taylor might be behind the earlier messages. I'd told her then I didn't think so. And the possibility seems just as unlikely now. After all, what motive would Taylor have had for wanting to hurt her? His problem wasn't that he hated Amelia or wanted revenge for something, like George, but that he didn't really have any feelings about her at all.

Mrs Lockwood drives off and I walk back inside. I can hear Jamie gabbling away to Mum and Poppy in the kitchen. I follow him into the room, deep in thought.

'So, Mummy, listen, me and Blakey went to the woods and did stick fighting just like in the best bit in *Warriors of the Doom Wood!*'

I glance at the floor. Mum and Poppy must have cleaned up as, thankfully, there's no sign that the dead bird was there. Jamie's still prattling on. It's funny, Mum says that Jamie's more talkative than Poppy and I were at the same age. I reckon it's because he's had the three of us chatting to him all his life. I wonder sometimes if he'd be different if Dad had hung around. And how it's going to affect him growing up without a man in the house.

Jamie's probably the most affectionate person I know. Right now he has his arms around Mum's hips, giving her an exuberant hug and still chuntering on. Mum looks over him and meets my eyes.

Thank you, she mouths, meaning about dealing with the bird.

I nod. It's not 'I believe you're innocent', but it is something.

It's the nicest evening we've had in ages. For once Poppy and I don't disappear to our rooms and the four of us settle down in front of the TV in the living room so that Jamie can watch his silly cartoons while Poppy makes us all laugh by posting on NatterSnap about how I dealt with the pigeon and giving a running commentary on the horrified responses she's getting from her mates.

'I've made you my Hero of the Day, Carey,' she giggles. 'All my male friends think you're boss.'

'Nice somebody does,' I mutter.

Mum gives a loud sigh.

A few moments later both she and Jamie have fallen asleep. I creep out of the room, intending to go upstairs, but Poppy catches up with me before I make it to the bottom step.

'I told Mum again earlier that you didn't do it,' Poppy says, lowering her voice. 'I think she wants to believe that . . .'

'. . . but she doesn't.' I feel flat again. I turn away.

94

'Wait.' Poppy catches my arm. 'It's hard for her. All the evidence points to you, the police are insisting it's you and she's doubting herself, like maybe it's *her* fault, that she's been a bad parent.'

'Right.' I don't understand why Mum would think that. 'She should still trust me.'

Poppy wrinkles her nose. 'I think she would if maybe you hadn't lied to her about other things.'

I shrug.

'Anyway that's not what I wanted to tell you,' Poppy says. 'There's something I need to let you know . . .'

'Yeah, what's that?'

'George came up to me today,' she says with a sigh.

My eyes widen. 'What did he say? Did he let anything slip about SweetFreak, or—?'

'No, nothing like that.' Poppy makes a face. 'He just wanted to let me know he was going out with someone else, that he'd "moved on".'

'Nice of him to keep you up to date.'

'I know.' She sighs again. 'I reckon he was trying to get a reaction out of me but I didn't rise to it, instead I just asked how Amelia was.'

'Oh?' I lean closer, my heart suddenly thudding. 'How is she? Is she all right? Did you say how much I miss her?'

'I didn't get a chance,' Poppy explains. 'George just said that how Amelia was, was none of my business but – and

95

this is what I wanted to tell you – it turns out she'll be back at school tomorrow.'

My breath catches in my throat. 'Really?'

'Yes, word is she's still depressed but her mum couldn't take any more time off work and they're worried about her missing any more school so . . .'

'OK,' I say, butterflies suddenly zooming around my stomach. 'Thanks.'

I head up the stairs, a massive smile on my face. I'm scared to see Amelia again, but I'm also hopeful. Maybe she'll be prepared to talk to me, to give me another chance.

To be friends again.

The next morning I set off early for school and walk through the cool autumn air with a real spring in my step. All I can think about is how great it will be to see Amelia again, how today could be the start of everything getting better. Maybe I'll even be able to persuade her to celebrate my birthday with me tomorrow night. I get to school stupidly early so I hang around behind the caretaker's hut near the entrance, waiting for Amelia to arrive.

She walks in on her own, just five minutes before registration is due to start. She's left it to the last moment, probably so that she doesn't have to answer lots of questions. I get it, Amelia, I think to myself. I know what it's like to want to avoid attention.

She's walking fast, head down, so she doesn't see me as she passes. Part of me wants to call after her, but a group of boys from Poppy's year are just behind her and I don't want to draw attention to us. Amelia goes inside. I hurry after her, but inside the entrance hall there's a group of year sevens, chattering at the tops of their voices and clearly about to head off on a trip somewhere. If I was taller I'd be able to see over their heads, but shortie that I am, it's impossible. I push through the group, but by the time I emerge on the other side there's no sign of Amelia.

My throat tightens. If she's gone straight to our form room then I'm going to have to see her for the first time in front of the rest of our class, which was *not* how I saw our reconciliation happening.

Hopefully she'll have chosen to dump her bag in the locker room first. I speed up. There are too many teachers about to run – the last thing I need is to get hauled over and given a time-wasting talking to for 'moving in a reckless rush' as Mrs Marchington likes to refer to it.

There're only two minutes left until registration when I turn the corridor that contains the locker room. Amelia is standing outside it, searching her bag for something. My heart thuds as I approach.

I open my mouth, just metres away, to call out to her. But before I can speak Amelia goes inside the locker room. I glance around me. The long corridor is almost empty now, everyone on their way to class. Amelia will have to hurry if she's going to make registration. Or perhaps she's been given a reprieve for today. I haven't of course. I'll be marked late if I'm not there, which is crazy considering how early I got to school and frankly the last thing I need.

It doesn't matter. Making up with Amelia is more important.

I take a deep breath and open the door. Amelia is standing beside her locker, her back to me, still fumbling in her bag. Rose Clones Minnie and Molly are in the room too. Their backs are turned and they're whispering to each other, presumably about Amelia, who is studiously ignoring them.

My heart goes out to her. I know what it feels like to have people gossiping and pointing behind their hands at you. The girls see me and turn away, busying themselves with their own lockers.

'Amelia?' My voice cracks as I say her name.

She spins around, blinking with surprise. 'Carey.' For a second I get a glimpse of the old Amelia, eyes full of fun and friendship. And then the wary mask comes down again.

I can't bear it. 'Hey.' Tears spring to my eyes.

Amelia offers me a weak smile. She tilts her head to one side, her fingers brushing over the heart on the end of her necklace.

'Hi.' It's just one word, but it leaves me feeling the happiest I've been in weeks.

Amelia turns back to her locker. It's unlocked – it was

98

cleared out the day after the death threat and has been empty and unused the whole time she's been away from school, a constant reminder every time I come in here of how much I've lost in losing our friendship.

But now, maybe, this is a first step back.

And then Amelia opens her locker and a second later her hands fly to her mouth and her bag drops to the floor.

'Aaagh!' She lets out an ear-splitting scream.

'What?' I run over but Minnie and Molly are there before me, blocking my view. Molly lets out a high-pitched shriek even louder than Amelia's.

'Oh, that's disgusting!' Minnie gasps.

'Aaagh! Aaagh!' Amelia is still screaming.

'What is it?' My pulse drums against my temples as Amelia swings round, a fresh fury in her eyes.

'How could you?' she yells.

I stare at her blankly. She swoops down, snatches up her bag and hares out of the locker room.

The other two girls are both talking at once. I don't hear a word they say. Because I'm now looking into Amelia's locker. And what I see, lying on top of the orange plastic bag I used to dispose of it yesterday, is the same bloodied, torn-winged, single-footed pigeon that Rumple brought in and that I put in our wheelie bin.

11

I stare, mystified, at the dead bird. Its scent drifts towards me: sweet and yet sour too. How on earth did it get from the wheelie bin outside my house to inside Amelia's locker? How did anyone even know it was there?

My first thought is Poppy, but I'd have seen her if she'd arrived at school while I was waiting outside so there's no way she could have got to the locker room before me. Anyway, I don't believe Poppy is SweetFreak any more. She wouldn't frame me like this; she's spent the past month defending me to anyone who'll listen.

The bell for registration sounds. As its sharp-edged note fades away I realise Minnie and Molly have stopped talking. The room is silent. I tear myself away from the pigeon and look around. I'm alone. Amelia and the others have gone, probably to find a teacher.

How could you?

Amelia's words echo around my head. She clearly thinks *I* put the bird here.

But I didn't. I didn't. My own panic rises. If anyone discovers this pigeon came from the bin outside my house . . .

I force myself to focus. There's no reason for anyone to make that connection. Amelia's made an assumption, but there's nothing to prove she's right. Only me, Mum and Poppy know about the bird. Well, whoever put it here does too but I can't think about that right now.

Right now I need to do something to protect myself.

For the second time in less than twenty-four hours I brace myself to pick up the wretched bird. The orange plastic of the bag sticks to my hot, clammy palms as I grab the edges and lift the bird. Another whiff of its decaying scent fills my nostrils. For a second I think I might puke, then I grit my teeth. There's a fire door just along the corridor with a bin outside. If I put the pigeon there, it will look like I'm trying to protect Amelia from having to see it again, won't it? The act of a good friend.

I need to hurry. The bell is the signal for registration. I should be in my form room right now. I take a step towards the locker room door, the bird and the bag balanced in my hands. As I reach the door it opens. Mrs Marchington sweeps in, Amelia in her wake. The teacher takes in the scene, her gaze darting from me to the bird held out in front of me, like an offering. She draws in her breath sharply.

101

'Come with me, Carey,' she barks.

I look down at the bird.

'And bring that with you.' Her voice is like ice.

Heart quailing, I follow Mrs Marchington along the empty corridor. Her footsteps tap briskly on the tiles. I glance at Amelia. She's hunched over, keeping her head down. Her little heart necklace catches the light, a silver twinkle against the grey of her jumper. She looks like she's put on weight since she stopped coming to school. I hadn't noticed when I went to her house, but our uniform shows every pound.

'Are you OK?' I whisper.

Amelia shrinks away from me as if I've punched her or am threatening to.

'I didn't do this,' I insist, my voice rising slightly.

Mrs Marchington glances over her shoulder. 'Silence,' she snaps.

A minute later we arrive outside the head's office. Mrs Marchington takes the dead bird from me and orders me to sit out here and wait, then she ushers Amelia into the room.

I sit, my stomach in knots, wondering what they're saying. I don't have to wonder for long. After just a few minutes Mrs Marchington and Amelia reappear. The teacher has her arm around Amelia's shoulders. It's obvious Amelia has been crying.

I stand up, feeling awkward. Part of me wants to comfort my friend. But I also need to protest my innocence.

'I didn't put the bird in your lock—'

'Sit down and wait.' Mrs Marchington's tone is positively vicious. I slump back into my chair and clench my fists. A moment later the bell goes for first lesson. I shift in my seat, instinct telling me to get up and go. But I stay put, as instructed, while around the corner the sounds of loud voices and stomping feet career along the corridor.

Two minutes later another bell goes and silence falls as first lessons commence. I wait. And I wait. And I wait. I'm starting to think the head has forgotten all about me, when Mum appears, charging along the corridor, her face white and tight with worry.

'What is this now, Carey?' she hisses.

I open my mouth to explain but at that moment the head opens his door and asks us to come in.

The dead pigeon has been placed on a small table to the side of the room, but it dominates the surrounding space. I have only been in this office once before, during the open day over three years ago, but I remember its long window and stacked bookshelves and smell of paper. I don't want to look at the bird or the head or Mum, so I stare down at the carpet. This is the only room in the school I've ever seen with a carpet. It's blue, with red flecks.

'Carey!'

My head jerks up as I realise Mr Emmett is speaking to me. The headteacher is a small man, only a few centimetres taller than Mum, with a thin, shiny nose. He's wearing a tightly knotted tie that matches his suit – and a deep frown.

'What do you know about this bird, Carey?' he asks, his tone all pompous and self-important.

An image of me laughing about the ridiculousness of this scene with Amelia flashes in front of my mind's eye. This would be funny if it wasn't so horrible. I glance at Mum. Her hands are over her mouth. She's staring at the dead pigeon, horror as well as recognition in her eyes.

I say nothing.

'Carey?' Mr Emmett repeats. He looks at Mum.

'Rumple ... our cat ...' She shakes her head and looks at me. 'I can't believe you'd ...'

'Carey?' Mr Emmett says a third time. 'The bird?'

I gulp. There's no point lying about it now. Mum has already given the game away. My best bet is to tell the truth and hope that someone believes me.

'I think someone must have taken it from our bin and put it in Amelia's locker,' I stammer. I'm aware of how unlikely this sounds as I say it.

Mum lets out a low moan. Mr Emmett tilts his head to one side.

'I wonder if you appreciate the impact of this on Amelia?' he asks. 'Devastated and terrified by the death threat she received, she bravely returns to school, only to find a continuation of the horrific bullying within just a few minutes of setting foot inside the building.'

'I didn't do it,' I mutter, feeling sullen. I've just given him and Mum the only possible explanation I can think of and they've totally ignored it.

Mr Emmett sighs. 'The very worst part of this is your refusal to accept any responsibility for your actions.'

'She's been seeing a therapist,' Mum blurts out. I'm not sure why, maybe she's trying to show the head that she's been attempting to deal with me and my supposedly psychotic ways.

Whatever, it's a fairly clear admission that I'm guilty in Mum's eyes.

'Well that doesn't seem to have done much good,' Mr Emmett says curtly. 'I'm afraid under the circumstances, considering our zero tolerance policy on bullying and the previous issues we've had with Carey, I really have no choice but to call the police.'

'Oh, no.' Mum lets out a strangled sob.

'Amelia's mother wants them involved too. My secretary has rung her and she's on her way to pick Amelia up.'

She'll love that, I think to myself. Just back to work and called away again.

'But ... but are the police absolutely necessary?' Mum pleads.

I stand beside her, ignored by both of them, wondering if

Mum is resisting another interview with the cops because she wants to protect me or, as I suspect, because it will make her feel like a bad parent, like Poppy said last night.

'Yes,' Mr Emmett says firmly. 'Apart from anything else the incident has happened on school property.' He pauses, a frown puckering his forehead. 'This is a clear violation of the second chance we gave Carey.'

'I didn't do anything.' I say it louder this time.

Mr Emmett and Mum look at me. It's obvious neither of them believe me.

'I think we also need to impose harsher sanctions,' Mr Emmett goes on. 'A fixed-term exclusion at least, maybe—'

'No,' Mum cries. Her voice cracks.

I look at the carpet again, now embarrassed she's getting all emotional on top of everything else. Mr Emmett clears his throat.

'I won't make any final decisions until the police have been informed,' he says. 'For today, however, I think it's best that you take Carey home.'

That's it. We're dismissed. Mum is trying not to cry as she stumbles out of the room. I follow her along the corridor towards reception and the exit. The bell sounds for the end of first lesson. I walk faster. The last thing I want is to be spotted getting chucked out of school. A couple of year eights fly past us, deep in conversation. We reach the reception desk as the sound of voices and footsteps rises up

all around us. Mum wipes her face and reaches for the visitor book on the reception desk in order to sign us out.

'Come on,' I urge. 'Let's go.'

'Stop it,' she snaps. 'Not one word.'

I hurry over to the main entrance. My hand is on the door, waiting for Mum to finish, as Poppy flies up. I can see from her confused and horrified expression that news of the pigeon has already spread to the sixth form.

She's panting for breath, she must have run all the way here from her classroom. 'What the hell? It's all over the school . . . Rumple's dead bird? *Seriously?*'

I nod. 'It's SweetFreak.'

'But how?' Poppy frowns. 'How would anyone even know the stupid bird was in our bin?'

My eyes widen as I suddenly realise what must have happened. '*You* told them,' I say, the whole thing now making sense. 'You told everyone on NatterSnap last night, remember? You made me your *Hero of the Day*, you posted about me dealing with the bird and—'

'. . . and I even said that you put it in our wheelie bin.' Poppy claps her hand over her mouth, lowering her voice. 'I'm so sorry, Carey.' She glances at Mum, who is standing awkwardly, clearly desperate to get away, as the receptionist talks to her. '*Jeez*, that means . . .'

'Oh, Poppy!' Mum turns, spots my sister and rushes over. She falls into Poppy's arms. Poppy's taller than Mum now.

She looks over Mum's head and meets my gaze. *Stay strong*, she mouths.

It strikes me again that Mum leans on Poppy a lot, far more than she does on me.

Thanks, I mouth back. A tiny thread of hope snakes through me. The fact that Poppy posted about me getting rid of the dead pigeon surely means George *has* to be SweetFreak. He would definitely have seen her posts – the two of them are in the same year, for goodness sake – and once he knew the bird was in our bin, he could easily have come to our house to steal it.

Maybe now I can persuade the police to investigate him.

Mum draws away from Poppy and wipes her eyes. The reception area is now full of people. Most of them are staring at us.

'Are you guys OK?' Poppy asks anxiously.

'We'll be fine,' Mum says in a small voice.

I squeeze Poppy's arm. My sister could easily have kept her head down and avoided meeting us here. Instead, she's on show along with me and Mum, tainted by association. I want to tell her how much her support means to me but she's already talking again.

'Carey didn't do this, Mum,' Poppy says.

Mum presses her lips together. Clearly she doesn't believe Poppy any more than she does me.

'You should get back to class.' She gives Poppy a kiss,

then turns to me. 'Come on.' She tugs my arm and starts walking away.

I wave at Poppy then turn and follow Mum out to the car park.

12

Mum and I don't speak on the way home. Mum sends me to my room as soon as we arrive, which suits me fine. My phone and laptop are still locked away somewhere, but Mum has let me use an ancient mobile of hers. It's supposed to be just for emergencies. And, frankly, it's not good for much else.

I send Amelia a couple of texts, but they bounce back, undelivered.

Angry and upset in equal measure, I pace around a bit, then lie on my bed with the first *Hunger Games* book. I've read it before, many times. It's an attempt at a comfort read, something to take my mind off what's happening. It doesn't work. Thoughts of the bird and Amelia's accusing face and Mum in tears keep flashing through my head.

About an hour into my read I sneak downstairs and check out social media by logging in on Mum's tablet.

There's plenty of chat about my latest alleged crime, most

of which is wildly inaccurate and suggests I killed the bird myself, in front of Amelia.

Shaking my head I turn to my private messages on NatterSnap. There's only one. It's from Rose.

Poor you. So sorry for you. If you want to talk, call me.

Her mobile number is underneath. I stare at the words, rereading them, bewildered. It sounds as if Rose knows all about the dead bird – well of course, Minnie and Molly were there and will have filled her in. I can just imagine their breathless tones and wide eyes as they described the scene in the locker room.

What really matters is that she seems to think I'm innocent. At least I think that's what her message means. My fingers tremble as I put her number into my mobile and then log off NatterSnap, closing the app so that Mum won't know what I've been up to.

I sneak back up the stairs and call Rose.

She picks up after just one ring. 'Hello?'

'Rose?' I say, my voice swelling with emotion. 'It's Carey.'

'Oh, Carey. I'm so glad you saw my message. You poor thing.' She sounds so sympathetic I almost start crying.

'I didn't do it. I didn't put that stupid bird in Amelia's locker.'

'Of course you didn't,' Rose says warmly. 'I know you wouldn't do anything like that.'

111

I hesitate. 'I didn't send the death threat or the other messages from SweetFreak either.' I hold my breath, desperate for Rose to believe me.

'I know,' Rose says. 'I know I've given you a hard time, but when I saw you in rehearsal the other day ... well, it was obvious how unhappy you were. There was no way you'd done what everyone thinks. And definitely no way you'd make things worse for yourself by putting something horrible in Amelia's locker.'

Relief floods through me. It's so good to have someone else on my side.

Even if it is Rose.

'That's right, I didn't, I didn't. And the worst thing is Amelia hates me and she's so unhappy, I can't bear it.' A sob rises in my chest, my voice cracking. 'I have to make her see I'm innocent. Make *everyone* see it.'

There's a pause on the other end of the line.

'Rose?'

'Do you have any idea who might be behind SweetFreak?' she asks.

I hesitate. It feels risky to tell her about my suspicions. But what do I have to lose? Right now things can't get worse, and Rose seems to be genuinely on my side now.

'I think it might be ... Amelia's brother, George,' I stammer. 'He hates us both.'

'You really think he'd go that far?' There's a shocked

edge to Rose's voice. 'Do you really think he'd do that to his own sister?'

I hurry on, determined to convince her.

'I know it's a terrible thing to accuse someone of and obviously I don't know for sure, but George has a reason to be angry with me and Amelia ...' I don't want to start trashing Poppy by explaining about her cheating on George, so I trail off. 'It's complicated, but there are reasons why he might want to hurt us and break up our friendship.'

'Wow!' Rose gasps. 'What a nightmare!'

'I know.'

Another pause.

'So what can I do to help, Carey?' Rose asks.

Is she serious? 'You mean help me find proof against George?'

'Sure,' Rose says. 'We could meet up tomorrow? Make a plan?'

'Thanks,' I say. 'That means a lot.'

'It's your birthday this weekend, isn't it?' Rose goes on.

'Yeah, it's tomorrow actually.' I frown. 'How did you—?'

'I remember from last year, it was the first good party of the term.' She laughs. 'We went for pizza, didn't we?'

'That's right,'

'So what are you doing this year?' Rose asks.

I shrug. 'I wasn't going to do anything, actually. I mean

before the whole SweetFreak thing blew up I was going to go to Nando's but—'

'Well let's meet there then,' Rose interrupts, her voice full of decision. 'Tomorrow night at seven, OK?'

'Yes,' I say, 'I'd love that. Oh, thank you, Rose, thank you.' As I put down the phone, a smile creeps across my face.

Maybe with Rose's help I can finally expose George, prove my innocence and win back Amelia's friendship.

The police turn up exactly when they say they will – on the dot of three p.m.. The same two officers as before.

I hurry downstairs, buoyed up by my conversation with Rose and eager to explain that Poppy's NatterSnap post means that loads of people knew the dead bird was in our bin. I explain my suspicions about George, but DC Kapoor dismisses my theory instantly.

'George Wilson was on an overnight Geography field trip to the South Downs yesterday, there's no way he could have been rummaging through your bin in the small hours.'

'Oh.' I frown. Fresh thoughts fire in my brain. 'Then maybe he got someone else to do it. In fact that would make sense, he'd *want* someone else to do it, in case he was recognised. He probably asked a friend.'

DS Carter gives a weary shake of his head. He glances at Mum and raises his eyebrows. 'As you know, Mrs Logan,' he says solemnly, 'last time we spoke we emphasised that we support local schools' zero tolerance approach on bullying with our early intervention initiative. We didn't feel then there was enough evidence against Carey to start a prosecution.' He pauses. 'After what happened this morning we're now far more worried that Carey does represent a credible threat to Amelia.'

'I'm *not* a threat. No way,' I say, incensed.

'In the light of Carey's persistent refusal to admit to her actions, we support her headteacher's decision to impose a one-week exclusion from school and we also recommend that you increase the subsidised counselling sessions Carey has been having to twice a week.'

'Oh.' Mum looks as if he's slapped her.

'We've contacted CAMHS, that's Child Mental Health Services,' DS Carter goes on. 'They're here to support you both and hopefully help Carey take responsibility for—.'

'I'm right here,' I say loudly. 'And I didn't do this.'

Mum nods. 'I'll do everything you suggest.' She looks at me and draws herself up. 'Carey is already grounded all the way through the rest of term right up until the new year and has no access to a smartphone or her old laptop. Basically she's not allowed to do anything or go anywhere outside the house without my express permission.'

'But I haven't *done* anything.' Frustration wells inside me. This is so unfair. So unjust.

Mum and the two officers exchange weary, irritated glances.

'If you would just stop lying, Carey,' DC Kapoor says tartly.

'I'm not lying.' My voice rises. 'I'm not a liar.'

Mum gazes at me, an expression of unbearable sorrow on her face. 'I'm afraid that's not true, is it?' she says softly. 'There was that party a few months ago that you lied about – and that wasn't an isolated incident, then you've repeatedly gone creeping out of your room at night, even after you promised you wouldn't.'

She's right of course. As was Poppy when she said Mum might find it easier to believe me if I hadn't lied before.

But those things were completely different. Why can't she see that? I sit back, feeling hurt and humiliated in front of the police They try, all three of them, to get me to talk some more but I'm done talking. I'm done protesting my innocence.

There's no point any more. They've all decided I'm guilty. I might as well be.

The rest of Friday passes slowly. I get a couple of sweet texts from Rose to say she's thinking of me and looking forward to meeting up tomorrow. The relief these messages give me is pathetically huge. A month ago I wouldn't have cared what Rose thought of me. It even crosses my mind to attempt to wrestle my curls into an approximation of her trademark long bob, but that really is a step too far, both for me and my unruly hair.

Poppy charges up the stairs to find me as soon as she gets

home. She is shocked that the police refused to credit the suggestion that George might have read about me putting the pigeon in the bin and asked a friend to steal it for him.

'They're convinced I'm guilty,' I say glumly. 'Nothing I say ever changes their minds.'

Poppy sighs. 'It's like that scientific thing where if you go into your research expecting a particular outcome, then that's the outcome you tend to get.' She sighs. 'Though it's still hard to imagine George being so mean, especially after all this time. You'd think he'd have moved on.' She paces up and down my room, lost in thought. She's grown taller in the past year and her face is longer, a perfect oval. She's always been pretty but now it's in a grown-up way, like she's comfortable in her own skin, at one with all aspects of her appearance, from her long slim legs to her almond-shaped eyes and her carefully messy blonde hair.

The way we've grown close since she accepted I wasn't SweetFreak isn't anything like the way Amelia and I were friends. That was based on sharp bursts of emotions where one minute we'd be in hysterical laughter over something and the next Amelia would be crying her eyes out looking to me for support and comfort. My friendship with my sister is far steadier, involving fewer displays of strong feeling, but for all that it's solid, based more on grit than glitz.

And apart from the first couple of days Poppy's faith in me hasn't wavered. I still don't really understand why she's

117

so convinced of my innocence, when everyone else thinks I'm guilty. For a split second I wonder again if maybe she's responsible herself and simply sticking up for me out of guilt. Then I push the thought away. This is the worst thing about being blamed for something I didn't do: no one trusts me and I trust no one.

'I'm excluded from school for the whole of next week,' I say and the words land flat in the room, as bleak as my mood.

'That sucks,' Poppy says.

She's right, it does.

But at least she's on my side. And tomorrow – my birthday – I'll meet with Rose and we can begin to plan a proper fight back against all the lies.

13

The next day is officially my worst birthday morning ever. For a start I'm plagued with memories of how much fun I had last year, when Amelia and I spent five hours at the mall, spending my birthday money on clothes. We bought matching tops and wore them when we went out that night.

Today is very different. Not only do I receive no money, but when Mum wishes me a 'happy birthday' her smile doesn't reach her eyes. I wasn't really expecting a gift, but it still hurts as she explains that my present will be the future return of my laptop and phone.

'You'll get them back once you've grown up enough to take responsibility for your actions,' she says miserably. 'And believe me, deciding not to celebrate your birthday this year is every bit as painful for me as it is for you.'

Yeah, right.

Jamie is excited at least. He proudly presents me with a

119

drawing of me and him acting out parts from *Warriors of the Doom Wood*. I get a card with cash inside from Mum's parents who she clearly hasn't told about my disgrace. Mum takes the money and pockets it without a word.

'I'll bank this for you for the time being.'

Awesome.

Poppy gives me a pretty necklace with pink beads. I give her a hug and put it on straightaway.

Nobody makes a cake.

The day slips past. I play with Jamie until I get bored, then I retreat into my room and focus on my lines for *The Sound of Music*. I'm almost word perfect in every scene now. I reckon I'll only miss two rehearsals over the coming week while I'm suspended from school. It's not a big deal. There are several scenes I'm not in that Mr Howard can work on while I'm away. He knows I'm well ahead on my part so I'm not worried about it.

Despite her decision not to celebrate my birthday, I overhear Mum telling Poppy that maybe she should forego her planned Happy Hour drinks on the high street. A few of her work colleagues are meeting up for someone's fortieth and Mum has flip-flopped over whether or not to go all week. Thankfully Poppy – who knows about my meet-up with Rose – urges her to go ahead and see her friends, saying that's she's going to microwave some popcorn and watch a movie with me.

Mum compromises by saying she'll go for a few hours. She comes into the living room to tell me and Jamie she'll be

back by ten and that Jamie better be asleep. She makes her eyes wide when she says this, which for some reason always makes him giggle.

As soon as Mum leaves I put on some lipgloss and my fave jeans and head out myself. It's not quite six thirty so I've got plenty of time before I meet Rose but I'm nervous so I hurry. I skirt around the park and take the road to the west part of town where the Nando's is situated.

I'm two streets away when I think I see Mum, across the street in a group of women. It's actually someone with a similar hair style, wearing the same Zara coat. I realise this later, but at the time I'm thrown into a panic and race in the opposite direction as fast as I can. I take a left turn, then two more, assuming this will bring me out back on the high street. But it doesn't. I wander around, cursing my lack of Google Maps and my poor sense of direction, until it gets to six forty-five and I have to acknowledge that I'm lost.

I swear under my breath, trying to take stock. I'm in a section of town I hardly ever come to: just to the north of the main drag. No one I know lives here. It's a weird mix of houses: a lot of run-down properties used as squats and a few streets with delis and those plantation blinds at the window, part of the Lower Cornmouth gentrification plans, according to Mum.

I turn a corner and almost trip over something on the pavement.

I yelp, stumbling. A strong arm yanks me upright. I pull

121

away and spin around. There's a canvas rucksack at my feet.

'Sorry, that's mine. Sorry.'

I look up. A boy stands in front of me, about my age. He's vaguely familiar, with a shaggy shock of thick dark hair and piercing blue eyes. He's dressed in an odd combination of clothes – a worn leather jacket that looks too big for him, over faded jeans and mismatching trainers.

It's the trainers – one grey Adidas, one yellow with a green Nike swoosh – that prompt my memory: this is the boy I saw the night I crept out to meet Amelia. He was with a girl wearing DMs with rainbow laces. I'm on my guard instantly, instinct telling me he's homeless and a million warnings from home and school making me afraid he's about to try and mug me. Or at least ask for money.

The boy must see my anxiety on my face.

'I don't want anything,' he says, smiling. 'Are you OK? You were storming round that corner like a bull.'

'A bull?'

He laughs. 'Sorry, that's not very flattering, is it? I mean you steamed round like a sleek missile, intent on your target.'

'I'm not sure being a WMD is any better than a bull,' I say, relaxing a little. The boy seems genuine enough. There's real kindness in those blue eyes and when he smiles they light up. He's not obviously good-looking – his face is too long and his lips on the thin side – but there's something intriguing about him.

122

'Actually, I'm lost,' I admit. 'I need to find my way back to the high street.'

'Yeah, there's loads of cul-de-sacs and dead ends round here,' he says knowledgably. 'So how long are you visiting Cornmouth?'

I laugh. 'Would you believe I've lived here all my life?'

The boy laughs too. It's a rich, warm sound. For a fleeting second I wonder if he really does live on the streets like I assumed when I first saw him and why he's wearing odd trainers. Then I remember Rose will be arriving any minute at Nando's. I need to hurry.

'So which way is it?' I ask.

The boy gives me directions and I thank him then hurry on my way. Turns out I'm only a couple of minutes away from Nando's, arriving at five to seven. The restaurant isn't busy right now, though I know it'll be heaving later. I explain I'm meeting a friend and the waiter puts me at a little table by the window.

I check my phone as I wait. I'm starting to feel nervous again. I try to reassure myself: Rose was so sweet yesterday, she believes in me, she's going to help me.

From tonight, everything is going to start getting better.

I check my make-up and adjust my top. It's now quarter past seven. The place is half full now and the waiter is eyeing me suspiciously. Where is she? I check my useless text-and-calls-only phone again. Rose and I definitely agreed on seven. It gets to twenty past and another group of teens

I don't know saunters in. Only three empty tables are left, none of them as nice as mine by the window. The waiter is openly throwing me dirty looks.

I send Rose a text:

I'm here. Are u on ur way?

No reply.

The waiter, who has managed with difficulty to seat a large group just next to me, comes over just before half past seven. 'I'm afraid I can't hold your table much longer,' he says. 'When is your friend going to get here?'

'Just a few more minutes,' I say.

'OK.' He looks doubtful, but leaves me in peace.

I text Rose again. Then I call her. Nothing.

And then a text finally arrives. The sender has withheld their number, but it's undoubtedly from Rose:

Hey SweetFreak. Check your NatterSnap

I stare numbly at the screen. She's not coming. She was never coming. I've been set up.

I was set up from the start. It's so obvious now I think about it: Rose was only been pretending to be friendly yesterday in order to humiliate me tonight, here in the restaurant.

I stumble out the restaurant door, too numb even to feel

the shock and shame of this latest slap in the face. I trudge home, too low to cry.

As soon as I get through the door I ask to borrow Poppy's phone to check NatterSnap. There's a photo of me from Nando's sitting alone at my table. It's been posted on the main feed by someone – presumably Rose – calling themselves CareyLFreako – which is *not* my NatterSnap handle. The caption underneath reads:

Big Saturday night with da gang. #popular #freak

All I want to do is get back and crawl into bed and stay there.

Which is what I do for most of the weekend. Poppy tries to talk to me, but what is there to say? Someone – most likely George – has set out to ruin my life. And there's nothing I can do about it. I cry every now and then, but mostly I just feel a dull, dead sense of despair. I no longer wonder or even care if George is SweetFreak. What does it matter? Even if he is, he's covered his tracks so well I'll never be able to prove it.

My week of being excluded from school begins and I'm glad I don't have to go in and face Rose and everyone. Mum knows she can't police my being grounded during the day, though she's threatened to make random calls on the house phone to check up on me. I don't really care if I stay put, to be honest. Where am I going to hang out if not at home? It's getting too cold for the park or the wood and I don't have any money.

*

125

I spend Monday trying and failing to lose myself in *The Hunger Games*, again. I watch TV and try a couple of movies but I can't concentrate. I think about how much I miss being online. It's the weirdest thing not being connected any more but of course I don't have any way of accessing my own devices and when Mum went to work this morning she locked all the other electrical items in the house away.

On Tuesday I have a morning session with Sonia the patronising therapist which is the worst yet, ending with her suggesting that my refusal to open up to her is a sign that I'm tussling with myself over being honest and that underneath she knows I want to confess my guilt.

That afternoon I run through all my lines from *The Sound of Music*. At least I know the part, though how I'm ever going to face everyone else in the play again, especially Rose, I've got no idea. And then Poppy arrives home from school with a letter for Mum about me. We steam it open, knowing Mum won't be back for another hour and that we can reseal it before she gets in.

The letter is from the head. It's the formal acknowledgement of my week-long exclusion.

We don't want to give up on Carey and we don't want her to give up on herself. Obviously the main condition of her returning to school is that there should be no further instances of bullying or

threats against any pupil or member of staff. And
of course we have already discussed increasing
Carey's counselling sessions to twice a week. It is
also important to stress that this is Carey's final
chance. Another incident and she will be permanently
excluded from school.

'Jeez,' Poppy breathes.

'I know,' I say with feeling.

You'd think that would be the worst bit – the threat of expulsion over things I haven't even done. But it isn't. The worst part of the letter comes right at the end, after all the warnings and heavy stuff.

I have discussed the situation with Mr Howard and
we both agree, very reluctantly on Mr Howard's part,
that it is no longer appropriate for Carey to take
the lead in the school's production of The Sound of
Music. *I'm sure you will understand our view that*
there should be no reward for bad behaviour and
it is inevitable that a role such as 'Maria' confers
celebrity status within the school. I also believe that
though Mr Howard has apparently been impressed
with Carey's application to her part, we are
concerned about putting her in the position of role
model to the younger years.

127

'In other words their parents have complained,' Poppy says, wrinkling her nose. 'I'm so sorry, Carey.'

I nod, tears pricking at my eyes. I'm too choked to speak. There's a dull weight in my guts. The bitter taste of despair in my mouth. Being Maria in *The Sound of Music* has been about the only thing keeping me going for the past few months.

'At least things can't get any worse,' Poppy says with a sigh.

But it soon turns out she is wrong.

FREAK

14

My week-long exclusion from school ends, half term comes and goes and the endless days of November turn into the interminable weeks of December. I have absolutely no social life so, other than when I'm dragged off for therapy sessions with annoying Sonia, I stay home, bored and resentful. After much begging on my part Poppy lets me borrow her phone so I can at least connect with the outside world. I'm excited to be able to get into my social media accounts, then crushed to discover that I'm still ignored – or abused – on everything. Any posts I make are met either with absolute silence or a torrent of nastiness in which the nicest word anyone has to say about me is: *Freak*.

I try again a few days later, hoping the bitchy gossip will have died down.

It hasn't. Even the boys from school who didn't ignore me after the SweetFreak death threat now clearly think I'm a psycho bunny boiler, thanks to that stupid pigeon in Amelia's locker. How do I know? There's one of those horrible chats between the boys on NatterSnap where they rate the hottest girls in our year. Mostly the posts are straightforward: a boy puts forward his choice of girl and the others either agree or not. I have an alert on my name, so I see when Aaron Price – a dweeby boy I barely know in one of the other classes – says he thinks I'm hot. And I see when, immediately afterwards, a whole bunch of other boys gleefully warn him to stay away from me, telling him and the entire world that I'm deranged, that if he doesn't watch out I'm liable to kill any pets he might have ... or start stalking him ... or chop off bits of his body ...

It's all ridiculous and I don't believe any of them seriously think I'd do any of these things. They're not really thinking about me at all, it's just a game to them, something to tease each other about. And they don't think about how I'm a real person, whose feelings might be hurt. Truth is, though, that I'm kind of past hurt feelings. Most of the time I'm just numb, existing in a strange limbo with my house and family – and perhaps the woods where I sometimes take Jamie to play *Warriors* – my entire world.

Mum softens a little as Christmas approaches. We never have lavish Christmases, there's not enough money for that, and Poppy and I long ago accepted that the focus of the day should be on our little brother, not ourselves. Jamie is, as ever, full of wonderment and delight at his presents: a tablet of his own, bought secondhand on eBay, from Mum and a new plastic sword set and *Warriors of the Doom Wood* dressing-up outfit from me and Poppy.

Poppy gets a secondhand tablet too and some perfume and cash. Mum gives me clothes, which Poppy has chosen. They're nice, though I'd far rather have got a proper phone or a new laptop – or even my old ones back. But Mum is carrying through on her pledge to deny me access to decent technology. I still have to make do with her ancient mobile that just makes calls and texts. At least I'm no longer grounded once January starts.

I go out on New Year's Day eager to take advantage of my regained freedom. It's the first time I've been anywhere other than school or Sonia's house for ages but I quickly realise I have absolutely nowhere to go. The places in town I used to hang out with my friends are just boring dumps with no one to liven them up. I miss Amelia more than I would ever have imagined: the way we could make a joke out of anything, the way we usually agreed on stuff and the way we'd talk and talk, processing every aspect of our lives and relationships.

I stroll around for a bit, bitter with loneliness, then return home in a grumpy mood.

I'm dreading the start of term, but in fact when school resumes a few days later, it isn't as bad as before Christmas. Perhaps I'm just used to being alone now, but I no longer feel picked on or pointed at.

It's more like I've become invisible, one of those girls nobody takes any notice of, who slinks around in the background of everything. People talk to me, but only superficially. Rose drops a few asides now and then about how awful I am, not just to hurt Amelia, who is still away from school, but also to attempt to blame George for what happened. But most people just act like I'm not there at all, leaving me hovering around the edges of school existence. If anything, what I sense off them is a slightly haughty indifference. They're all better than me, I can see them thinking: I'm the girl who gave her best friend a breakdown.

News filters through that Amelia is being homeschooled by a series of expensive tutors. It seems that she and Rose have become good friends and, along with the Rose Clones, have formed a little social group that I am entirely excluded from. Whenever I'm close enough to hear her, Rose takes great delight in talking about how she and Amelia hang out together.

It hurts. A lot.

Occasionally someone forgets my lowly status and asks if I'm going to some activity or other out of school. But mostly I'm left to my own devices, too self-conscious now to speak up much in lessons and in the habit of taking my sandwiches outside where I can huddle under the eaves at the very back of the school and spend my lunch breaks alone.

Perhaps the single worst thing is watching as rehearsals

134

for *The Sound of Music* become more frequent. Mr Howard pins notices every week, saying who is required for each of the three weekly sessions. By the last week in January, I'm sure most people have forgotten I was ever involved but every time I see the call list on the board I feel a fresh twinge of resentment.

Especially when I see Rose's name.

Yep, guess who got upgraded to the part of Maria once I was chucked off the show? That's right. Rose was the first person to approach Mr Howard – at the time frantic with worry at not having a Maria – and told him she already knew most of the lines. He saw a few other girls, for appearance's sake I reckon, but there was never any doubt that Rose would get the role. And no doubt in my own mind that she's the most grasping, manipulative chancer I've ever met. It even crosses my mind that she could be the one behind the nasty messages and the dead pigeon in the locker. The only problem is, I can't for the life of me see why she would go so far. She wasn't ever really part of Amelia and my friendship group – though we all got on well enough – and it's not as if Rose is envious and unpopular. She's always surrounded by the Rose Clones, is generally liked by everyone and usually seems to have a boyfriend. She even dated Heath Sixsmith at the start of term – proving I was right about her being after him. But, according to the snatches of conversation I overhear, they fizzled out pretty quickly.

So I don't think she set out to wrangle the part of Maria from me, she just took the opportunity to grab it with both hands when it became available. She's a nasty piece of work, but more into conniving behind people's backs than the deep secret of anonymous messages and fishing dead birds out of wheelie bins.

By the beginning of February I realise that my situation, though hard, is at least livable with. And when I leave school the following Wednesday I'm not, for once, thinking about how I've been abused and tricked. I'm wondering instead if I have time to pop into the chemist for a new nail varnish on my way to pick up Jamie from his after-school club. Mum is at a late meeting and Poppy has a guitar lesson so I'm in charge of my little brother and I really want that pot of polish. I've taken recently to making an effort with cheap, but time-consuming beauty routines – nails and hair are something to do at least.

I take longer in the chemist than I expect, so I'm now hurrying down the road towards Jamie's school, my scarf and coat flying out behind me, when a male voice calls out.

'Carey!'

I spin around. A boy wearing the smart black blazer and red tie of Bamford House, the local private school, stands in front of me. He's tall with extremely close-cropped hair. If he was frowning he might look intimidating. But his eyes are soft – a beautiful shade of green with velvet black lashes – and there's a huge smile on his tanned face.

I have no idea how he knows my name. Perhaps he's a friend of Poppy's. I nod, feeling embarrassed, and quickly turn away.

'Hey, Carey!' The boy's tone shifts from amazement to consternation. 'Aren't you going to even say hello?'

I turn back and look at him again. Which is when I recognise him at last.

It's Taylor, Amelia's ex, the one she was so upset over when he dumped her, only with far shorter hair than he had last autumn.

'Taylor?' I stammer. 'Er, you cut your hair.' I blush, embarrassed to have stated the blindingly obvious and expecting him to either point this out or else roll his eyes.

But instead Taylor nods, clearly delighted. 'Yeah, buzzcut. Soldier style.' He grins, and I notice how white and even his teeth are. My stomach does a weird little skip. 'You like?' he asks.

'Sure,' I say. 'It looks great.' How bizarre is this: me standing in the street giving my opinion on a virtual stranger's hairstyle? I only met Taylor a few times when he was linking with Amelia, and then just in passing. Years ago I used to see him sometimes when I'd go with Mum to pick up Jamie from playdates with Taylor's little brother Blake, but really I barely know him – just what I've heard from Amelia. Which, let's face it, hardly adds up to a flattering personality profile. I bite my lip. Amelia would hate it if she

137

knew I was talking to Taylor and though she might have walked out on our friendship, I still feel loyal to her.

'I have to go,' I say, shuffling my feet. 'I've got to pick up my little brother.'

'You mean from Cornmouth Primary?' Taylor asks. 'Yeah, that's where I'm going too. To get Blake.'

A memory of a heartbroken Amelia asking me to fix a playdate between Jamie and Blake to give her an excuse to go round to Taylor's house flits through my mind.

'Oh,' I say. 'Right.'

Taylor falls into step beside me, chatting away, asking me a million questions about where I live and whether I've heard a new band called Bon Wheel and how my hair is amazingly, wonderfully curly. I've never met a guy who talks as freely as Taylor does. He never seemed to notice me much when Amelia and his friends were around, but now I'm getting the full force of his attention I'm starting to see why Amelia liked him so much. He's charming and . . . just so *interested* in everything I have to say.

After three months of being virtually ignored by almost everyone, his attention is like water on parched earth. And by the time we reach the school gates I realise that I'm actually enjoying myself.

And then I remember Amelia again. Taylor hasn't mentioned her, hasn't even asked how she is. Does he know what I'm supposed to have done to her? Surely he must. OK so he wasn't going out with Amelia when it all kicked off, and he doesn't go to our school, but the scandal was all over NatterSnap and he's got to be on that.

We stand together, like a ludicrously young couple alongside all the mums and dads, as the kids in Blake and Jamie's year swarm out of after-school club and into the playground. Maybe Taylor's talking to me so he can go gossip about me to his friends.

'So how come you're here?' I ask, as Taylor falls silent at last, his eyes roaming the chattering kids, looking out for his little brother. 'I mean you don't normally pick Blake up from school, do you?'

'Nah, it's ... family stuff,' Taylor says awkwardly. He hesitates a moment. 'The truth is that my dad left home a few weeks ago – he's splitting up from my mum – and he used to pick up Blake on Wednesdays but now he's gone so I'm just trying to help out.'

I stare at him, aghast. 'Oh, I'm so sorry, that's awful.' I grimace. 'I had no idea ...' I trail off, my cheeks burning.

Taylor looks at the ground, clearly as embarrassed as I am. I feel horrible.

'I'm really sorry,' I say again. 'I know what it's like. My dad left years back. We never see him now.'

'Oh, my dad's still around,' Taylor says with real bitterness. 'He can't do Wednesdays any more, but he takes Blake every other weekend.'

Around us children are milling and chatting. I catch Jamie running across the playground out of the corner of my eye, but I keep my focus on Taylor. 'What about you?'

Taylor looks up and his eyes glisten with angry tears. 'I don't want anything to do with him.'

I nod. 'I get it,' I say.

'Do you?' Taylor asks. 'Really? Because everyone else keeps telling me I should keep seeing him, as if nothing's happened. Like, they're all, "he's still your dad, Taylor", but he isn't. At least, he isn't the dad I thought I had.'

'I know exactly what you mean,' I say, as Jamie runs up and hurls himself at me.

I stagger backwards, returning his hug.

'I forgot it was you, today, Carey. Can I play with Blakey? Can we go to woods, Carey? *Please?*'

I glance across at Taylor. He's rubbing furiously at his eyes, clearly upset over his dad. My heart goes out to him.

'Another time,' I say, but Jamie is not so easily deterred. He turns to Blake, now trotting over to us. He's a smaller, rounder version of Taylor with an equally dazzling smile. 'D'you wanna go to Bow Wood, Blakey?'

'Yeah! Yeah!' Blake leaps up and down.

'It's *February*,' I protest. 'It's too cold and it'll be dark in an hour.'

'Aw, come on, Carey.' Taylor looks at me and smiles. 'We can use our phones as torches. How about it?'

140

My stomach gives that weird little flip again. Not only is Taylor gorgeous and nice, but he really doesn't seem to have any idea about the SweetFreak messages or the fact that I'm supposed to be behind them. I'm tempted to go to the woods with him. *Seriously* tempted.

I sigh. Which is all the more reason why I shouldn't go. Amelia was heartbroken when Taylor dumped her. It's one thing chatting to him while we're picking up our kid brothers, but quite another to extend the chat into an impromptu playdate.

'We can't,' I say, trying to inject a note of regret into my voice. I guess I must sound like I'm making an excuse because Taylor's face falls and I say without thinking: 'But maybe we could do something next Wednesday after school?'

'*Next* Wednesday?' Jamie grumbles. 'That's years away.'

'Yeah, like light years,' Blake adds.

'Like a *million* light years,' Jamie says.

'I think next Wednesday would be OK.' Unlike our brothers, Taylor is grinning, the cloud lifting from his face. 'See you then.'

I bustle a still complaining Jamie away. Once I'm home and Jamie is settled with a snack and a cartoon on the TV, I lie on my bed and think about what just happened.

I shouldn't have arranged to see Taylor next week, but at the same time I'm excited that I have. It's confusing. I feel guilty that Amelia would hate me spending time with Taylor,

141

but also resentful that I'm worrying about her feelings, when she's cut me off so easily.

'It's just a kids' playdate,' I mutter under my breath. 'Taylor's going through a hard time – one that I've been through too. Why shouldn't I talk to him about it? Why shouldn't I talk to him about anything? It's not like he's asked me out or that we *like* each other.'

But, as the light fades outside my bedroom window, I know that somewhere inside me I wouldn't mind it if Taylor *did* like me.

15

At least I've got a week to prepare for seeing Taylor again. Well, that's what I think on Wednesday evening. Two days later I'm trudging out of school and there he is, all handsome in jeans and a black leather jacket, leaning against the iron gates.

'Hi, Carey,' he says, a big grin on his face.

'I thought we were meeting next week,' I stammer. He looks sooo gorgeous.

'Mmn,' he says, his eyes glinting with excitement. 'I couldn't wait until next week. Do you want to get a coffee?'

'Oh.' I remember Amelia telling me about his leather jacket, gushing about how fit he looked in it. The thought of her makes me squirm with guilt. I really should say 'no'.

I open my mouth. 'Sure,' I say. 'That would be cool.'

We walk along the street. Taylor's far longer legs mean he can saunter while I have to hurry to keep up. I glance over my shoulder to make sure no one from my form has seen us – this really is the last thing I'd want getting back to Amelia.

Taylor chats away like he did before, all easy and funny and charming. By the time we reach the high street I realise I'm no longer feeling guilty.

There's no room for guilty. I'm too excited about what Taylor said outside the school gates:

I couldn't wait until next week.

Which means he *is* interested. And, as we settle ourselves down in a booth at the Cornmouth Corner Café and Taylor brings over two caramel frappuccinos, I admit to myself that I'm seriously interested back.

Taylor's as chatty as he was before, asking questions about my day at school and getting me to listen with him to a couple of tracks on his phone. Sharing earbuds with him sends a shiver down my spine. What is happening to me? I remind myself this is Amelia's ex and we *still* haven't mentioned her, which means she's kind of overshadowing everything we do and say.

I can't let anything happen between us. I *mustn't*.

And then Taylor stops talking and runs his finger along the inside of my arm, resting his hand on mine. My heart bumps against my ribs as his green eyes fix on mine.

'I can't stop thinking about you,' he says, his voice all husky and serious. 'You look amazing: it's everything, your

144

face and your eyes and your hair.' He smiles. 'Your hair is *beautiful*. I've never seen curls like those before.'

'Thanks.' I shift awkwardly in my seat, giving my unruly hair a self-conscious pat. It's no good, I've *got* to say something. 'Amelia.' I squeak out her name at last. 'What about Amelia?'

Taylor frowns but he doesn't take his hand off mine. 'Amelia was *months* ago,' he says, as if baffled why I've brought up something from the distant past. 'I know she's a friend of yours but we only hooked up for like, ten minutes or so.'

I meet his gaze. Emotions collide inside my head: mostly I feel an awkward sadness that Taylor clearly felt so little for Amelia when she was so loved-up over him. But mingling with the sadness is delight that he likes me and (though I don't want to admit this to myself) a small, mean, relieved feeling that he's obviously way more into me than he was into her. He certainly doesn't seem to know about SweetFreak. Or that Amelia and I don't see each other any more.

'She was bare upset when you dumped her,' I say, determined to at least try to stay loyal to my friend. Taylor is still holding my hand. Part of me wishes he would stop. Most of me is glad he hasn't. 'Devastated in fact.'

Taylor wrinkles his nose. 'I don't see how she could ...' He sighs. 'Look I didn't realise she was taking it all so seriously. I told her that I wasn't looking for a relationship.'

145

'You did?' This is news to me. Amelia always made it sound like they were desperately in love.

'Yeah, I mean, I thought Amelia was nice but I always kind of wished ...' Taylor looks away. 'I wished it was you.'

My mouth gapes. '*Me?*'

'Yeah, don't sound so surprised. I mean, Amelia's pretty and fun to be around, but next to you she's like ... like I dunno, a *thumb.*'

'What?'

'You know.' Taylor's tanned cheeks are pinking. He picks up the café menu and points to the picture of the Cornmouth Cornerburger Deluxe, complete with cheese, tomatoes and brioche bun. 'She's like a bit of gherkin while you're the actual steak.'

I burst into giggles and now Taylor does remove his hand. He looks embarrassed – which I didn't mean him to be. Buoyed with confidence, I grasp his fingers and squeeze. 'I'd be happy to be your hamburger.'

I don't know what makes such a stupid line fly out of my mouth, but Taylor's grin is back on his face in an instant.

'Really.' He leans forward and it's as clear an invitation to kiss as I've ever seen.

I want to lean forward too and just let it happen, but there's something I need to say first, something that has to be said, if Taylor is going to be any serious part of my life.

'You need to know ...' I trail off under the intense gaze of those green eyes.

Taylor raises his eyebrows. 'Know what?' he whispers.

The hum of the café fades as I keep my eyes fixed on his. 'Maybe you haven't heard, but last September someone called SweetFreak sent horrible messages to Amelia, including a ... a death threat. Then a few weeks later they left this disgusting dead pigeon in her locker. She really flipped out over it all, hasn't been at school since.'

Taylor nods slowly. 'Yeah I did hear something,' he says. 'Not from Amelia though.' He grimaces. 'I hope it doesn't sound mean but I blocked her when she started messaging me all the time after we stopped seeing each other ...' He frowns. 'Why? What does all that have to do with you?'

I take a deep breath. 'Almost everyone thinks that *I'm* SweetFreak, but I'm *not*. Honestly, I didn't do any of it.' My voice rises as I realise how vital it is Taylor believes me. 'I *couldn't* do any of it, especially not to Amelia. But she thinks it was me. So do the police. And my mum. She grounded me and took away my phone and my laptop.' Tears prick at my eyes as I speak. I blink them away. 'I swear I didn't do any of it, but the messages came from my laptop and the pigeon came from our wheelie bin which—'

'Which proves nothing,' Taylor interrupts. 'Laptops can be hacked and your bin would have been in your front garden, so anyone could have raided it.'

147

'And then put it in Amelia's school locker?' I say. It's hopeless. When Taylor hears all the details he's going to think I'm as guilty as everyone else. Better to leave right now, before I see the look of disappointment on his face.

I get to my feet.

'Please don't go,' Taylor says.

But I'm already heading for the door, cheeks burning and stupid tears bubbling up out of my eyes.

I only get halfway down the high street before Taylor catches up with me. Breathless, he spins me round to face him. A soft rain is falling like a mist. It has settled on his long lashes, making them seem even darker than usual, the perfect frame for his eyes.

'Why are you running away from me?' he gasps.

I shrug, feeling embarrassed and stupid. 'Look,' I say. 'Now you know about SweetFreak ... the messages ... the death threat ... that stupid pigeon ... you're going to think the same as everyone else, that I'm guilty and—'

'I don't think that.' Taylor tugs at my arm and I let him draw me into the shelter of a shop doorway. A couple of elderly ladies glance at us as they pass by and roll their eyes. 'If you say you didn't do those horrible things to Amelia, I believe you.'

'Really?'

'Really.' Taylor frowns. 'For a start, how do you know Amelia didn't send herself all the messages, including the death threat.'

148

'My mum asked the police the same thing,' I say. 'The earlier messages were all deleted, but they found out exactly where and when the death threat was sent and it couldn't have been Amelia.'

'They were sent from your laptop?' Taylor says.

'Yes, they were posted at the exact time Amelia was halfway across Cornmouth waiting for me at a bus shelter. Nowhere near my laptop. The police tracked her movements through her phone. Unfortunately my phone was switched off at the time, so I couldn't prove it wasn't me.'

'I see.' Taylor leans back against the wall. 'So definitely not Amelia, then. There's no way she could have hacked your laptop. Still . . .'

There's clearly something he's not telling me.

'Why did you even think Amelia might have sent the messages to herself?' I ask. 'Because she was really freaked out over them . . . it seemed genuine to me.'

There's a pause, then Taylor blows out his breath. 'OK,' he says. 'Well from the time I spent with her, I got the impression she's not really the person she pretends to be.'

'What do you mean?'

'It was at this party we went to,' he says. 'There was a girl there from Amelia's school. *Your* school. I can't remember her name, but Amelia was really annoyed about her being there, said she couldn't stand her.'

'Really?' I wrinkle my nose. Amelia was always very

easy going about people – a bit quick to take offence maybe, but also quick to forgive and forget. 'You're sure you don't remember who it was?'

'No, but Amelia was convinced this girl hated her as much as she hated the girl.'

This sounds even more unlikely. Surely I'd have noticed that kind of bad feeling? 'She never said anything like that to me.'

Taylor frowns. 'Really? But you're her best friend.'

'*Was* her best friend,' I correct with a sigh. 'So what did Amelia say? What did this girl do to her?'

'It was more what Amelia did to the girl when they were at primary school.' Taylor runs his hand over his cropped hair.

Now it's my turn to frown. I'm certain Amelia never mentioned knowing anyone from her old primary school. Most of our class, including me, went to Cornmouth Primary, the same as Jamie and Taylor's brother Blake. But Amelia had gone to a tiny primary school way over on the other side of the town.

'Amelia was upset when she told me, it was … like a confession,' Taylor explains. 'I think she wanted me to say it wasn't so bad, that she'd just been a little kid at the time, that she hadn't realised how hurtful she must have been.'

I stare at him. 'How *hurtful* she was?' It doesn't make sense. Amelia was … is … a gentle person: neither outspoken nor mean.

'Amelia admitted that she made this girl's life a misery – pretended to be best friends then ignored her, told lies about her, said a bunch of stuff behind her back. I don't remember the details. To be honest, I wasn't really interested, but Amelia was upset so . . .' Taylor rubs his forehead.

The rain is getting harder, drumming down on the pavement. The high street is virtually empty. Most people have, like us, taken shelter under doorways and in shop entrances.

'Do you remember anything about the other girl?' A gust of wind whips a damp curl across my face and I shiver. 'Was she pretty? Dark hair? Blonde?'

'Dark hair I think.' Taylor smooths back the curl, his finger soft on my cheek. I shiver again. This time not from the cold. 'I remember noticing that she was pretty, but there was something else too . . . something to do with the girls she had come to the party with.'

'Were they from my school too?'

'I don't know.' There's a short pause, then Taylor's eyes widen. 'Hang on, maybe she's in one of the pictures.' Taylor digs his phone out of his pocket. I glance up and down the high street. The pavements are glistening, wet under the street lamps. Cars whoosh by. The rain patters down all around us. A pair of older teenage girls hurry past. One of them clocks Taylor, then glances at me, a look of naked admiration on her face.

I blush, glad that Taylor is still absorbed in his phone and can't see my red face.

'Look. She's in this one.' Taylor holds the mobile so I can see the screen. We huddle together, watching the little video of people dancing. The camera pans around the room, from a clearly drunk Amelia, stumbling about as she tosses her hair wildly, to the other girls with their short skirts and their waving arms. 'There she is,' Taylor says as the little clip zooms in on a slim girl with a long brown bob. She's wearing a long-sleeved top with cutaways at the shoulders. Two girls sway beside her, also with long bobs and dressed in similar style tops.

My breath catches in my throat.

It's Rose.

16

'Oh my goodness,' I gasp.

'Do you recognise her?' Taylor asks.

'Yes, that's Rose from my school.' My mind races. I can't get my head around it: Rose and Amelia were at primary together? Amelia pretended to be best friends then was horrible to her? Yet neither ever mentioned that they knew each other?

How is any of that possible?

'I remember noticing the girl, mainly because those two . . .' Taylor points at Minnie and Molly, '. . . had obviously copied her look, but she was clearly the one in charge. And I remember thinking it was weird when Amelia told me how mean she'd been to her, that girl – Rose – just didn't look like a victim of bullying.'

'She isn't one. At least she isn't one *now*.' I draw in my breath sharply, an idea occurring. 'Do you think *she* could be SweetFreak?'

'I guess,' Taylor says.

My head spins. On the one hand it makes perfect sense that Rose might have sent Amelia nasty messages as revenge for what Amelia did when they were younger. And when it comes to the pigeon – Molly and Minnie, the Rose Clones, were both in the locker room just before Amelia arrived. They could easily have planted the dead bird on Rose's behalf. Framing me for everything makes sense too, from Rose's point of view. Quite apart from the fact that she envied me over *The Sound of Music*, it would have added a particularly satisfying twist to her revenge: breaking up *my* friendship with Amelia would be a great way of getting back at Amelia for ending *her* friendship with Rose.

On the other hand . . .

'No,' I say, my heart sinking. 'It's crazy. I mean why would Rose wait over three years? If she wanted to get back at Amelia for the bullying surely she'd have done it in Year Seven, not waited 'til the start of Year Ten? And, anyway, Rose and Amelia are friends now. Why would Rose want to be mates with her if she hates her so much?'

Taylor shrugs. He pockets his phone.

'It's more likely it was Amelia's brother, George,' I carry on. 'Me and Amelia upset him just before the messages happened.'

Taylor snorts. 'I've met George. He's way too thick to think it all up. Anyway, nasty messages and dead birds are more girl things to do, don't you think?' He peers out at the high street. The rain has worn itself out and shoppers are starting to emerge from their shelters. 'All Rose needed to do was hack your laptop and—'

'It wasn't hacked,' I interrupt. 'My sister wondered about that too, but the police were adamant. They said the death threat was inputted in person – and that mine were the only fingerprints on the keyboard.'

'What do the police know about it?' Taylor scoffs. He wanders onto the street and takes a deep lungful of damp air. I hurry after him. 'Seriously, my dad's an IT consultant. He's always saying that the public services are light years behind the private sector, that the police are way too easy to fool on stuff like that.'

'OK, but I'm pretty certain Rose isn't capable of that level of hacking. Certainly not of covering her tracks afterwards so no one even realises the laptop *was* hacked.'

'You can't know that for sure,' Taylor insists. 'Seriously, there are a couple of geeks in my IT GCSE class who could *easily* do that stuff. Amelia couldn't, for sure, but maybe Rose is a secret IT genius.'

Or maybe she knows someone who is and who is prepared to do her dirty work for her. I fill up with fresh hope. If Rose really is guilty then maybe I'll be able to clear my name at last.

'Whatever.' Taylor takes my hand, drawing me out to join

155

him on the gleaming pavement. 'I don't believe *you* did those horrible things, not for a second.'

'Thank you,' I say, beaming up at him. It feels so good to have a friend again. Maybe more than a friend from the way he's smiling back at me.

'Hey, do you fancy going park?' he asks. 'You can give me your phone number on the way.'

As we stroll to the park, I explain how Mum is still making me use one of her crappy old phones. I feel hot under his gaze, embarrassed about the phone, and fall silent as we reach the swings. They're empty, thanks to the recent rain. It feels like a million years since I waited here for Amelia last September. I lean against the metal post, lost in memories.

'What are you thinking?' Taylor asks, then groans. 'Sorry, that was such a girly question. It's just . . .' He pauses.

'What?' I straighten up. The wind gusts past, bitingly cold on my face.

Taylor slides his arm around my shoulders and squeezes me awkwardly towards him. My heart pummels at my ribs as Taylor pulls away and looks into my eyes. 'I didn't expect this,' he says.

'Expect what?' My voice is barely audible over the sound of the wind in the trees. Taylor bends closer to hear me, his face just centimetres from mine.

'How you make me feel,' Taylor says, his breath hot on my ear.

I shiver. 'How ... how do I ... ?'

'Like I want to kiss you,' he says softly. He winds one of my curls around his finger.

My stomach flips wildly over and over. A little voice in my head is screaming that this is Amelia's ex and by all the rules of friendship ever invented it's wrong for me to get involved with him.

She's your best friend, the voice shrieks.

Not any more, I reason back. *And they broke up months ago. And Taylor never led her on, he's told me. And Amelia doesn't care what I do anyway. She hates me.*

It's this last thought that finally does it, as Taylor's hands run down my arms, pulling me closer. His lips hover over mine. *Amelia already hates me. Kissing Taylor can't possibly make her hate me any more than she already does.* And pushing all thoughts of my former friend finally to one side, I stretch up to meet Taylor's lips and give in to the long, lush kiss that follows.

Of course I feel guilty again later. But when Taylor sends me a text, complaining he wants a pic of me, which of course my rubbish phone can't provide, my heart still skips a beat.

I shouldn't like him. He dumped Amelia and she was ... for all I know, still is ... heartbroken. Anyway, he was hers, which means he mustn't be mine.

Except ... except ... he likes me. And I like him. And

after months of having no friends and no one to talk to outside my own family, it's bliss to have Taylor calling me, eager to see me.

I meet him in the park on both the Saturday and Sunday of that first weekend. It's still only early February, the weather is cold and there's no one else much around, but we huddle under the shelter of a tree and make out and talk.

I ask more questions about what Amelia said about Rose. Taylor answers as best he can, but all he really adds to what he's already told me is that after Amelia met me at secondary school she was 'inspired' to reinvent herself. It sounds far-fetched, but Taylor insists it's true. 'She told me that she turned over a new leaf when she met you, that you inspired her to be a better person.'

His words fire a mix of pleasure and pain inside me: delight that my friendship with Amelia meant so much to her and fresh misery at its loss.

My mood improves when, amazingly, Taylor gives me a PAYG smartphone that he's loaded with credit. 'It's an old one of my dad's, so we can private message on NatterSnap or whatever,' he says, nuzzling into my neck.

I can't believe it. I mean I know that Taylor's family lives in a massive house in the posh part of town – East Cornmouth – but even so giving me a phone is beyond generous.

'Oh, wow,' I gush. 'Thank you.'

'It's nothing,' he says, running his hands down my back.

'You're worth it . . . you're amazing.' And he kisses me again and I squirm with delight.

By the time Monday morning comes I'm full of confidence, determined to find out if Rose really is SweetFreak. I march up to her in our form room as soon as she arrives.

'Can I talk to you outside?' I ask.

Rose looks me up and down coolly. 'S'pose.' She saunters out into the corridor.

I follow, my heart beating fast.

There's no point beating about the bush so I launch straight in.

'Did Amelia bully you back at Primary?' I ask.

Rose instinctively recoils, clearly shocked, then she recovers herself.

'Who told you that?'

'Is it true?'

Over our heads the first bell screeches out.

Rose tilts her head to one side. 'Why are you so interested, Freak?'

Now it's my turn to recoil. It's the first time she's used the name directly to my face. Part of me itches to tell her to take it back, then it occurs to me this is probably what Rose is hoping I'll do, so that she can avoid answering my questions.

'I'll take that as a yes, then,' I say. And the flicker of fearful annoyance in Rose's eyes tells me I'm right. 'So I'm guessing you don't like Amelia very much?'

'Actually I do. We're good friends now, whatever happened in the past,' Rose says.

'Right,' I say. Is it possible that Rose sent the nasty messages not just to get back at Amelia and to break up her friendship with me, but also to become BFFs with her again?

The second bell goes, as Mrs Marchington appears at the end of the corridor. Two boys rush into the form room past us. Rose takes a step towards the door. 'Wait,' I say.

Mrs Marchington's heels tap towards us. Rose looks around.

'Are you SweetFreak?' I demand.

The slightly fearful look vanishes from Rose's eyes, replaced by naked contempt. 'You're pathetic,' she says.

She disappears into the form room as Mrs Marchington strides up, chivvying me inside.

I take my seat, lost in thought.

Rose had the motive *and* the opportunity to post the messages *and* organise the dead bird in Amelia's locker.

I think Taylor is right. I've been looking in the wrong direction all along, Amelia's brother, George, isn't the one behind everything, it's Rose.

17

I rush out of school at the end of the day. Taylor has promised to meet me in the park again, and I can't wait to tell him how my confrontation with Rose went, how I'm sure she's the one who set me up.

But Taylor doesn't come and I end up shivering under the trees for ten minutes before I receive his apologetic message telling me he can't make it. He can't see me the next day, either. Which is Valentine's Day. I pretend I'm cool about the whole thing – after all it's very early days for us to be thinking about Valentines – but I'm still a bit gutted.

Taylor insists we'll have more time the day after, Wednesday, when we're due to pick up our little brothers from Cornmouth Primary together. Mum is delighted that I've volunteered to collect Jamie from after-school club again and happy for me to take him to play at Blake's for

161

a couple of hours – which means of course hanging out at Taylor's house for a bit.

After his sketchy behaviour earlier in the week, I'm reassured by how into me he seems that Wednesday. I try to get Taylor to open up about his dad leaving, but he says it's too painful to talk about. I almost feel I could talk about *my* dad – certainly more than I can with Sonia – but before I can say very much it's time to go home. I'm really looking forward to seeing Taylor the next day, but he cancels again and on Friday tells me he is really sorry but he has a family supper he can't get out of.

It's hard to hide my disappointment, but at least we meet on Saturday – this time in the woods near the park. Taylor tells me about an abandoned hut he's discovered on the other side of town.

'It's a couple of miles from anywhere, past the industrial estate down a dirt track,' he says, eyes lighting up. 'I reckon it's haunted. I can't wait to show you. The Haunted Hut, like the Shrieking Shack in Harry Potter.' He laughs.

I try to join in, but I'm having a disturbing memory of Amelia mentioning this very hut and how she and Taylor had gone there and let themselves in with the key with the skull painted on the end.

'One day we'll run away there,' Taylor says, his lips drifting over mine. 'It'll be so romantic.'

Like it was with Amelia?

I don't say this out loud. Instead, I try to talk about Rose again.

'I'm convinced she's SweetFreak but I can't see any way of proving it,' I complain.

'Well there probably isn't a way,' Taylor says. 'Rose has got what she wants, hasn't she? Back friends with Amelia *and* the lead in that stupid play.'

He's right, of course, but it still rankles that I can't call her out on what she's done.

'You need to let it go,' Taylor urges, and maybe it's my imagination but I'm sure there's a hint of impatience in his voice. 'Everyone's forgotten what you're supposed to have done, haven't they?'

I shrug. 'Mostly, I guess.'

It's true that school gossip has moved on. I'm no longer pointed at or whispered over. And yet my position at school is transformed: whereas at the start of the year I was included in everything, now I am ignored, my status downgraded from popular to invisible.

It hurts but when I turn to Taylor for comfort, I'm not sure he really understands. He tells me I just have to 'be myself', that I'm so great everyone will come around eventually and, when I keep talking about it, that I'm being oversensitive and the situation isn't as bad as all that.

'It's not like you're actually getting picked on any more, is it?' he asks with a tinge of impatience in his voice.

163

And I have to agree that I'm not.

The following week I hardly see Taylor. We meet after school on the Monday, but it's already starting to get dark and the rain is heavy and we're soon soaked through and running for home. We pick up our brothers together on Wednesday and I'm hoping for an invite back to his, but Taylor says he's busy. He doesn't call later either and I'm just starting to worry that he's totally lost interest, when he calls to ask me to go to a party on Friday night.

I have to slip out of the house to meet up with him – Mum might have relaxed her sanction that I'm grounded, but I'm still under a strict curfew – and my heart bubbles with excitement as I let myself down from the bathroom window and patter across the extension roof next door to the pavement below. I race to the edge of the woods, where I'm meeting Taylor, and we catch a bus to the party.

It's being thrown in a massive house, by a friend of Taylor's from his private school. I don't know any of these posh Bamford House teenagers – they all seem super confident, the boys showing off to impress the girls and the girls themselves uniformly slim, pretty and groomed like models in designer dresses. I feel self-conscious in my cheap jeans and high street top and wish I'd tied my wild hair back so it was less obvious.

The boys at the party greet Taylor like a hero.

'It's Super H,' one of them says in his upper-class accent.

'Yeah, yah, Super H. Super H,' the group around him chant.

Taylor blushes modestly.

'What are they talking about?' I ask.

'Just a nickname,' Taylor says smoothly. 'Come on, let's dance.'

He drags me over to the centre of the living room. The boys at this party outnumber girls by about three to one and I can feel many pairs of eyes on me as Taylor and I move to the loud dance track.

I pull the black strappy top I 'borrowed' from Poppy self-consciously over my hips.

'Don't.' Taylor grins. 'You look amazing.'

I glow in the warmth of his pleasure. I must have been wrong about him losing interest. He's just busy with his life. Which, unlike me, he still has.

We dance until we're both sweating and panting for breath. Taylor heads in search of drinks and the boy who called him 'Super H' sidles over to me.

'I'm Jack. I go to school with Taylor.' He has an earnest face, with round-rimmed glasses and a snub nose. It's hard to believe he and Taylor are the same age. Jack looks and sounds much younger. 'How d'you meet Taylor then?' he asks.

'Through a friend,' I say, not wanting to mention Amelia's name. 'How well do you know him?'

'Not that well. Taylor's like a shark, always moving on.' Jack laughs, though I don't see that he's said anything particularly funny. 'He gets through people ... girls mostly, like you wouldn't believe. Not you, though.' Jack touches my arm. 'He's obviously mad about you.'

I'm not sure if he's saying that sarcastically or not, so I ignore it.

'You make him sound like a bit of a player,' I say. The music soars around us. A taller, bigger boy barges past unheeding and knocks beer over Jack's arm. He wipes it away with a string of swear words.

'Not at all,' he says and, again, I'm not sure if he's being sarcastic or not. 'Did he tell you about Mooney?'

'What's that?'

'Not what. Who. This guy in our class Taylor got excluded.'

'What?'

'Yeah, Taylor was messing about with his posse which Mooney was in. They set fire to the sixth form block after school one evening. No one was hurt, but a couple of the sixth formers had to be rescued by the fire service. They made a big deal of the investigation. Mooney's fingerprints were on the can of petrol Taylor used. I dunno if Mooney was even with Taylor, but he went down for the fire.'

'He went to prison?' I stare at Jack, aghast.

'No. *Course* not.' Jack shakes his head solemnly, to emphasise the point. 'People like us don't go to prison.

Permanent exclusion, that's what they call it.' He shrugs. 'Mooney's probably up at some other private school by now.'

'Right.' I frown. 'Does that have something to do with why you call Taylor "Super H"?'

'No,' Jack starts, 'we call him that because—'

'Hey!' Taylor breaks across Jack's sentence, our drinks in his hands. He glares at Jack who presses his lips together, makes the zip sign, then gives me a wink as he slips away.

'What did he want?' Taylor asks, suspiciously.

'Nothing. He told me about someone called Mooney. Says you got him permanently excluded from your school.'

Taylor shrugs. 'Mooney got himself excluded,' he says. 'It wasn't my fault he got caught. I told everyone to wear gloves so they wouldn't leave fingerprints. It was just a stupid prank that got out of hand, Carey. No big deal.'

'Sounds like it was a big deal for Mooney,' I say, wondering how Taylor can sound so casual about letting another person take the blame for the fire, not to mention the terrible risk to the lives of everyone in the building that burnt down.

'He'll just have moved to another school,' Taylor says.

'That's what your friend Jack said.'

'Well that's what happens,' Taylor says, with a dismissive wave of his hand.

'So tell me about the Super H nickname?' I ask.

'No,' Taylor says, sounding cross. 'I told you, it's just a

167

stupid thing, I don't even remember how I got it.' He smiles. 'Come on, we're here to have a good time, not talk about stuff that happened a zillion years ago.'

'Course,' I say, smiling back.

We swig our drinks, then get back to dancing and making out. But something has changed between us. Taylor seems somehow distant. As if the party was a test which I have failed.

168

18

I'm still obsessing over how Taylor feels about me the following morning as I lie in bed. I can't make sense of his behaviour: all interested one minute, distracted or withdrawn the next. Can I really trust him? Amelia's experiences bob uneasily at the back of my mind. She thought he was really into her, but he obviously wasn't. Is it the same with me? Surely it can't be, Taylor's made it clear several times that he always liked me far more than he liked her.

Jamie bounds in in the midst of my musings. He demands a story and I shout at him to leave me alone. Later, feeling guilty, I go in search of him to make up, only to find Poppy's taken him out to the woods and it's just me and Mum in the house.

'Are you all right, Carey?' Mum asks, her tone gentler

than usual. She's stretched out on the sofa, her laptop in her hands. She normally uses it for work but right now she's on a clothes website – rows of flowery dresses fill the page.

'Sure,' I ask. 'Mum, how can you tell if someone really likes you?'

Mum peers at me over the top of the laptop.

'Boy "like" or friend "like"?'

'Either,' I say, unwilling to give away any information about Taylor. I've kept his existence and our burgeoning relationship a secret from everyone apart from Poppy.

'Well I'd say being honest and reliable and respectful, those are good indicators.'

I nod and drift away, back up to my room.

Is Taylor those things? I'm not sure. He doesn't contact me all that day, Sunday. I'm relieved. It gives me time to think about what I learned about him last night.

According to Taylor, this boy Mooney only had himself to blame for getting caught while Taylor was just along for the ride. But I saw the way the boys from his school looked at him: part fear, part awe. I suspect Taylor was the ringleader of the fire. And even if it was a prank that went wrong, like Taylor claimed, it was still a terrible thing to do and horrible to let someone else take the blame for it.

I can't stop thinking about it. Or about Taylor. My relief at having time to myself on Sunday turns into anxiety when Taylor doesn't call or message until Tuesday night, when he asks if I want to bring Jamie over to his house after our usual little brother school pick-up the next day.

Relief washes over me. And then renewed uncertainty. It's starting to dawn on me that maybe I like Taylor more than Taylor likes me. More than he *says* he likes me. I try to talk to him about his feelings the next day, but he just yawns and changes the subject. I don't bring up the story of Mooney and the fire, or of Taylor's strange nickname, but both things prey on my mind.

I roll the nickname around my head. It seems weird. There's no 'H' in Taylor or his middle name or surname, so what does 'Super H' mean?

A couple of weeks ago Taylor had promised we'd spend the whole of half term together, but now the week off school is coming up, he is unwilling to make any definite plans.

'Mum wants to go to her sister in Nottingham for a few days,' he explains. 'So I might go with her, or I might just stay with friends in Cornmouth while she's gone. I'm not sure.'

'If you leave town, when would you go?' I don't mean the question to sound like a whine but I can't seem to get the needy edge out of my voice.

It clearly irritates Taylor. 'I don't know,' he snaps. 'Sometime over the weekend I guess.'

I gulp, afraid to push him further, especially on the phone, so I change the subject. There's no point discussing my suspicions about Rose any more; he's made it clear that he's bored of the whole SweatFreak thing now. Instead I chat about Bon Wheel – which I've totally got into since Taylor introduced me to their music – trying not to let the disappointment sound in my voice. Taylor is soon chatting away too, as warm and sweet-natured as I've ever heard him.

When we meet the next day, Wednesday, at the Cornmouth Primary school gates, I am careful not to mention the upcoming half term again and am rewarded by Taylor in a particularly affectionate mood. He snogs me in the playground, much to the obvious irritation of half the mums gathered to pick up their kids, and on the way back to his house he makes our little brothers laugh with his silly faces and voices.

We reach Taylor's house – which is three times the size of my own – where his Mum says a smiley 'hello' to me then ushers Jamie and Blake into the kitchen for juice and cookies. Taylor takes my hand and leads me up to his room. He's grinning as he sits me down on his bed and I can't help but grin back, in spite of the little coil of anxiety that seems to have settled permanently inside me these days. Taylor's smile is like the sun, all-consuming in its light and warmth, devastating when taken away.

'So what shall we do for the next two hours?' Taylor asks, eyes sparkling.

I wander around his room. It's cluttered and messy, though the floor is clear, as if someone has shoved everything back against the walls. The top drawer of his desk is open. My eye lights on a stash of old phones inside.

'Wow, look at all these.'

'They're old ones of my dad's,' Taylor explains. 'I told you before, he works in IT.'

'Right.' Perhaps Taylor giving me that phone wasn't such a significant gift as I'd imagined.

It's not a happy thought.

I rummage among the mobiles. In the corner of the drawer I spot the end of a long old-fashioned brass key. I pull it out. A black skull has been hand-painted on the head. My insides contract as Amelia's voice echoes in my head.

The last time I saw him he took me to the Haunted Hut outside the industrial estate with the key with the skull painted on the end and it was really spooky and I was all freaked and Taylor was really nice and we made out and it was so romantic . . .

'What's that key for?' I ask, assuming an air of curiosity.

Taylor follows my gaze. 'That's the key to the Haunted Hut I was telling you about,' he says. He sits up, eyes sparking. 'Hey, how about we go there on Friday night?' he asks. 'I've never gone there with a girl before, it could be our special place.'

My heart thuds painfully in my chest. He's lying to me. I should challenge him, but I'm scared he'll spin into a bad mood again.

173

'Won't it be really creepy going there in the dark?' I ask, feeling torn. Part of me hates the idea of following in Amelia's footsteps and of playing along with Taylor's lie. But part of me is excited at the prospect of going on a night-time adventure with him.

'Nah,' Taylor says. Then he opens his eyes wide in mock horror. 'Well, maybe a little, but it's OK, I'll protect you from the ghosts . . .' He finishes with a fiendish-sounding cackle.

I giggle. Maybe Taylor isn't mentioning the fact that he took Amelia to the hut because he doesn't want to upset me. Maybe the hut *will* be a special place for us.

'Come on, Carey,' Taylor urges. 'I'll meet you at the bus stop on the Bamford Road, you know? The one just before the industrial estate? We can go there together, it's not far really, all the way through the estate, then maybe ten minutes or so along a dirt track. Whaddya say? *Please?*'

I stare at his gorgeous face, all lit up with excitement. How can I possibly refuse? 'Sure,' I say, 'I'd love to.'

The next two days pass slowly. I can't wait for Friday evening and neither, it seems, can Taylor. He messages me about our planned trip five or six times, full of enthusiasm.  He even says how going to the Haunted Hut with me on Friday will be a wonderful way to spend time together in case he has to go away afterwards, for the rest of half term. It seems a bit strange to me that he doesn't yet know whether he's leaving Cornmouth with his mum, or staying in town with friends, but I don't want to irritate him by pushing, so I leave the subject alone.

I'm almost giddy with anticipation as I do my hair and make-up on the Friday night. I might be dressed for a hike along a dirt track in the dark – in sweater and boots – but I'm determined to look as great as possible when we get to the Haunted Hut. I put on my black satin jacket with the flower embroidery on the back, apply Mum's expensive eyeliner and finish my look with several slashes of Poppy's favourite plum-coloured lipgloss. Poppy herself is babysitting Jamie tonight, while Mum goes out to her book group, so there's no need for me to creep out of the house. I catch the bus straight away, having double-checked the timetable on the phone Taylor gave me. I get off at the stop just before the industrial estate, as Taylor instructed. His own bus from East Cornmouth is due in ten minutes. I check my make-up and huddle in a corner of the shelter. I'm suddenly reminded of the night back in September when I met Amelia in the bus shelter by the rec. I don't feel like I have anything in common with the Carey I was then. She existed in a different world, a different life.

It's drizzling outside, with a chill wind that matches the turbulence inside me. Am I in love with Taylor? I've asked myself that several times over the past week. I certainly feel out of control when he's around. His bus arrives and

I straighten up, gazing away from the door, determined to look as indifferent to his arrival as possible. A middle-aged woman gets off, then two twenty-something guys in suits.

There's no sign of Taylor.

The bus roars off along the gleaming tarmac. I examine my phone. No text or missed call or NatterSnap message. Perhaps he'll be on the next bus. I have no idea when it will get here but I don't fancy heading into the industrial estate by myself, so I sit tight, tugging my arms around me. The rain picks up, driving against the shelter wall. I'm just shuffling along, trying to find a patch of shelter from the wind, when a vaguely familiar voice says:

'Hey.'

I look up. It's the boy with the piercing blue eyes and the mismatched trainers who helped me when I was looking for Nando's on my birthday last October. His thick dark hair is wet, plastered to his head, and his thin jacket drenched with rain.

'I remember you,' he says. 'The girl who got lost in her own hometown.'

I gulp. There's a real intensity to his eyes. It's pretty creepy out here in the dim street light and my nerves are already all jangled. He seemed totally harmless before, but now I'm wondering if he's some sort of teenage psychopath.

'Are you waiting for a bus?' he asks. Considering how rough he looks, his voice is surprisingly soft.

'Yeah,' I lie, too embarrassed to say what seems increasingly clear is the truth – that Taylor has stood me up.

The boy frowns. 'No,' he says. 'No, you can't.'

What is he talking about? He takes a step towards me.

Fear rises inside me. I shuffle back on the bus shelter seat, flattening myself against the perspex wall behind.

'Who are you?' I squeak. 'What do you want?'

'Please.' The boy's takes another step towards me. 'Listen.'

And this time I scream.

19

The boy's mouth falls open in horror. His hand is still outstretched, pointing at me.

No, not at me, at something over my shoulder.

'I ... I ... was just trying to show you the timetable,' he stammers. 'There won't be another bus along here for three hours. The last bus comes then. I'm sorry I frightened you.'

I glance over my shoulder at the back of the bus shelter. The faded timetable is set inside cracked and grimy plastic.

'Oh,' I say, feeling both relieved and foolish. 'Er, thanks.'

'Blue? *Blue?*' It's the girl in the DMs with the rainbow laces. She's running up the road towards us, scowling furiously. 'Come on!' She glares at the boy, whose face under the street light is the colour of the tomatoes Mum insists on putting inside my packed lunches.

'Yeah, I'm coming,' Blue says, now scowling himself.

His hair is shaggier than when I saw him a few months ago. He looks thinner too, his cheekbones sharp in his face.

The girl folds her arms and studies me. She's tall and skinny, with loads of thin plaits cascading over her shoulders and three little studs in her right nostril. There's something effortlessly superior about the way she holds herself. She's certainly looking down her nose at me.

'Sidetracked by a pretty face, Blue?' She rolls her eyes.

'I said I'm coming.' Without a glance at either me or the girl, Blue stomps off.

The girl looks at me again and, this time, there's the hint of a smile in her eyes. I smile back, stupidly eager to look cool in her eyes. Then she turns and runs off. Soon both of them have vanished into the darkness.

What kind of lives do they lead? The girl is at least two or three years older than Blue . . . what's he doing with her? And where did he get that hippy name? Or those odd trainers?

It's now over twenty minutes since Taylor was due to meet me here. I spend a few moments examining the timetable behind me. Blue was right – there's only one more bus tonight and it doesn't even come from Taylor's direction.

I check my phone again. He hasn't left any kind of message, which, I'm forced to admit, is not entirely out of character. It's now over an hour since we were due to meet.

'You've stood me up again.' I say the words out loud,

trying to accept what this means: that Taylor cannot possibly be as into me as I want him to be or as I am into him.

I tug my jacket around me and begin the long trudge home. I'm angry at Taylor. He can't treat me like this, just cancelling at the drop of a hat without even letting me know. Unless something's happened to him? I allow myself a little worry over this possibility, but even as I do I know how unlikely it is that anything bad has happened. No, this is typical Taylor: flaky and unreliable.

It takes nearly fifty minutes to get home. I pass several taxi companies but don't have enough money to hire one. I would use Mum's Uber account – she gave me and Poppy the details ages ago for emergency use – but she'll see the fare and ask awkward questions so instead I hurry back on foot. At home I find Poppy curled up like a cat on her bed watching something on YouTube. Mum, of course, won't be back for another couple of hours.

I tell Poppy that Taylor couldn't make it – leaving out the fact that he stood me up – then I get into bed, feeling numb with misery. Taylor still hasn't called. He doesn't overnight. Or first thing in the morning.

By eleven the next morning I'm beside myself. Perhaps he's lost his phone? That is certainly more likely than a terrible accident. And, if that is the case, Taylor is probably as gutted about missing last night's adventure as I am.

Jamie is pestering me to take him to the woods to play *Warriors* again.

'Please, Carey, you're better at it than Poppy. She doesn't like running through the bushes cos it messes her hair. And Mum won't run at all.'

I eye my little brother thoughtfully. He's waving his sword, a stained tabard hanging cockeyed over his skinny little chest.

'How about I take you to play at Blake's?' I ask.

Jamie tilts his head to one side. 'Could you take *both* of us to the woods? Me *and* Blakey?'

'Sure. If his mum lets me,' I say, though privately I've got no intention of going to the woods. Instead I'm hoping to see Taylor, while our little brothers romp around in Blake's massive playroom.

'OK,' Jamie says.

'Good.' I pick up an eyeshadow brush. If I'm going to see Taylor I want to look my best. 'Go and check it's OK with Mum, then get your shoes on.'

Jamie races out of the room, almost colliding with Poppy who I hadn't noticed standing in the doorway.

'He hasn't called you, eh?' she asks, leaning against the jamb.

I shrug, not wanting to get into it with my sister.

Of course this doesn't deter Poppy. 'One of the boys in my class knows someone at Taylor's school, says he's a bit of a nutter.'

'What?' I stare at her. 'I've never even seen him swat a fly.'

'Not a violent nutter, stupid, but definitely ruthless. And he takes things to extremes. And he doesn't care about people. That's what this boy said anyway.'

'Well he doesn't know Taylor then,' I protest.

'Mmm.' Poppy wrinkles her nose. 'You're really into him, aren't you?'

'No,' I say. But I'm blushing as I say it.

'Liar.' Poppy grins. 'Anyway, be careful.' She wanders away and I carry on putting on my make-up. Could she be right about Taylor? He is selfish, that's true. And that story about the fire at his school was kind of extreme. But the way he listens to me and the way he's so upset about his dad ... those are surely signs that he's a sweet, genuine person underneath.

'Ready!' Jamie yells from downstairs.

I grab my black satin jacket, check myself in the mirror one last time and hurry out. Mum materialises in the hall just as Jamie and I are leaving.

'Thanks so much for taking Jamie. Just so you know, I've got a hair appointment later and Poppy's got a shift at the café,' Mum says. 'I'll be back about three.'

'Sure,' I say. Hopefully I'll be able to spend the whole afternoon at Taylor's house.

'Come on!' Jamie hurtles out the front door.

*

Butterflies zoom around my stomach as we reach the gravel drive in front of Taylor's house.

I ring on the doorbell. I can hear voices inside but it takes nearly a minute before the door opens. Taylor's mum stands there. She looks harassed, with no make-up on and a DKNY sweatshirt over artfully ripped jeans.

'Jamie!' She looks from my brother to me, clearly searching for and failing to find my name.

'Carey,' I say.

'Yes, er, hello.' She frowns. 'Did we have a playdate that I've forgotten about?'

'No, but Jamie was hoping he could hang out with Blake for a bit.' This is true of course, but also such a lie that I feel my neck growing hot. I'm suddenly reminded of the night Amelia asked me to take her and my brother round to Taylor's house, just as I am doing now, using a suggested playdate as a cover for an attempt to see Taylor. At the time I'd refused, hurt that Amelia would try and use me like that, appalled at the idea of using my brother and at how pathetic and needy Amelia seemed.

And yet here I am, just as pathetic and needy as she was.

'Oh dear,' Mrs Lockwood says. 'I'm afraid—'

She's drowned out by a commotion in the hallway behind. A middle-aged couple and two little girls with white-blonde hair appear. The little girls are fighting over something. At the sight of them Jamie shrinks slightly into my side. I put my arm around his shoulders, feeling ashamed of myself.

183

'I'm sorry,' I say, 'you've got people over.'

'Friends of the family.' She pauses. 'They've come to pick up Taylor. He's staying with them while I take Blake to my sister's for a couple of days. We were supposed to leave half an hour ago.' Mrs Lockwood indicates a jumble of bags under a pile of assorted jumpers and jackets.

'Right,' I say. A seedling of hope roots itself in my chest. Perhaps Taylor was distracted last night because he was going away. Maybe that's why he didn't show up.

On the other side of the hall the two little girls have stopped fighting. Their parents have squatted down and are talking to them in low, serious tones – I can't hear what they're saying but it's obvious the girls are being told off.

'Mum!' Blake calls from somewhere high up in the house. '*Mum!*'

His mother rolls her eyes. 'Coming!' she yells back. She turns back to us and I can see she's desperate to get rid of us and finish her packing.

'I'm afraid it's not a good time,' she says with an apologetic smile. 'We're running late as it is.'

'But Taylor isn't going with you?' I ask, hating myself for the needy edge to my voice.

'That's right,' she says absently, glancing at the messy pile of bags again. 'Taylor and Abi are such great friends.'

Who the hell is Abi?

184

As I think the question, the answer walks into view: a girl about my age in a skin-tight mini dress and expensive-looking leather boots. She has the kind of hair I've always envied: long and shining like a gold sheet. It's clear that she's related to the two little blonde girls and their parents. There's a shared air of designer chic radiating off all of them.

'Mum!' Blake yells again.

'I'm afraid I have to go,' Mrs Lockwood says. 'Oh, Abi, hello.'

She hurries away as the girl, Abi, wanders over. She looks me up and down with a critical and appraising gaze. 'Are you looking for T?' she drawls.

I gulp, torn between repeating my cover story about bringing my brother here to play with Jamie and admitting the truth in an attempt to get information.

I settle for something half way between the two. 'I was wondering if he was here,' I say, blushing at the note of desperation I can hear in my voice.

'I see,' the girl says. She looks down her nose at me. Jamie she ignores completely. He tugs at my hand, trying to drag me away. 'Well,' the girl says slowly, as if I'm a total idiot, 'T *is* here. He's coming to my house in a minute so he's busy packing a bag. Who shall I say was asking after him?'

It's an oddly formal phrase to use, but it sounds authentic

185

in the girl's mouth. She's so poised, a real beauty with slanting eyes and those long, long legs. My own legs feel like jelly; I'm beyond intimidated.

'How come you call him T?' The question slips out of me like an accusation.

A slow smile spreads across the girl's face. I can see she has sussed my jealousy and is enjoying it. My face burns. Jamie's yanking on my hand becomes more insistent.

'I call him "T",' she drawls, 'because we're *close*,' she lowers her voice, 'if you know what I mean?'

She's inferring that they're a couple, isn't she? Or at the very least that they've linked in the past.

'Taylor has lots of nicknames,' she goes on. 'T is just the one *I* use.'

What a bitch. She must know she's upsetting me.

'I know he has nicknames,' I say, my whole face burning. 'Like Super H.'

I still don't know what that nickname refers to, but at least it's a way of proving I'm close to Taylor too.

'*You* call him Super H?' The girl raises her elegantly plucked eyebrows. 'I thought that was just at his school.'

Defeated, I look away. Jamie is pulling on my arm with real effort now. I take a step away from the house.

'I bet you don't even know what Super H means,' the girl hisses.

I meet her gaze. I know I'm giving away my feelings but I

186

don't know how to shut them down, how to stop transmitting how helplessly I've fallen for Taylor.

'H for Hacker,' the girl says, conspiratorially, then she straightens up. 'I'll tell T you were here.'

And with that she shuts the door in my face.

I let Jamie drag me down the path and along the street. My mind reels. Super H means Super Hacker? I think about what Poppy said earlier and how Taylor put the blame for the fire at his school on that other boy, Mooney.

My breath catches in my throat as a horrific thought flashes into my head. Could Taylor be SweetFreak?

It's unthinkable, isn't it? And yet he's told me plenty of times that his dad works in IT and there was loads of tech in his room. And you don't get a nickname like Super Hacker for nothing. It sounds like he could have easily hacked my computer and covered his tracks. And, if he's as ruthless as Poppy said, maybe he wouldn't care about me getting hurt in his attempt to hurt Amelia. Maybe he even enjoy toying with me, knowing he'd ruined our friendship.

I tell myself it can't be true. That I know Taylor, that he's a kind and thoughtful person who likes me. He's my *boyfriend* for goodness sake, not that either of us have ever used that label.

And yet what if it *is* true? What if Taylor, having bumped into me on the way to his little brother's school, thought it would be fun to play games with me. The fact that he forgets

187

when we're supposed to meet and ignores my calls shows that I'm hardly always on his mind. Maybe he decided to play games with Amelia too, once he got bored of going out with her. Nasty, evil games ... No. Wait. He couldn't have known about the dead bird. Poppy posted about it on NatterSnap but Taylor goes to a different school and probably wouldn't have seen that.

And then I remember how Taylor's mum dropped Jamie at home just as I was putting the pigeon in the bin outside our house. She could have clocked what I was doing and mentioned it to Taylor. I don't know how he could have got the bird into Amelia's locker, but he definitely had a potential motive. I remember clearly that he said he had blocked Amelia because her messages annoyed him. Suppose they annoyed him enough to make him want to punish her? He didn't care about the boy who got framed for the fire at his school, maybe he didn't care about framing me?

'Carey! Carey!' I'm suddenly aware of Jamie jumping up and down beside me.

I stop pacing along. We're closer to home than I've realised. Almost at the point where the woods intersect with the park. I am desperate to get home and think about all this.

'Carey!' Jamie shouts.

'What?' I turn on him, irritation flaring.

'You said we could go play in the woods,' Jamie pouts.

'But we've just walked past the entrance. He points to the pathway just a few metres behind us.

I frown. No way am I in the mood to play *Warriors of the Doom Wood*. 'We're going home,' I snap.

'No.' Jamie stamps his foot. 'No, you promised.'

I boil over, a horrible swear word erupting from my mouth. 'We're not going to the woods, d'you hear me? You're so annoying sometimes, Jamie Logan. I can't stand you!'

I want to bite back the words as soon as I've uttered them. But before I can speak, Jamie's mouth wobbles, his eyes fill with hot, angry tears and he turns and rushes away.

'Jamie!' I yell after him. 'Jamie, come back!'

But he's already out of sight along the path into the woods.

Irritation rises inside me again. What's he playing at? He knows he's not allowed to go into the woods without me or Mum or Poppy. I know the way through the trees, right through to the cliffs on the other side, but Jamie is too little. He'll get lost.

'Jamie!' I shout again. I walk back to the pathway and peer into the dark forest. There's no sign of him. He's probably hiding nearby. 'Jamie, I'm sorry I shouted. Come back, please!'

I stand and wait. The sun goes behind a cloud, leaving the air damp and chilly. I shiver. 'Jamie?'

I run into the woods. Where on earth has he gone?

'Jamie?' A finger of fear hooks itself around my heart. 'Jamie, stop mucking about.'

No reply.

'Jamie, you win, we'll play *Warriors*. I didn't mean what I said. Please come out.'

I stand, waiting. A car whooshes past, whipping up the leaves at the edge of the trees. I go deeper into the woods. It's quieter here, just the sound of the wind in the branches.

'Jamie!' I call again. *'Please!'*

But though I shout and shout, my little brother does not reappear.

20

Fear chases reason as I race through the wood, retracing my tracks over and over, even though it's obvious Jamie isn't here. I'm panting for breath, sweat dripping down my face and my back. Where is he? He can't have just vanished. I crash over twigs and leaves, pushing past branches, my throat hoarse from yelling his name. I widen the scope of my search until I'm almost at the point where the woods narrow, close to the sea.

There's no way Jamie would have come this far. I turn around and take a circuitous route back to the place where I last saw him, the entrance to the woods close to the park near our house.

It starts to rain as I call Jamie's name one final time. Nearly fifty minutes have passed since he ran into the woods and there is still no sign of my little brother. I imagine that he's lost, wandering among the trees. I imagine he's run through

191

the woods and down to the cliffs on the other side. I imagine him falling, terrified, into the sea below. I don't know what has happened or where he is, all I know is that I've lost him.

I hurry home, not bothering to wipe my damp hair from my eyes. It's just after three o'clock. Poppy and Mum should be back by now. How am I going to face either of them? Jamie is the very heart of our family, the only pure and innocent element.

What if someone's taken him? Maybe the same person behind SweetFreak? Taylor? Abi would have told him I'd come to the door, he could easily have followed us to the woods. Maybe he took Jamie as the price of my silence.

I'm being crazy now. Taylor doesn't even know I suspect him of being SweetFreak. I stand, shivering, at the traffic lights on the road past the park, waiting to cross as cars swoosh past, sending spray over my already wet legs.

At last the traffic comes to a halt. I fly across the road then up our street. I'm soaked through, but I barely notice. Terror for Jamie coils around the guilt that feels like it's splitting me into fragments. My heart is beating so hard I actually think it might explode. I raise my key to the lock with trembling fingers. The wood is damp as I push the door open. I step inside. Voices drift across the hall from the kitchen. Mum is laughing, Poppy saying something in that low-voiced, sarcastic way of hers. In seconds I will have to deliver the most devastating news of our lives.

'And yay, I present thee my sword and swear myself to thy service!' Jamie's excitable squeal sends Mum into giggles again.

I stop in my tracks, my drenched satin jacket dripping onto the carpet. For a second I can't actually process what I've heard. Then I break into a run and storm into the kitchen. Jamie is right there, his plastic sword in his hand as he kneels before Mum at the kitchen sink. He looks up and sees me, slack-jawed, staring at him. A guilty look flashes across his little face.

'Carey, for heaven's sake!' Mum exclaims.

'The wet look was very last year, actually,' Poppy drawls.

'Jamie! Where've you *been*? I thought you were lost,' I say, not taking my eyes off my brother. 'I thought you'd been kidnapped or . . . or . . .' My voice shakes and all of a sudden I'm in floods of tears. It's the relief, washing over me in huge waves. I sink against a chair. 'What happened? I was looking everywhere for you.'

Jamie stands up, shuffling from foot to foot.

'Jamie said he turned around and you'd gone,' Mum says, her voice half accusatory, half concerned. 'I tried to call you, but there was no reply.'

My hand strays to the phone Taylor gave me. It is still in my pocket but of course Mum would have called me on the rubbish mobile she gave me. And I left that at home.

I look at my brother. I'm guessing he hasn't told Mum

about our argument or that he ran away. He knows that would get him into trouble.

'No,' I say, my voice still shaking. 'I turned around and *Jamie* had gone. I've been looking everywhere for him.' I wipe my eyes and focus on my brother again. 'Thank goodness you're all right.'

'Well it sounds like you were both extremely careless,' Mum says, sounding a little bewildered.

I nod. I'm just beginning to accept that nothing bad has happened. Which is, frankly, so amazing I don't have the slightest desire to drop Jamie in it.

'So ...' Mum goes on. 'Jamie, you shouldn't have run off, but I understand you wanting to come home when you couldn't find Carey. And Carey, obviously you should have kept a better eye on him, but it looks like you've suffered enough.' She eyes my wet clothes and hair. 'So why don't you go and change and I'll make us all some hot chocolate.'

I nod again, slowly. Jamie darts across the room and throws his arms around me. It's a hug not just of affection but of gratitude.

I hug him back, tears sparking at my eyes again. Suddenly I feel wrung out and exhausted. I hang my damp jacket on the peg by the door and trudge upstairs. I shower and change into leggings and a baggy jumper. Warm and cosy at last, I brush leave-in conditioner through my curls, eyeing myself in the mirror. The world feels like it's shifted on its axis, just

194

a little. I didn't lose Jamie, but I could have. It makes me see what's important: keeping the people you love safe, or even more simply: keeping the people you love.

I detangle my hair, strand by strand. I'm determined to sort things out and get my life back. I've let myself be buffeted about by the terrible things I was accused of, allowing those things to dictate how people behave towards me.

Well, all that is going to change.

First, I'll call Taylor and ask him what's going on between us. I won't mention the whole SweetFreak thing. Instead I'll keep the focus on us and whether or not he actually wants to go out with me.

Then I'm going to try and speak to Amelia again but this time, instead of blaming other people for SweetFreak, I'll simply insist that it isn't me, that I'm her good friend and that I always have been.

I should never have given up on our friendship and if I can get Amelia on my side then everyone else will come round in time. My friends will start talking to me ... Mum will stop looking at me through wary eyes ... I'll be liked again. Most important of all, I'll get my best friend back.

The rain has stopped outside and the sun is out, making a rainbow that curves over the horizon. Downstairs I can hear Mum and Poppy discussing a dress Mum is thinking of buying. Toots and whistles blare out from the living room where Jamie must be watching a cartoon.

This is my world, my family. We're all here. Safe. For the first time in ages I actually feel happy.

I put down my comb and take out the phone Taylor gave me. I plug it in to charge, then idly open NatterSnap. Mum calls up to say the hot chocolate is ready and I'm about to head downstairs, when a deluge of posts all with the hashtag LostGirl catches my eye. Why are there so many pictures of Amelia flooding the screen?

Mum calls up to me again, but I am glued to NatterSnap, my heart pounding, the glow that had lit me just a moment earlier evaporating.

Because all the posts are full of just one bit of news: Amelia is missing.

21

Downstairs the doorbell rings.

I hear Mum answer, then the low rumble of voices.

'Carey? Come down please,' Mum orders. Her voice sounds different from when she was calling me for my hot chocolate just a minute ago: heavier and harder.

I set down the phone.

'*Carey!*' Now she sounds distraught.

I hurry downstairs. DS Carter and DC Kapoor are standing in the hall with Mum. They're examining my black satin jacket, poring over the flower embroidery on the back. Their faces are deathly serious.

My insides drop away. Nobody speaks as the four of us walk into the kitchen. Poppy is making toast in the corner. She keeps her head down, focusing on scooping a slide of butter onto her knife, but I can tell she's listening.

'What's happening?' I blurt out.

Mum mutters something, but her voice is all strangled.

'We need to ask you some questions about where you've been this afternoon,' DC Kapoor says. Her voice is cold and hard.

'Is this about Amelia?' I demand.

The two detectives exchange a glance.

'I just heard she was missing,' I say quickly. 'I didn't have anything to do with it if that's why you're here.'

DS Carter sighs. 'Let's not get ahead of ourselves. But, yes, Amelia Wilson is missing.'

Mum claps her hand over her mouth.

'And,' DS Carter goes on, 'we have reason to believe you, Carey, may have seen her just before she disappeared.'

'What?' I stare at him. 'I *didn't*.'

'Why do you think that?' Mum demands. 'What makes you think this has anything to do with Carey?'

The detectives look at each other. DS Carter clears his throat. 'An eyewitness called the station. He says he saw you and Amelia arguing at the edge of the cliffs just past Bow Wood about an hour ago.'

Mum gasps.

'Someone says they *saw* us?' I ask, bewildered. 'But I wasn't with Amelia.'

'What kind of person calls the police because they saw an argument?' Mum asks suspiciously. 'Who was he?'

'It was an anonymous call,' DS Carter admits, 'but the

198

witness described Amelia and Carey in detail: hair, build, height difference, what both of you were wearing ...' He glances out into the hallway, towards my black satin jacket. 'He also reported what was being said: threats. Abusive language. *That's* why he felt he needed to call us.'

'*What?*' My jaw drops. 'He's lying. I told you, I wasn't with Amelia.'

Mum looks stunned.

'So you can see why we need to get an idea about Carey's movements this afternoon.' DC Kapoor is now speaking to Mum, as if I'm not even in the room. 'We need a timeline.'

Mum nods, her forehead creased with anxiety. She and I sit down at the kitchen table. Poppy is still lurking by the toaster but no one takes any notice of her. Mum holds my hand as the two police officers sit opposite.

'In your own words, Carey,' DS Carter says, 'can you walk us through your day, please? What time did you leave the house?'

I start talking, my voice a dull monotone, like something I'm only vaguely connected to. I think back to the morning and how I worried for hours that Taylor hadn't called to explain why he hadn't met me.

I don't say this to the police. Apart from anything else, I don't want Mum to know I've been linking with Taylor. This, I realise later, is a mistake, as it makes my turning up at Taylor's house with Jamie in tow look like an attempt to give

199

myself an alibi, instead of what it actually was: a desperate desire to understand why he'd stood me up.

'I took my little brother to play with his friend Blake,' I explain. 'Er, to see if Blake could play with him.'

'And?' DS Carter raises his eyebrows.

'Blake and his mum were busy getting ready to go away for a few days, so we left.'

'Is it usual for Carey to organise Jamie's playdates?' DS Carter glances at Mum, a puzzled expression on his face.

'Er, no.' Mum squirms in her seat. 'I imagine Jamie was pestering for Carey to take him. He loves playing with Blake.'

She looks at me and I nod.

'And where were you, Mrs Logan? At lunch then the spa, was it?' DC Kapoor smiles, but there's a hard edge to her voice. Mum blushes. I bristle at the implication that perhaps if Mum spent less time gadding about with her friends indulging in beauty treatments her children wouldn't have turned into feral delinquents.

'I was at the hairdressers.' Mum's cheeks are deep pink with shame. My tongue feels thick in my throat.

'Carey and I often help out with Jamie,' Poppy snaps from across the room. 'Just because Mum's on her own it doesn't make her a bad parent.' We all turn in her direction. Her eyes glitter dangerously. 'We're family and we look out for each other. OK?'

A tense silence descends on the room. DC Kapoor looks deeply affronted, but before she can speak DS Carter spreads his arms and smiles.

'Now come on, let's all calm down a bit, eh?' he says, his voice low and soothing. 'It's understandable nerves are frayed, but let's keep it civil.'

Poppy gives a harrumph, but doesn't speak. I tighten my hold on Mum's hand.

'There's something I don't quite understand,' DS Carter says patiently. 'Why didn't you call Blake's mother before going over there?' He pauses. 'Or his older brother, who I understand you've seen quite a bit of recently?'

I gulp. How on earth do they know about me and Taylor?

Mum is staring at me. I'm sure she doesn't want to look like she has no clue about my romantic relationships in front of the police, but it must be obvious to them anyway from her shell-shocked expression.

'I was hoping maybe I'd see Taylor if I just turned up,' I admit, my face burning. I sound like a jerk, a loved-up idiot of the kind I used to laugh at.

'Again, why not call first?' DS Carter asks.

'I . . . I . . .' The last thing I want to do is talk about all this in front of Mum and the police. 'Taylor and I were supposed to meet yesterday,' I confess, 'but he didn't show up so . . .'

Mum shifts uncomfortably in her seat.

'So, have you been *dating* him, Carey?' DC Kapoor asks. 'Taylor Lockwood?'

I squirm. Mum puts her hand over her forehead.

'You weren't aware of the relationship, Mrs Logan?' DC Kapoor asks. Again, there's the implication that Mum isn't aware of what's going on with her own daughter.

'It's not Mum's fault,' I jump in. 'I just hadn't got round to . . . me and Taylor, it wasn't a serious thing, it hadn't been going on long . . .'

'How about Amelia? Was she aware that you and Taylor had been seeing each other? I believe they were dating until a week or so before Amelia received the death threat?' DS Carter consults his notes.

Now I look like a terrible, boyfriend-stealing friend, on top of everything else. 'Amelia and Taylor did go out, but obviously it was ages ago so—'

'Were you jealous of Amelia and Taylor's relationship?' DC Kapoor enquires. Her voice oozes with triumph, like she's totally sussed out my motive for wanting to hurt Amelia. 'Had you hoped he'd go out with you all along? Were you delighted when he did, then perhaps angry over the past few days, when he seemed to lose interest?'

'No, I only met him a couple of times when they were seeing each other.' My hackles rise. 'If you're trying to say—'

'OK, OK.' DS Carter pats the air with his hands in a

calming gesture. He frowns at DC Kapoor, who purses her lips. 'Let's go back to today.' He clears his throat. 'Did you see Taylor when you arrived at the Lockwood house?'

'No,' I say. 'Like I told you before, his mum was about to set off with Blake for a few days and Taylor was going to stay with friends. When I got there he was upstairs packing a bag.'

DS Carter nods. 'So you and Jamie left and then—'

'Before I left I spoke to a girl from the family Taylor was going to stay with,' I blurt out. 'We talked about Taylor. She told me that one of his nicknames is Super H, meaning Super Hacker. It . . . It made me wonder if my laptop *was* hacked to make it look like the SweetFreak death threat was sent from it. If Taylor's been behind it all.'

The officers exchange a look.

'As I believe we've already explained,' DS Carter says evenly, 'our examination of your laptop shows clearly that the messages were made manually, not remotely.'

'But someone clever could have hacked in and done it without you realising.'

'No, Carey, that's not possible,' DC Kapoor says firmly. 'So back to this afternoon. You're saying you left Taylor's house just after two p.m.'

I nod, my frustration rising.

'Then where did you go?'

'Jamie and I went home,' I say sullenly. This is hopeless.

The police have already decided what the story here is: I sent the nasty messages and the death threat because I was jealous Taylor chose Amelia instead of me months ago. And then, after having finally got Taylor to ask me out, I was tipped into a fresh fury against Amelia when he lost interest.

'Did you and Jamie go straight home?' DC Kapoor pushes.

Mum is staring at me again. I know how guilty I'll look once the police know I was in the wood on my own. I want to make up a story, to say that Jamie and I did come home together, but Mum will call me out on the lie. And, anyway, there's CCTV on the main roads between Taylor's house and mine. It won't be hard to place where I was. Or when.

'No. We stopped at the edge of Bow Wood,' I explain. 'Jamie wanted me to take him in there to play, but I wanted to go home. We argued a bit, then he ran off into the trees. I looked for him for a while, but he'd vanished. I was really worried.'

DS Carter leans forward.

'So you admit you *were* in the woods this afternoon?' he asks.

I squirm. 'Yes.'

'Did you go near the cliffs?'

'Sort of, but only for a moment. When I realised Jamie wasn't there, I went back through the woods and headed home.'

'Did you see Amelia in the woods or by the cliff?'

'No, absolutely not.'

'Did you argue with her?'

'I'm telling you, I didn't see her.' My voice rises. 'When I got to the edge of the trees I looked out towards the sea for a few seconds. I wasn't properly on the cliff. Like ... from where I was standing I couldn't even see whether the tide was in or out.'

'It was in.' The way DS Carter says it sounds ominous.

A shiver snakes down my spine. He's already confirmed that Amelia is missing. What has happened to her? Where is she? Is she all right?

'So how close did you actually get to the edge of the cliff?' DC Kapoor asks.

'Why are you asking that?' Mum snaps.

DS Carter frowns, as if the younger officer has said too much. I stare at their worried faces as a new realisation dawns on me: they seriously think I might have pushed Amelia over the cliff. She could have fallen to the sea many metres below. At high tide the water washes onto the rocks, sweeping everything that falls out to sea.

A tornado of anxiety sweeps through me. For the first time it occurs to me that something really awful may have happened to my best friend.

'Please answer the question, Carey,' DS Carter insists.

'Where is this going?' Mum demands, her voice icy. 'Does my daughter need a lawyer?'

'It's OK, Mum,' I say. Because it is, isn't it? It has to be. Surely if I just explain what happened, they'll see I couldn't possibly have hurt Amelia and start focusing their attention on finding her – and tracking down whoever is guilty.

'Like I told you, I only went to the edge of the trees. I glanced across the coastal path, along the cliff, but I still couldn't see Jamie so I had another look in the woods, then I left and came straight home,' I say, eager now to get my story out, to explain everything that happened, to prove my innocence. 'I was worried about Jamie, but when I got home I found he'd run back here from the woods without me.'

'That's true,' Mum says.

'And what time did Jamie arrive back here?' DS Carter asks Mum.

'Mum was still out, but I was here,' Poppy interjects. 'It was just after two thirty, I'd just got in from the café where I work on Saturdays.'

'I got back from the hairdressers' at three,' Mum adds.

'And when did Carey arrive?' The officer looks from Mum to me.

I shrug.

'About ten minutes after me,' Mum says. 'Maybe less.'

The atmosphere tenses. 'So what were you doing between the time you separated from Jamie at about two twenty and the time you arrived home at roughly ten past three?' DS Carter asks.

'I told you,' I mutter. 'I was looking for Jamie.'

'In Bow Wood?' DS Carter says. 'Through the trees, down to the cliff, though you say you didn't actually get close to the edge?'

'Yes.' A fresh panic whirls inside me. Why is he asking me again?

DC Kapoor narrows her eyes. 'So where exactly were you when you were arguing with Amelia?'

'I wasn't arguing with her,' I insist. 'I haven't seen Amelia today. I haven't seen her for weeks!'

Both officers stare at me. Their silence is somehow more unnerving than their questions.

'Come on, this is ridiculous,' Mum says. 'What would Amelia have been doing in Bow Wood or on the coastal path? She doesn't live anywhere near there.'

'Amelia was last seen by her mother at home this morning,' DC Kapoor explains. 'When she didn't appear all afternoon, her mum went to check on her and found a handwritten note saying she was going out to meet someone – Amelia didn't say who – and would be back by 3.30 at the latest. When she hadn't turned up by four her mother called her phone, which was answered by someone who said they were on the coastal path and heard the mobile ringing and found it lying on the ground.'

'Another anonymous witness?' Poppy asks, her voice heavy with sarcasm.

207

'Not at all,' says DC Kapoor. 'The rambler was happy to give all her details to Amelia's mother, who naturally became very concerned that Amelia wasn't with her phone. At about the same time as Mrs Wilson was speaking with the rambler, we received our anonymous call about two girls arguing near the cliff edge.'

'It wasn't me,' I protest. 'You need to be trying to find whoever *was* there. You need to be looking for Amelia.'

'Well, the eyewitness described you perfectly,' DS Carter says with a sigh.

'What exactly did he claim Carey was saying?' Mum asks. She stares at DS Carter, her grip on my hand tightening. I squeeze her fingers, my throat tight with fear.

DS Carter exchanges a glance with his colleague, then gives a self-conscious cough as he looks back at me and Mum.

'The eyewitness said you were yelling at Amelia, saying that you hated her.' He pauses. 'And that you were going to kill her.'

208

22

Mum gasps. 'Oh, Carey,' she breathes.

'No!' I'm on my feet now, unaware of anything except this latest attack on my innocence. 'Somebody's set me up. Again. There couldn't have been an eyewitness because there wasn't anything *to* witness. The call was a hoax.'

Out of the corner of my eye I can see Jamie in the doorway. He must have heard us and crept closer to see what was going on.

'I'm telling the truth,' I say, desperate for them believe me. 'What about Taylor? Maybe he did all the SweetFreak stuff and Amelia found out. He could have gone to Bow Wood to meet her and—'

'Knowing Amelia's feelings for and previous relationship with Taylor, we've already been in touch with the Lockwood family,' DC Kapoor interrupts. 'Taylor was with the daughter of family friends in East Cornmouth all afternoon.'

So Taylor was with Abi? Jealousy flares inside me. I fall silent. Mum turns to me. There's terrible pain in her eyes.

Worse, there's a flicker of doubt. 'Carey?' she whispers.

I shake my head, too overwhelmed to speak.

'I'm afraid we need to take Carey to the station,' DS Carter says. 'The existence of previous threats linked to Carey plus the fact that Amelia is still missing make this a very serious situation.'

'But Carey *can't* be involved in something like this,' Mum protests. 'Anonymous threats and upsetting gestures like the dead bird are one thing but this ...' She trails off.

'You should be out looking for Amelia.' I insist, my voice cracking with emotion. 'Not wasting time here with me.'

'We just need to ask you a few more questions,' DS Carter says smoothly.

'Before you arrest her?' Poppy snarls, striding over.

'Come on, Carey,' DS Carter insists.

'No.' I clutch the edge of the chair in front of me. 'I'm not going anywhere.'

'You don't have a choice,' DC Kapoor says.

Meaning that if I don't go with them willingly, they will arrest me.

Mum's face pales. She picks up her handbag. 'Let's go. The sooner we finish answering all these questions, the sooner we can get back home again.' She turns to Poppy. 'Will you mind Jamie until I'm back?'

Poppy nods. She touches my arm. 'It'll be OK.'

I shake my head, shot through with panic. Thoughts pile into my mind, one on top of the next. I must look guilty as anything: first the death threat from my laptop, then the dead pigeon from our bin and now an eyewitness saying I was threatening Amelia right next to the cliff edge. I close my eyes, imagining the waves smashing against the rocks at the bottom. I've heard all the local rumours about people falling – or jumping – from that cliff: occasionally, when the tide is out, their bodies can even be seen mangled on the rocks beneath. Nobody ever survives.

Terror for Amelia sears through me. I can't bear the idea of her being hurt. Or worse.

'Do you think Amelia might be dead?' I ask, my voice shaky and small. 'Do you think this is SweetFreak, carrying out their death threat?'

'Right now Amelia's status is missing,' DS Carter says. His voice is softer than DC Kapoor, almost kindly. 'We're just following all possible leads in order to find her.'

Missing. My best friend. Gone. Fresh pain twists the terror in my chest.

I take a step towards the kitchen door, away from the two officers. I can't let them take me to the station and arrest me. I've been set up, right from the start, but nobody believes it. Nobody apart from Poppy even really thinks I'm innocent.

211

Killing Amelia will seem to everyone like the next step, something I planned to do. I'll go to prison.

Which I can't, I just can't.

'Carey, we need to go.' DC Kapoor's voice is stern and forbidding.

I stare at her in blind panic. I want to run, but she would catch me before I reached the front door.

There's no way out. I'm trapped.

'I'll get our coats,' Mum says. She walks past me into the hall, avoiding my gaze.

'Carey?' Jamie runs across the room and hurls himself at my legs, giving them a big squeeze. 'When will you be back?'

'I don't know.' I bend down and kiss the top of his sweet, blond head. 'I love you, Baby Bear.' I haven't used that name for him in years. Jamie hated it once he started Big School, but now he submits with another hug.

As he releases me, Poppy takes his place.

'Stay strong,' she whispers in my ear.

'I can't do this,' I whisper back, my voice cracking.

'There's cash under my mattress, at the bottom of my bed,' Poppy whispers. 'Take it.'

I draw back and look her in the eye. What is she suggesting?

She meets my gaze, her eyes intense with meaning. And in that moment I see what I need to do next.

I turn to the officers. 'Can I use the loo before we go?' I say.

DS Carter nods. 'Be quick,' he says.

I give Poppy another squeeze and pat Jamie on the head, then I turn and race upstairs. I go into my room, snatch my phone from its charger and a jumper from the floor, then into Poppy's next door. I feel under the mattress at the end of the bed. *There.* My fingers curl around a thick roll of notes. I shove them in my pocket, then race along the corridor to the bathroom. I'm out the window in seconds, easing myself onto the shed roof, then over the fence to next door. Moments later I'm tearing along the pavement, jumper swinging from my hand. I run until I'm in the heart of Lower Cornmouth, well away from the main roads, then I stop to catch my breath.

There's a chill wind and now I've stopped running I'm cold, but I barely notice. I pull Poppy's money out of my pocket and count the notes: it comes to £220. How far will that get me?

I gulp.

What on earth do I do now?

RUN

23

I count the money again then take stock. I'm on the run from the police, with just over two hundred pounds in cash and the clothes I'm wearing. I don't even have a jacket and the wind is bitterly cold.

What am I going to do? Where am I going to go?

I take out the mobile Taylor gave me. Apart from him, only Poppy has the number. The police are bound to ask her if there's any way of contacting me but I'm sure she won't give me away. Taylor, on the other hand, might – which means the police would then be able to trace me. Still, I reckon I'm safe using it for the next few minutes.

So what? The thought descends on me like a dense fog, swamping all hopefulness. What am I going to use my phone to do? Who am I going to contact? My life has been so miserable and lonely lately, none of my actual former friends are even online friends with me any more. And it's clear that Taylor no longer wants anything to do with me.

I still have to try. I log on to NatterSnap. Maybe there'll be someone there I can turn to . . . someone who might help me. The news of Amelia going missing has spread like wildfire, it's all over the public messages. My heart sinks as I follow thread after thread and discover that all the people I know from school have made comments: Rose. Both the Rose Clones. Heath. Even Lauren.

I reckon Carey knifed her.

She must have been planning it for months.

Total psycho . . . Amelia's dead FOR SURE.

At first I don't understand why they are all so convinced I must be responsible, then I find the source: two posts from Rose, the first saying (truthfully) that there's a police car outside my house and the second (completely made up) that I've been arrested and charged with Amelia's abduction.

My hands tremble as I scroll through more messages. The level of hate against me is overwhelming. I put the phone in my pocket and slump against the wall behind me. Part of me wants just to turn around and go home. But of course, I can't. The police are convinced I was with Amelia this afternoon thanks to the person who lied about seeing us arguing. Could that have been Rose? No. They said it was a man.

Whatever. All the venom directed at me doesn't matter. Amelia is missing. That's what really counts. I wipe my face, anxiety rearing up again, mingling with the fresh hurt of being accused. I am powerless to help Amelia. In fact, I'm totally alone. And the police aren't even looking for whoever might have actually hurt her, because they think *I'm* responsible. I shiver as a light drizzle begins. And then, just as I'm thinking things really can't get any worse, they do.

'Hey, Curly Wurly!' a voice calls, muffled by the wind and rain.

I look up. A car has slowed to a crawl on the road in front of me. A young guy in a silver shirt is hanging out of the window, waving at me.

Blinking, I turn and hurry away.

'Hey, come back!' Laughter from inside the car. My heart beats fast. I quicken my pace. 'You have amazing hair!' More laughter.

With a crunch of gears the car stops. I hear the engine switched off then footsteps running up. The guy in the silver shirt is grinning, walking beside me. Another man with spiky hair and a half-bottle of vodka dangling from his hand hurries into place on my other side. I speed up again, but they are far taller than me and have no problem keeping up.

'Where are you going, Curly Wurly?' Silver Shirt slurs.

'Yeah, we're going to a club,' Spiky Hair adds. 'Wanna come?'

'No,' I mutter. Age-old warnings about getting into cars with strangers flit through my head. At least these guys are

219

smiling, but I'm aware how easily the situation could turn. I want to face them down, tell them to leave me alone, but they're grown-up men, not like the boys from Poppy's class. I'm scared.

'For God's sake, you two, get back here!' someone shouts from inside the car.

Silver Shirt and Spiky Hair ignore him. They're talking rapidly over the top of each other, trying to convince me to go with them to their stupid club. Suddenly I feel like crying. All I want to do is go home and let Mum look after me. But if I go home I'll be arrested and maybe even sent to some awful juvenile prison. By running away I've made myself look even more guilty than I did before. The thought sends a throb of fear and anger spiralling up through me. The two guys are still walking beside me, talking and laughing.

'Go away!' I yell so loudly that they are shocked into silence.

I break into a run, tearing away from them. I race across the road – thankfully there aren't any cars because I don't look before I dart out – and down the street opposite. I don't stop to see if the two guys are following me, I just run as hard as I can.

A few minutes later it's clear that the men have given up their chase – and also that I am utterly lost. That is, I know I'm in Lower Cornmouth but otherwise I have no idea, though I'm possibly close to the bus stop where I waited for Taylor last night. That seems a lifetime ago.

I don't recognise the street where I'm standing. There's a church on the corner. I hurry towards it, my head clearing slightly. I can look up the church's name on my phone, work out where I am, maybe even find a cheap place to stay. I should try and get a message to Mum somehow, before it gets really late, let her know I'm OK.

As I get closer to the church I see it has a long, dark porch. It's still drizzling and, though the rain is light and misty, I'm starting to feel damp through my jumper. Maybe I should just take shelter under the porch. It's dark there, I'll be completely hidden from the street – and I can work out what to do next.

I hurry up the steps and along the brick path. The church looms overhead. Under other circumstances I'd be scared, spooked by the silence and the gloom. But right now I'm just glad to have got away from the drunk guys and to have found shelter from the rain. And then I reach the porch.

A soft, shuffling noise echoes towards me.

What is that? An animal?

I gulp.

'Hi, please don't be scared.' The boy's voice is vaguely familiar, but it's the uncertainty of his tone more than its familiarity that stops me from running.

A second later he emerges from the shadows. It's the boy with the mismatched trainers and bright blue eyes. He's smiling – a nervous smile.

221

'Hi,' I say, still wary, though reassured by his cautious expression.

'Do you remember me?' he asks. 'You were waiting for a bus just around the corner yesterday evening? I freaked you out by mistake.' He stops, his face flushing slightly in the dim lamplight.

'I remember,' I say.

The night air is still, the wind dropping as suddenly as it whipped up. The drizzle is still coming down though, a fine, wet mist on my face and hair.

'I'm Blue,' the boy says.

'Carey.'

'Hello, Carey.' He smiles properly this time and there's real warmth in his eyes.

Instinct tells me I can trust him but I'm still wary. Anyway, if he's taken the church porch, then I need to find somewhere else to hide out.

'Bye,' I say, then turn away.

'You don't have to go,' Blue says earnestly. 'That is, if you were looking for a place away from the rain you can . . . I mean, that's what I was doing, I just stopped here on my way home so as not to get wet and . . . and to think for a bit.'

'To think?'

'Yeah, I'm living just a couple of streets away but it's super-crowded, so it's hard to get any space . . .'

'Oh, you have a big family then?' I ask.

222

Blue laughs. 'No, I don't live with my family. It's a squat.'

'Oh.' I'm not sure what to say. I'm only vaguely aware of what a squat is – basically a place people stay that they aren't supposed to, like 'borrowing' somebody's house without permission. Whatever, I'm certain it's against the law.

'My friend Seti found the place through the main guy who lives there,' Blue explains. 'But he let me crash there too. People are always coming and going. I mean, it's OK, but . . .' he stops again. 'Please come under here, you're getting wet.'

I shuffle uncertainly from side to side. If I take a couple more steps forward I'll be out of the rain, properly inside the shelter. Blue doesn't seem like he's going to hurt me. Perhaps it's worth the risk. Steeling myself, I take a deep breath and move inside. In the dim light I can make out the low, wooden benches that run on either side of the porch, up to the church door.

I perch on the bench nearest me. Blue sits down opposite.

'What about you?' he asks. 'Where do you live?'

'Other side of Cornmouth,' I say. 'But I've run away.'

'Really?' Blue leans forward. He's wearing ripped jeans and a black jumper with holes in the sleeves. His hair doesn't look like it's been brushed in weeks, but he seems clean. I want to ask how come he doesn't smell, if he lives in a squat, but I don't want to seem rude so I press my lips together.

'It's OK if you don't want to talk about it,' Blue says. 'I ran away too.'

'Did you?' All the tension of the past couple of hours swells inside me. 'Then would you mind telling me how you managed it, because right now, I've got a phone with about twenty pounds credit and not enough cash to survive more than a week or two, even if I sleep rough, and basically I . . . I have no idea what I'm doing. I just need to . . . to disappear for a bit.' I stop before I burst out crying. Furious with myself for showing so much emotion, I blink away the tears pricking at my eyes.

Blue frowns, his whole expression darkening.

I've said too much. What was I thinking, telling this strange boy all of that? For all I know he might decide to snatch my phone and my money. I tense, ready to run. But Blue just studies me carefully. In spite of my reservations, there's a seriousness about him that I like, something weighty and reassuring about his presence. He seems somehow older than I am, though he's shorter than Taylor and doesn't look much different from most of the boys in my year.

'If you don't want people to find you, you need to ditch the phone you were talking about,' he says.

'Oh, that's OK,' I explain breezily, delighted to be able to show him that I'm not as naïve as he thinks. 'I know the police can trace phones, but hardly anyone knows I have it, so I reckon I've got a few more minutes. My mum definitely doesn't know about it, so—'

'Have you ever used your phone to go on social media?' Blue asks.

I nod, thinking of all the NatterSnap messages between me and Taylor and the occasional, pointless attempts I've made recently to 'like' or 'follow' or 'join' other people's profiles, images and conversations.

'Then they'll be able to trace it from that without getting the number off anyone. You need to dump it.'

'Not just switch it off?' I stare at him, aghast. The phone feels like my only link to home.

'Write down anything you need, like useful numbers or NatterSnap handles or whatever, then get rid of it,' Blue says. 'Seriously.' He hands me a little notebook and a pen. 'I use this for doodles, I used to have a tablet but it got nicked. Take a sheet.'

The notebook is well worn, the edges curled and grubby. I open it up. Even in the dim light coming off the street I can see that it's full of drawings. Mostly people's faces. I flick through, sensing Blue is watching me.

These aren't just 'doodles'. The pencil sketches are beautiful – a world away from the graphic collages Amelia used to do for her art projects. There's something raw and simple about them. Several faces appear again and again – an older woman with a gentle smile, then the girl I saw Blue with before, Seti I guess, instantly recognisable with her long thin plaits snaking out of her head and her imperious glare. I turn the next page and find a picture of a girl with wide-set eyes and a halo of curly hair. Her expression is one of anxious shock, like she's just been startled.

'Is this me?' I ask, looking up. 'At the bus stop?'

Blue nods, clearly embarrassed.

'Your drawings are really good,' I say, fishing out my phone and scrolling to the two numbers stored.

'Thanks,' he says gruffly.

I scribble down Poppy's number. I hesitate before writing down Taylor's. I can't imagine why I'd call him, but if I'm going to dump the phone it seems silly not to take it just in case. I fold the paper with the sketch of me and the two numbers and shove it into my pocket. Then I hold up my phone.

'So what do I do with this?' I ask.

'Keep it,' Blue says. 'It's just the SIM you need to destroy.'

'OK.' I take the SIM out. I hesitate for a second, then snap it in two. I expect to feel an overwhelming sense of loss – or liberation – but neither feeling comes.

'Now we need to get out of here,' Blue says. 'In case your parents have already reported you missing and the police are trying to trace you right now.'

'OK.' I don't ask where we're going or why Blue appears to have taken me under his wing. I just follow him out of the church porch and back onto the street. It's stopped raining, thankfully, and I'm no longer as cold as I was before.

'You should keep your head down when we get to the main road,' Blue cautions. 'You need to cover your face from the CCTV.'

A dim recollection of DS Carter explaining that Cornmouth only had CCTV on the main drags flitters into my mind. 'Why don't we just stay off the main road?' I ask.

'Because we need to cross it,' Blue says, matter-of-factly.

A worm of anxiety coils up in my chest. 'To get where?' I ask.

'The squat,' he says, as if it's obvious. 'Unless you *want* to stay out on the streets all night?'

I say nothing, turning the prospect over in my head. Blue really doesn't seem like he'd want to hurt me. Anyway, where else am I going to go?

'Here, take this.' Blue tugs off his black jumper and hands it to me. He is wearing another jumper underneath. Both have hoods. 'Put it on and pull the hood up.'

I do as he says. We stroll along the main road, our hoods low over our faces. I glance at Blue's mismatched trainers again. The question I've wanted to ask since I first saw him months ago finally pops out of my mouth.

'How come you have shoes that don't match?'

'My second night on the streets someone nicked one of the sneakers I'd run away in,' Blue explains. 'When I woke up and realised, it felt like the last straw. I was cold and hungry and angry and I felt stupid too. I'd heard about this

soup kitchen so I went there in my one shoe. Seti was there too. She came over and we got talking and I told her how my trainer had been taken and the next thing I knew she disappeared then came back about twenty minutes later with a replacement. "Sorry it's yellow," was all she said. I was so grateful I didn't even ask her where she got it from. We've hung out together ever since.'

I wonder if he means like a couple. She seems a bit old for him, but you never know.

'Truth is I would never have survived this long without Seti,' Blue says.

'Why did you run away from home?' I ask, curious.

'That's a long story,' Blue says.

I fall silent again. It's fair enough he doesn't want to tell me. I don't really want to tell him how I've ended up here either.

My thoughts turn to Amelia. Anxieties whip through my head: is she OK? She's been missing for hours now. What can have happened to her? The police said she left a note saying she was going to meet someone in Bow Wood. But who? And why did someone – the same person, perhaps – claim to have seen me with her? Presumably they must have known I was there, otherwise the accusation wouldn't stick.

We turn off the main road. Blue and I remove our hoods. The rain has stopped and I run my fingers through my wet hair, which is hopelessly tangled.

'I'm thinking maybe you should cut that,' Blue suggests.

'My hair?'

Blue smiles at the horrified look on my face. 'Or else cover it up,' he says. 'It's very distinctive.'

'You mean odd?' I grin.

'I mean pretty,' he counters straight back.

There's an awkward silence.

'The squat's down here,' Blue says, pointing along the street. 'Like I said, the house'll be full of people and some of them won't want another person there, but don't worry, I'll talk to Seti and she'll fix it.'

'OK.' My stomach churns with anxiety.

'Also . . .' Blue hesitates. 'Quite a few of the people there are like these mad political activists, like they go on demos and believe in bringing down the government, like extreme stuff, so . . . so don't let them bully you and don't be scared. Most of them are all talk and no action.'

'I'll be fine,' I say, though inside I'm quaking.

'I'm sure you will be.' Blue laughs and his face lights up. 'I wasn't saying you couldn't stand up for yourself. I just wanted to warn you.'

'Thanks,' I say and, buoyed unexpectedly by his confidence in me, I follow him along the road towards the squat.

24

It's a huge house, even bigger than the one Taylor lives in, but it's in a terrible state: the brickwork is crumbling off the outer walls and the wood around the windows is rotten and splintered. The front garden is a mess of overgrown plants and weeds and there's a huge, dirty puddle by the blistered and swollen front door.

Blue gives the door a shove to open it.

'No key?' I murmur.

'No key and no hot water,' he says. 'But we do have electricity.' To prove the point he flicks a light switch by the door and the dilapidated hallway comes into view.

It's as big a mess as the front garden – piles of old cloths and cardboard boxes and flaky paint on the walls. The bit of floor that's visible is made up of stained, warped floorboards.

'Whose house is this?' I ask.

Blue shrugs. 'No idea. But Tommo says it's ethical

squatting because we're not taking a home that anyone else wants. This one's been derelict for years.'

'Who's Tommo?' I ask.

'I am.' A thin snarl of a voice echoes towards us and I look up to see a skinny, wiry guy of about nineteen or twenty sauntering down the stairs. He has a shaved head, a long brown beard and about twenty piercings across his ears, nose and lips.

'Hi,' I say nervously.

'Who's this, Blue?' Tommo asks with a sneer. 'Another charity case?'

Blue tenses slightly. I'm guessing he doesn't like Tommo much.

'This is Carey,' he says. 'She's in a heavy situation at home, just needs to crash for a couple of nights.'

Tommo nods. 'From each according to his means ...' he says.

'Sorry?' I glance at Blue.

'He means he'd like you to help out,' Blue explains. 'Right, Tommo?'

'We're a community,' Tommo says. 'Everyone makes a contribution.'

'Sure,' I say. 'What do you want me to do? I can cook – basic stuff anyway – or I can clean up a bit.' I stop, worrying that I'm sounding like my mum, not to mention stereotypically girly.

231

'Are you saying this place is dirty?' Tommo grins. He has a mean little rat-like face. I'm not sure if he's joking or not . . . surely it's obvious that the house is filthy, but I don't want to sound rude.

'Give her a break,' Blue snaps.

'She can help with the placards in the morning. Second floor, it's got great light. She can sleep in that room you and Seti and that tattoo-face one and her mate are using.'

Tommo stands back to let me pass. I can feel his eyes on me as I walk up the stairs, Blue right behind.

'Is Tommo in charge?' I whisper, as we reach the first floor.

Tommo himself is still watching us, along with two other boys with similar beards who have emerged from downstairs rooms.

'Likes to think he is,' Blue says with a sniff. 'Under the guise of it all being a co-operative.'

I frown, not really understanding. The first-floor landing is empty – faded paint on the walls and a threadbare carpet – with doors leading off on all sides. I glimpse a dingy bathroom with stained tiles on the floor.

'That's the shower,' Blue says with a wry smile. 'Luckily I don't mind it being permanently cold.' We carry on, up to the second floor. Raucous male voices float out from a room to the left. I glance over, my anxiety building.

'Is it all blokes here?' I ask.

'No,' Blue says. 'Come and meet Seti.' He opens a door on the right. The room beyond is as tatty as the rest of the house, but far cosier than I expected. The floor is covered with rugs in reds and browns. Another rug hangs on the wall and sheets are gathered at the deep windows. Seti herself is sitting with a small group of people, propped up against a pile of moth-eaten cushions in the far corner. She's picking at a plate of biscuits, nodding intently as one of the other girls speaks. They glance around as Blue and I come in, but the girl doesn't break off from what she's saying.

'So, like, it's a global thing, run by big corporations and stuff.'

'It's so unfair,' one of the guys says.

'They just really want to keep the masses in their place.'

'Yeah, under their steel boots.'

Murmurs of agreement.

'Hey, Blue.' Seti acknowledges us at last. She smiles at me, flicking her long, thin plaits over her shoulders. 'Who's your friend?'

'I'm Carey,' I say. All eyes fix on me. I give an awkward smile. 'Blue said I could stay here for a couple of nights, if that's OK?'

'She can't have my space,' a girl with a tattoo of a spider's web on her right cheek says to no one in particular.

Beside me, Blue stiffens.

'If Carey's a friend of Blue's then she's cool,' Seti says. 'Carey's welcome.'

And this seems to settle it. The others nod and smile at me, making room for us as Blue leads me over. We sit down. I feel desperately self-conscious, but luckily I don't have to speak. Blue is doing the talking, explaining how he met me in the church porch and how I've run away from home.

Thankfully nobody asks me to explain what I'm running from. I wonder how they have all ended up here. None of them look older than nineteen or twenty, though Blue and I are definitely the youngest.

The small group carries on chatting, mostly about political stuff I don't understand. Music and loud voices echo occasionally from the room across the landing, but no one from there comes into our room.

'How many people live here?' I ask Blue quietly.

'I don't know exactly,' he says softly back. 'Seti and I only moved in a few weeks ago. It's much nicer than our last place.'

'I see.'

'Tommo was already here with I reckon about twenty mates. I think he let us move in cos he fancied Seti.' Blue grimaces, then a slow grin spreads across his face. 'Not that she's interested in him.'

'So is Seti your girlfriend?' My stomach gives a twist. For reasons I don't quite understand, I'm hoping the answer to my question is 'no'.

'No way,' Blue says with a chuckle. 'I mean I like Seti all

right, but not like that. She's taught me plenty of tricks for getting by on the streets but she's definitely not—'

'Are you talking about me?' Seti herself cuts in, her voice arch and imperious.

Blue meets her gaze. 'Just saying how you begged me to date you but I turned you down.'

Seti laughs, flicking her long, thin plaits over her shoulder. 'Yeah right, like I'd look twice at you, you're half my age for a start.'

'I'm fifteen,' Blue says in mock outrage.

Seti looks over. Her almond-shaped eyes sparkle with life as she smiles. She's really pretty in her blue jumper and skinny jeans. There's something haughty and intimidating in her expression as she turns to me but there's warmth too.

'Don't worry, Carey, he's all yours.'

I can feel my face reddening, the burn deepening as everyone else, apart from Blue, laughs.

'Shut up, Seti,' Blue mutters, clearly embarrassed.

'Whatever.' Seti stretches out her long, slim legs and leans back against her cushions. 'Go next door, Bobs, and see if they've got any booze, yeah?'

One of the guys immediately gets up and trots out of the room.

'Seti the slave owner,' murmurs Tattoo-face.

'I can't help it if I'm a natural leader,' Seti says with a smug grin.

I glance at Blue again. Despite the fact that he's several years younger than the others, I get the impression that he would never let anyone tell him what to do. There's a steely quality about him. Perhaps that's what makes him seem so much older. I have a sudden intuition that Seti likes him precisely because she can't push him around.

Of course I don't say this. Or anything. I carry on sitting there in silence while Bobs comes back from the room next door with a bottle in his hand and passes it round so everyone can take a swig.

I refuse the bottle when it comes to me. I want to keep a clear head among all these strangers. Blue doesn't drink either, nor does he join in the heated political debate that ensues. He slips out of the room in fact, returning a few minutes later with a fresh plate of toast and some lumps of rubbery cheese to share with me. I devour as much of the plateful as I can get my hands on, while the older teens talk around us.

As far as I can work out, Seti and most of the others think that their protests and those of other anti-capitalist demonstrators around the world will lead to new governments run as co-operatives, with everyone looked after by everyone else.

'Like with bartering for food and no greedy bankers,' Seti explains with conviction.

''Better to have a revolution, clean and quick and simple,'

Tattoo-face says with a contemptuous sniff. 'Start with a proper clean slate.'

Blue rolls his eyes at me. It's clear he thinks they're talking rubbish.

I have no idea what time it is now, but I'm struggling to keep my eyes open so it comes as a relief when Tattoo-face and her friend wander off and Seti lies down on her cushions and closes her eyes. The others left in the room take this as a sign to either leave, or go to bed themselves.

Blue fetches me a blanket from a pile in the corner and I grab a frayed and faded velvet cushion for my head. It's hard on the thin carpet of the floor, definitely the strangest place I've ever slept. Blue falls asleep on the other side of the room way before me. No one has changed into night things or cleaned their teeth. I feel suddenly lonely and miss home desperately. Mum will be furious and scared that I'm gone. Jamie will be worried and confused too. How will Mum and Poppy explain to him why I'm still not home?

My thoughts turn to Amelia again. Is she all right? I really hope that she's turned up safely at home, but without my phone I have no way of checking online to see if there's any news.

Whoever made the anonymous call claiming I was arguing with her yesterday afternoon was clearly trying to frame me. That *has* to be the same person who was behind the SweetFreak messages *and* the dead bird in Amelia's

locker. Which means whoever's responsible for Amelia going missing can't be a random stranger but someone known to us both.

It can't be either of the people I've seriously suspected so far: George is Amelia's brother, so Amelia wouldn't need to leave home if she was going to meet him, and it's seems very unlikely that Rose would have known I'd be in Bow Wood yesterday afternoon.

Which brings me back to Taylor.

I dismissed my earlier suspicions that he was SweetFreak as far-fetched but maybe I should think it through, step by step. It's certainly possible from a practical point of view: Taylor has the IT skills to hack my computer and cover his tracks, his mum could have told him about the dead pigeon, which he could easily have arranged to be dumped in Amelia's locker, and I'm certain Abi would be prepared to lie to protect him, so his alibi for yesterday doesn't count for much.

But *why* would he go to all those lengths? I frown, trying to work it back to the start. Taylor told me that he blocked Amelia after they split up because she was pestering him online. Which was exactly the time SweetFreak started sending messages. That surely can't be a coincidence. Suppose instead of just blocking Amelia he also sent her nasty messages to get back at her for annoying him? Breaking up her friendship with me would have just been part of the revenge. All of which he totally got away with . . .

Until, perhaps, Amelia discovered what he had done.

My breath catches in my throat. *Yes.* It makes sense now: if Amelia recently found out Taylor was SweetFreak, she might well have called him out on it. Perhaps she even said she was going to tell everyone. How far would Taylor have gone to stop her? Under those circumstances it's not hard to imagine him totally losing his temper – or getting violent.

I shiver at the thought. And yet it doesn't seem so impossible as it would have once. People are capable of anything if pushed far enough. Look at me. I could never have imagined just a few months ago that I would run away from home and end up sleeping in a derelict house.

As for Taylor framing me . . . it would have taken a clear head and some quick thinking to pull it all together, but if he'd overheard Jamie and me on the doorstep talking about going to Bow Wood, he could have easily arranged to meet Amelia there too. Then all he'd have had to do – after he'd attacked her – was make that phone call claiming I'd been arguing with Amelia at the cliff edge.

It all seems to fit.

The only thing I don't understand is why he'd want to hurt me when he barely knew me back in September, and then go out with me months afterwards. Or perhaps he's never really cared what happened to me either way . . . perhaps all I've ever been is collateral damage.

I mull it over as the grey sheets at the window start to

lighten. They are patchy with stains. Mum would be shocked to see them, even more shocked to see me here, lying under a grubby blanket surrounded by strangers. As I lie in the dark, my fears threaten to overwhelm me: for Amelia and for myself.

It's a long time before I fall asleep.

25

I wake with a start to find bright winter sunlight streaming in through the window. I squint at the glare and a figure moves to block the stream of light. Tommo is staring down at me. I'm suddenly aware that there are other people beside him. I look around. Four men and two women – none of whom I recognise from last night – are watching me.

Gasping for breath I scramble to sit up, scrabbling back across the room.

'What do you make of our commune?' Tommo asks.

I gaze up at him. He's smiling, though not in a kind way. One of the guys he's with laughs.

'What's going on?' It's Seti, pushing her way between the laughing guy and the woman next to him. She glances down at me. 'You OK, Carey?'

I nod, relieved to see her. Where is Blue? I glance around

241

the room. Blue and all the other people who were here last night appear to have vanished.

'I was just asking Carey what she thinks of the place,' Tommo says, a touch defensively.

I sense the atmosphere changing, the others hanging back, watching Tommo and Seti. Tommo's in charge, that's obvious, but Seti seems like a leader sort of person too, a challenge to Tommo's authority.

'I'm sure Carey's happy to have had a roof over her head,' Seti says with a haughty shrug. 'Aren't you, Carey?'

'Yes, er, I am, er . . . thank you.'

'Any other thoughts?' Tommo asks lightly.

Seti folds her arms, shaking her head at Tommo.

'It's . . . interesting to be here,' I say, trying to think of something to say that will satisfy Tommo and show my loyalty to Seti who is trying to defend me.

A murmur of laughter, not unfriendly, ripples around the group.

'So what's so fascinating about us?' Tommo asks.

'For Pete's sake,' Seti mutters.

I look from her to Tommo. Where on earth is Blue?

I clear my throat. 'Um, well one thing is that everyone has interesting names.'

The others roar with laughter. I blush. That sounded stupid.

'What's going on?' Blue strides over, pushing into the group to stand beside Seti.

242

Feeling braver now that Blue is here, I stand up.

'Just saying hello to our newest housemate.' Tommo turns and strides away.

Blue looks suspiciously around the group. 'I've made some breakfast,' he says to me. 'It's next door.'

He takes my hand and leads me out of the room.

More laughter erupts behind us. Blue's face is flushed with irritation. 'I'm sorry they were hassling you,' he says.

'They weren't all,' I say. 'Seti actually stood up for me.'

Blue nods. 'Seti's OK. That is, I don't agree with all that property is theft rubbish she believes in—'

'Property is theft?'

'Yeah, but she's been good to me,' Blue says as we reach the room across the landing. 'And she's not afraid of Tommo.'

We go into the next room. It's very different from the one in which I spent the night. There are actual mattresses on the floor, for a start, and a big TV in front of the far wall. A cookery programme is on at low volume. Nobody is watching it. Tattoo-face and her friend are sitting on a rug next to the TV, talking quietly. Two guys squat beside them, setting up an Xbox. The floor is littered with empty beer cans and food wrappers. There's a low table in the middle with a kettle and a collection of mugs. Steam rises out of two of them, next to a plate of buttered toast.

'Thanks,' I say to Blue, walking over and picking up one of the mugs.

243

'I wasn't sure if you took sugar in your tea,' Blue says. 'There's a bag on the table.'

'You're such a host,' Seti giggles from the door. She must have followed us across the landing.

Blue scowls and joins me by the table. The guys setting up the Xbox start arguing over which cable plugs into the big TV. Seti comes over and takes a slice of toast. I sip at my tea, wondering how long I'll be able to stay here. It's not particularly that I *want* to stay, but at least there's food and shelter here. And I don't want to think about the future.

'It's her!' Tattoo-face's voice cuts across all the others in the room. She turns to me, her arm outstretched, her finger pointing. 'It's you! Look!'

She turns back to the TV. Everyone else follows her gaze, including me.

She's right. There's a picture of me on the screen, beside the programme's presenter.

'*Sssh*,' Tattoo-face snatches up the remote control and the volume rises. I recognise the local news programme, one that Mum sometimes watches. The presenter is speaking:

'A warrant is out for the arrest of local schoolgirl Carey Logan, wanted by the police in connection with the disappearance of fourteen-year-old Amelia Wilson.' The presenter carries on talking, explaining how I ran away from the police and giving a number, plastered across the screen, for anyone with information on my whereabouts to call.

244

The room falls silent. Beside me, Blue is staring at the screen, his mouth open and a piece of half-eaten toast forgotten in his hand. Everyone else is looking at me, their eyes wide.

Painful thoughts thunder against my skull:

Amelia is still missing.

The police are ramping up their efforts to find me.

Everyone at the squat now knows why I'm here.

'You're on the run from the pigs?' The sophisticated drawl has gone from Seti's voice. '*You?*'

I gulp. 'I didn't have anything to do with Amelia going missing,' I bleat, feeling a guilty flush creeping up my neck.

Blue gulps down his toast. 'Course you didn't.' He stares at me, a look of naked astonishment on his face. 'But still . . .'

'You're not the only one here in trouble with the police,' Tattoo-face snarls.

'It's not a competition,' Seti snaps. 'Well it just goes to show. You never really know about people.' She sounds almost impressed, as if I've gone up in her estimation.

'I didn't do anything,' I repeat.

'We know,' Blue says stoutly.

'Yeah, you're safe from the pigs here,' Seti says. 'Isn't she?' She glares around the room, her eyes resting on Tattoo-face a moment longer than on anyone else.

'Course.'

'Sure.'

245

Voices echo around me.

'No one's turning Carey over to the cops,' Blue adds emphatically.

'You and I need to talk.' Seti prods me lightly on the arm. 'Everyone else: out!'

I expect Tattoo-face to argue, but she gets up and leaves without a word.

'She won't say anything, will she?' I ask.

'Not if she wants to stay on in this squat,' Seti says.

The room is empty now, apart from Seti, me and Blue.

'So what happened, Carey?' Seti asks. 'With this Amelia girl? Seriously.'

'I was framed,' I explain, figuring my only option is to tell the truth. A bunch of lies will almost certainly tie my tongue in knots. 'Amelia is . . . was my best friend and she was being bullied online by this weirdo. It kept getting worse and then there was a death threat and she . . . she kind of flipped out. Anyway, someone made it look like I'd sent the threat from my laptop, but I didn't. Then there was another incident . . . and basically Amelia's been off school for months and yesterday she went missing and someone made  an anonymous call to the police, saying that he'd seen me arguing with her just before she vanished. Which I swear I wasn't doing, I didn't even *see* her yesterday. But the police don't believe me and were going to arrest me and . . .' I hold my arms out in a gesture of helplessness.

'You gave the cops the slip,' Seti says.

'Cool,' Blue adds.

'My sister helped,' I acknowledge.

'So who made the call about you, pretending you'd been arguing with Amelia?' Seti asks.

'I don't know for sure,' I say.

'Logically whoever it was must be the person who's been framing you all along,' Blue points out.

Seti nods. 'Yeah.'

I nod. Do they really believe me? After so many months of being mistrusted it's hard to accept their support is genuine.

'That's what I figured. I think it might have been Amelia's ex-boyfriend, Taylor,' I say, eager to test out my theory. 'He dumped her just before she was sent the threat. I reckon Amelia worked out it was him who was behind everything and went to confront him yesterday and he's done ... something to her to shut her up.'

'Whoa.' Seti is open-mouthed, her almond eyes alive with excitement. 'You mean you think he's *killed* her?'

I shrug.

Blue wrinkles his nose. 'This Taylor ... who is he? A guy our age? At your school?'

'Yes, well no, he goes to Bamford House.' I roll my eyes. 'It's a posh private school. Taylor messes people around a lot, someone told me that he once got another boy expelled. So it's not the first time he's framed someone ...'

247

'Scumbag,' Seti breathes.

Blue falls silent as Seti pesters me for more details. I tell her a little more, mostly about Taylor and how flaky and unreliable he is.

'He's from this rich family,' I explain. 'And I think he takes lots of things for granted, from money to people.'

I'm too embarrassed to reveal that Taylor and I were dating. It's partly because, for some reason, I really don't want Blue to imagine I still have feelings for Taylor. But it's also because I don't want either him or Seti to realise how stupid I've been in letting Taylor manipulate me. So I simply say that Taylor and I were friends. However, I can see Seti's sharp eyes narrowing as I speak and wonder if she's guessing the truth. Blue just frowns, pacing up and down.

'What do you think, Blue?' Seti asks at last.

'It sounds far-fetched to me,' he grunts. 'I mean why would—'

'Carey!' The door flies open. Tattoo-face stands in the doorway. 'Tommo just called the police,' she says. 'You need to leave. Now.'

26

'Tommo called the police?' I gasp.

Blue spins around. 'Are you sure?'

Tattoo-face nods. 'I overheard him boasting about it—'

'We need to get out of here,' Seti cuts in. She grabs my arm.

'OK,' Tattoo-face says. 'I'll keep Tommo talking, give you a chance to get out without him seeing.' She vanishes.

I grab my shoes and tug them on my feet.

'Wait,' Blue says. 'Perhaps you *should* talk to the police.'

'What?' I stare up at him.

'If you didn't do anything wrong . . . why not let the cops sort it out?'

'You have to be kidding.' Seti's eyes widen dramatically. 'You heard what Carey said, it's this rich guy Taylor, he's set her up and done something to her friend and—'

'You don't know any of that,' Blue interrupts. 'Come on,

it's crazy. This Taylor might be an idiot, but … Anyway, you're better off telling the police what you think he did, letting them work it out. If you're innocent, you'll be OK.'

Seti snorts. 'Like you were, you mean?'

Blue glares at her. 'I'm just—'

'Excuse me,' I interrupt. 'But it's my decision.'

Seti and Blue look at me. Blue's expression is one of exasperated concern, but Seti's eyes are wide with excitement.

'What do you want to do?' she asks.

I think it through. A while ago I would have totally agreed with Blue about trusting the police to work out who was setting me up, but I've lived for months with no one believing a thing I've said and I have no faith that anyone in authority will listen to anything I have to say. They certainly haven't up to now. That's why I ran away in the first place. Plus, I already mentioned Taylor to the police and they totally dismissed the idea he might be SweetFreak.

'If we're leaving we need to go now,' Seti urges.

'Don't go, Carey.' Blue touches my arm. 'Please, you haven't given the police a chance to investigate Amelia's disappearance. Whatever happened, there will be clues, things the police can follow up on. If it was Taylor there'll be evidence somewhere – he's only a kid, he can't have covered all his tracks. And by running away you make yourself look—'

250

'You are such a hypocrite, Blue,' Seti blurts out. She turns to me, all impatience. 'Well?'

'I'm leaving.' I throw Blue an apologetic glance. He still looks deeply concerned. 'I have to go. I'm sorry. Thanks for everything.' I hurry out of the room, Seti at my heels.

We fly down the stairs. I'm half hoping Blue will follow us, but he doesn't. Seti leads me along the street and into an area of Cornmouth I don't know at all. It's a bright, sunny day and I'm soon warm, jogging along in my jumper. The roads are busier here, with little shops and cafés. Several heads turn as Seti passes. It's not just how pretty she is, it's also her air of absolute self-confidence. Her conviction that I'm right to run and the way she's striding purposefully ahead give me a new strength. I don't know how or where, but somehow I will get through this.

We stop under a little stone bridge. There's a sign explaining the maximum height of vehicles that can pass. Seti leans against the wall under the sign and blows out her breath.

I lean over, panting, then straighten up. 'Why would Tommo grass me up?' I ask.

Seti shrugs. 'Probably thinks you're a privileged cow who doesn't deserve a place in his house.'

'*His* house?' I ask. 'I thought it was a squat?'

'It is, technically,' Seti explains. 'That is, we're not all supposed to be living there, but it actually belongs to

251

Tommo's granddad. Tommo's parents let him stay there because they don't know what else to do with him.' She snorts. 'He's as posh as you are.'

'I'm not posh.'

'Whatever.' Seti pushes herself up from the wall. 'Tommo likes to pretend it's a proper squat but it isn't really, not for him. I sussed him on day one. I haven't told anyone, not even Blue.'

'Where are we going to go?' I ask.

Seti thinks for a moment. 'You know, Blue was right about one thing.'

I raise my eyebrows.

'This guy who set you up?'

'Taylor?'

'Yeah, like Blue said, if he's guilty of hurting your friend there'll be evidence somewhere. Taylor's your age, right?'

I nod.

'So he's an amateur, unless . . . what's his background?'

'He lives in a big house in East Cornmouth, his parents just separated, he's got a younger brother called Blake—'

Seti holds up a hand to stop me talking. 'You know where he lives?'

'Yes, but he's not there. His whole family is away.'

'If you could take a look at his things, his room, do you think there might be evidence there? Anything at all?'

'I guess,' I say. 'But, like I said, his family is away which makes it impossible to get inside and snoop around.'

'On the contrary,' Seti says, a mischievous grin on her face. 'If the house is empty, it makes snooping around all the easier.'

'You mean break in?'

'Why not? It's for a good cause. Listen to my idea at least.'

We stroll around the edges of Cornmouth, while Seti explains her plan for getting inside Taylor's house. She brushes away my concerns about house alarms and nosy neighbours and causing damage by breaking doors and windows.

'I wouldn't want to cause Taylor's mum any more stress,' I say. 'Her husband only left her a couple of months ago. The last thing she needs is to have to deal with a break-in.'

Seti tilts her head to one side. She has a small, pointy little face and looks, right now, like an inquisitive sparrow. 'But you agree that if Taylor is behind Amelia's disappearance – or knows anything about it – there might be some sort of proof in his room?'

'Yes, but—'

'Then let me worry about how we get inside. I promise we won't do any damage. And I can easily deal with the alarm. With a bit of luck Taylor's mum won't even know anyone's been inside.' Seti pauses. 'Think of Amelia.'

I nod. I *have* to do this, however overwhelming it seems. For my best friend. Because I'm certain that Taylor knows

253

more than he's letting on about her disappearance and, if the police won't investigate him, then I have to.

'OK,' I agree. 'We'll search his room, look for clues that will help find Amelia. When should we go?'

'Soon as it's dark,' Seti says. 'We'll need to buy a couple of bits and pieces first though. Have you got any cash?'

I let her take me to the DIY superstore on the outskirts of town where, under Seti's instructions, I use some of the cash Poppy gave me to buy wire cutters and a screwdriver.

'Why do we need these?' I ask, alarmed, as I put the big roll of notes back into my pocket.

'Just to help us get in without causing any damage,' Seti explains. 'The screwdriver is the main thing, the wire cutters are only in an absolute emergency.'

Reassured, I spend another few quid on some cans of pop and a couple of hamburgers. Seti wolfs hers down, but mine sticks in my throat.

Are we doing the right thing? Blue's anxious face keeps appearing in my mind's eye. Maybe he's right that I should turn myself over to the police and tell them my suspicions about Taylor. Surely if I really explain everything they'll *have* to investigate Taylor themselves.

'You can't rely on them listening to you, but if you can provide proof from Taylor's house then they'll be forced to act,' Seti insists. 'Anyway, it's not like we're going to steal anything or hurt anyone. And you can hardly get into any more trouble than you're already in, can you?'

She's right.

An hour later, as the sun begins to set, Seti and I make our way towards Taylor's house. It's been a bright, sunny day and my anxieties ease as we stroll across the park a few streets away from where he lives. It's a smaller park than the one near my house and far better maintained, with smart patches of shrubs and trees dotted artistically at regular intervals. There's a children's play area too, with freshly painted swings and a climbing frame in the shape of a bumble bee.

'Posh part of town,' Seti comments. She sounds like she hasn't been here before.

'Where are you from?' I ask.

'Hornchurch,' she says. 'Essex.'

'So how come you're here, in Cornmouth?' I ask.

'Oh, this and that,' Seti says airily. 'Got in a bit of trouble when I was younger, spent some time in care. I was with a lovely foster family for a few years but I had to leave when . . . Anyway, I moved about, came to Cornmouth a few months ago . . .'

I ask a few more questions but Seti sidesteps them neatly, turning the conversation back to the squat and to Tommo's hypocrisy. After a while she pauses. 'So what do you think of Blue?' Her eyes twinkle as she speaks.

255

'He seems nice,' I say, not quite sure what she's getting at. 'He helped me when he didn't need to. Not that I really know him of course.'

'He likes you,' Seti says with a chuckle. 'I can tell.' She taps her nose. 'I'm good at reading people.'

I bet you're good at lots of things, I think, feeling intimidated again. I've never met anyone as effortlessly cool as Seti. She studies me with her almond-shaped eyes. 'So?' she says. 'Do you like him?'

'Blue?' The heat rushes up my neck to my face. 'No,' I say. 'Not like that.'

'Mmm.' Seti laughs. 'If you say so.'

I change the subject to our impending break-in of Taylor's house. We are at the edge of the park and Seti reassures me, yet again, that we won't damage anything and that we'll just look in Taylor's room and not go anywhere near the rest of the house.

We wait another thirty minutes or so until it's properly dark, then we pull up our hoods and leave the park. Seti falls silent as we reach Taylor's house. Her sharp eyes take in the long sweep of the gravel drive.

The house is dark, just a little light over the front door. I can't believe that I stood here with Jamie only a day and a half ago. My little brother will be missing me. I miss him badly. And as for Mum, I can't bear to imagine how worried she must be. When we're done here I'm going to ask Seti if

she has a phone I can borrow so I can call home and let them know I'm all right.

Seti creeps across the drive. I follow her as she crouches down, frowning, and examines the wires that surround the door frame and flow along the base of the brick wall on either side. Without speaking, she takes the cutters and snips the wires close to the ground.

'What are you doing?' I hiss. 'I thought we weren't going to cause any damage?'

'It's just a little cut,' she protests, sweeping her plaits over her shoulder with a flourish. 'We don't have a choice. We'll set off the alarm otherwise.'

'OK,' I say, 'but that's it, we're not damaging anything else.'

'Course not,' Seti says with a grin, then steps smartly across to the hall window and smashes the glass at the bottom with the end of the wire cutters. As I gasp, she sweeps the glass away, then leans inside, flicks a catch and levers up the window. In less than ten seconds the window is open enough for us to crawl through.

My mouth hangs open. 'You said we wouldn't break anything.'

'Well it's done now,' Seti says with a giggle. 'We might as well go in.'

I stare at her, an uneasy feeling creeping over me.

'There's no point *not* going in, is there?' she goes on.

My heart is beating fast. I'm wishing we hadn't come, but

Seti is right, the damage is done. We might as well look at Taylor's stuff now we're here.

Seti scrambles deftly inside. She's disappeared by the time I've clambered over the sill and am standing, terrified, in the hall.

'Seti!' I whisper. '*Seti*, where are you?'

'Here!' She's already halfway up the stairs. 'Come on.'

I follow her up to the first floor.

'Which is his room?' Seti asks.

'Second on the left,' I say.

Seti peers into the other doors as we pass: there's just enough light from the uncurtained windows to make out the other bedrooms: the row of bottles and boxes ranged across the dressing table in Taylor's mum's room and the toys on the floor of Blake's.

'Don't turn on any lights,' Seti warns as we reach Taylor's bedroom. Her sharp eyes dart all over, taking it in. I follow her gaze, clocking the big heap of clothes, the football posters on the walls, the big-screen TV with both an Xbox and a PS4 attached. It's such a rich boy's room: twice the size of mine, with a king-size bed and a massive walk-in wardrobe at the far end.

'Try under the bed,' Seti suggests. 'I'll look in the wardrobe.'

I crawl under Taylor's bed. There's nothing here apart from a collection of muddy football boots, some empty deodorant cans and a stray sock. I shuffle back out again. There's no sign of Seti, who must still be looking through the walk-in closet. I turn my attention to the desk under the window. A stack of text books and folders are piled, higgledy-piggledy, on the top; the drawers beneath are so crammed they won't close. I pull them fully open one by one, scrabbling through their contents. The top drawer is still full of old phones, just as it was when I came here before. The drawer beneath is all USB sticks and cables and wads of tissue and bags of half-open sweets. I push a handful of cables to one side of the drawer, revealing a pair of phone chargers. I'm about to turn away when I catch a glint of silver peeking out from underneath one of the chargers. It's a chain . . . a necklace with a heart on the end. I hold it up to the moonlight that streams in through the window. My throat tightens as I turn the little heart over. There on the back someone has scratched the initials 'A' and 'T', entwined. I gasp. This is the necklace Taylor gave Amelia, the one she never took off. It's proof at last that he must have had something to do with her disappearance.

'Seti?' I hiss, hurrying over to the closet. I peer inside. There's no sign of her, just a load of messy shelves and clothes half off their hangers. My heart skips a beat. Where is she? I hurry out on to the landing. 'Seti?' I call as loudly as I dare. 'I've found something. Where are you?'

No reply. I dart from room to room. I can't see her anywhere, but the elegant wooden dressing table in Taylor's mum's room is scattered with upturned bottles and what looks like a jewellery box tipped on its side. A shell necklace and a handful of chunky bangles trail onto the table. I stare at the mess. I'm certain the bottles and the box were neatly placed to the back of the table when we passed this room earlier. I hurry over to the box. It's almost empty ... I stagger back as the truth hits me.

Seti has stolen Taylor's mum's jewellery and run away.

A light filters up from the ground floor. I rush to the top of the stairs. People are outside, crunching on the gravel. Torchlight flickers over the broken window.

'See that?' It's a woman's voice. 'I knew I heard breaking glass.'

'And those wires have been cut.' It's a man. 'D'you think they're still inside?'

I freeze.

'Let's go back to the road and call the police from there,' the woman says. Their voices fade away along with their footsteps.

I grip the bannister. The quiet of the house presses down on me. Seti is long gone. I need to go, too, before the police get here. The thought propels me down the stairs and across the hall. I fling open the door and race across the drive. The couple with the torch are just ahead of me on the pavement. Their light swings around, into my eyes. I shield my gaze and race on, head down.

'Aagh!' the woman shrieks.

I tear past them and swerve on to the pavement beyond. I run hard, pounding past the park Seti and I waited in earlier and on in the vague direction of the squat. As I stop at last to catch my breath, a freezing-cold rain starts to fall. In seconds I'm wet through, the droplets driving against my face like tiny knives. I keep moving, jogging now, without much sense of purpose. It's not quite eleven o'clock, but it feels like the middle of the night. Tears stream down my face, and my heart, already in my stomach, plummets to my shoes. I can't believe Seti tricked me like that. She did exactly the opposite of what she promised. And now Taylor's mum has had her house broken into and jewellery stolen and it's all my fault.

I can't go back to the squat. And I can't go home.

The police already think I'm a criminal. Now I've turned myself into one.

27

I shove my hands in my pockets. My fingers curl around Amelia's necklace. Even though this is proof against Taylor, it doesn't really bring me any closer to finding my best friend. What's to say the police will even believe I found the necklace in Taylor's house?

I trudge along the empty backstreets, rain and tears mingling on my cheeks. I feel so despairing that I don't even bother to wipe them away. After about half an hour, I realise I'm just a few streets away from the church porch where I tried to shelter last night. Tugging my hood low over my face I make my lonely way there. It's as good a place as any to get out of the rain and to think about what I should do next.

I slump against the wall of the porch on the cold stone seat. Seti will be long gone now, with the jewellery in her bag. I'm in bigger trouble than ever, with the police coming after me at home *and* at the squat. Blue was right. I should have turned myself in while there was still a chance that I might persuade them I was innocent. Now I don't have a leg to stand on, because I'm guilty of breaking in and, though I didn't take the jewellery myself, I'm the one who brought Seti to the house. I'm responsible for the crime that's been committed.

I won't be able to talk my way out of that.

Which means I can't go back.

I look out into the dark, damp streets. Despair washes over me again: bleak and black and brutal.

A familiar figure turns the corner and comes loping along the road. I gasp as he hurries up to the porch.

It's Blue.

'Carey?' he calls. He steps inside the porch, blinking, his eyes adjusting to the gloom. 'Are you here?'

'Yes.' My heart swells with gratitude and relief and I rush into his arms. He hugs me tightly. 'How did you know where I was?'

'I've been looking for you since you left, I had a feeling what Seti might be planning.' He draws back, his face clouding with anger. 'When she turned up at the squat I knew I'd been right.'

'She went back to the squat?' I flush with shame, sitting down on the church porch bench. 'Oh, Blue, I've been such an idiot, I helped her break into Taylor's house and—'

'I know what she did.' Blue grits his teeth, sitting beside me.

263

'And now the police will think I'm a thief on top of everything else.' I look up. 'What happened when they came to the squat looking for me?'

'I said I'd only met you yesterday – which was almost true.' He gives me a shy smile. 'Tommo talked to them most, told them how you spent the night.'

'I can't go back there,' I say.

'I know.' Blue sighs. 'I can't go back either. I had a big row with Tommo over grassing you up to the police and then when Seti turned up I had an even bigger row with her.'

'Is she still there?' I stand up. Perhaps I can talk her into returning the jewellery.

'Nah, she only came to get her stuff. She's gone again now. She wanted me to go with her but I refused. I can't tell you how mad I am at her. I mean I knew Seti'd stolen food before, shoplifted and stuff, but I didn't think she'd take advantage like that. I'm so sorry.'

I sit back down. 'I can't tell you how much it means that you stood up for me.'

'I did more than that,' Blue grins. 'I took this out of her rucksack while she wasn't looking.' He holds up a plastic bag and hands it to me. 'Then I ran like hell.'

I peer inside and see two diamond necklaces, a string of pearls and assorted earrings and rings. It must be the jewellery Seti stole.

Tears prick at my eyes as I take the bag. 'Thank you.'

Blue beams at me and I hug him again. How is it, I wonder, that I feel so comfortable when he's around? I never felt like that with Taylor. Blue just seems to understand me and accept me as I am.

'What are you going to do with the jewellery?' Blue asks.

'I don't know,' I say. 'I mean I know I should take it all to the police, but I'm worried they'll think I stole it.'

Blue opens his mouth but before he can speak I hurry on.

'I know you're going to say that I should tell them everything and it's true that I've got proof against Taylor now. I found Amelia's necklace in his bedroom.' I pull the silver chain out of my pocket and show Blue the scratched initials on the back of the heart. 'Amelia *never* took this off. If Taylor's got it, he must have seen her recently. But I don't know if the police will even believe I found it at Taylor's.'

I'm expecting Blue to argue back, to insist as he did before that I should definitely go to the police with everything. Instead he wrinkles his nose.

'Yeah, you're probably right,' he says.

I sink back against the cold, damp stone wall, suddenly deflated. Part of me, I realise, had been hoping Blue would insist I went to the police whatever the risks. After all, what other alternative do I have?

'Well that's just great,' I say bitterly. 'Looks like I'm totally out of options.'

'No you aren't.' Blue leans forward, suddenly earnest. 'You're free right now. We can go wherever we like.'

'We?' I raise my eyebrows. 'You mean you want to come with me?'

'Sure.' Blue shrugs, suddenly self-conscious. 'I mean, after what I said to Tommo I'm not going back to the squat, so ...' He clears his throat. 'Do you have any friends or family that might help? Lend us money? A place to stay?'

I dig my hands into my back pocket and draw out what remains of the money Poppy gave me. To my horror there's only a couple of ten pound notes and a handful of coins. The main roll of cash is gone.

'Seti must have seen where I put my money and pickpocketed it,' I wail. 'I've got less than twenty-five pounds left.'

Blue and I stare at each other.

'OK, well, that's enough for bus tickets, so long as we don't go too far,' Blue says. 'I can probably find us a squat or a shelter if we need it, but do you know anyone who would take us in for a bit? Anyone who lives nearby?'

'Only my dad,' I say with a hollow laugh. 'He lives in Broadcombe, at least he did last summer. Camber Avenue.'

Blue gives me a quizzical look. 'So when did you last go there?'

'I've never been there.'

'But you're in touch with him?' Blue persists.

'Not really,' I admit, my cheeks burning. I wish I hadn't mentioned Dad now. It's stupid, I know, because lots of people's dads aren't around, but talking about him always makes me feel rubbish: a mix of embarrassment and anger and a weird kind of emptiness. 'Don't *you* have any relatives?' I ask, trying to shift the emphasis of the conversation.

'Not that I have anything to do with,' Blue says. He's still frowning. 'I don't understand about your dad. You know where he lives and you obviously saw him six months ago, so what's happened sin—?'

'I *didn't* see him, he just sent a . . .' I draw in my breath. 'I don't want to talk about it.'

Blue now looks baffled. 'I'm just trying to work out if he could help us.'

'He couldn't,' I say.

'Why not?' Blue persists.

I grit my teeth. Why is he pushing this?

'Carey?'

I turn on him. 'My dad has a new family, OK?' I spit. 'I haven't seen him since he walked out five years ago. The only time he even bothered to contact us was to send us a picture of his new baby. *That's* why he got in touch last summer. But he didn't want to see me or my sister or my brother. All right? Can we drop it now?'

Blue studies me. 'How do you know he didn't want to see you?' he asks.

267

'Because he hardly wrote anything in the letter with the picture of Teddy – just "hope you're well" and his address.' I pause, remembering Jamie's face when he saw the photo. 'It really upset my little brother.'

Blue hesitates. 'I'm sorry. Maybe he put his address in because he *wanted* you to contact him?'

'No way,' I say with a sniff. 'You don't know my dad.'

Blue shrugs. 'OK,' he says.

'What's *your* dad like?' I ask, more aggressively than I mean to.

'He's dead.' Blue looks away, but not before I see the flicker of pain cross his face.

'Oh,' I say, wincing. 'Sorry.'

'So . . . if you really don't want to see your dad and there aren't any other family or friends who could help . . .' Blue tails off.

'. . . we're out of options,' I finish. 'Just like I said.'

We look at each other and there's such warmth and kindness in Blue's eyes that I have to swallow hard to stop myself from crying.

'I guess I'll have to go to the police then. Tell them everything. Hand in this.' I hold up the bag of jewellery again. 'And hope they believe me.'

'I'm sure they will. And the fact that you'll be returning stolen goods has *got* to count in your favour when it comes to everything else.' Blue grins.

I smile back.

'So we'll go to the police in the morning, yeah?'

I nod, relieved to have made a decision, though uneasy about how the police will react. I have to use everything I've got to convince them they have to properly investigate Taylor.

Amelia's life may depend on it.

28

We spend the rest of the night huddled together for warmth in the very back of the church porch. I sleep badly. Images of Amelia's face – alternately weeping and accusatory – drift around the edges of my dreams. I wake with a start, just before dawn. Fear for my friend sears through me.

As soon as it's light we set off for the police station. I'm stiff and sore and cold to my bones though it's a warm morning, almost spring-like and much milder than yesterday. Blue buys some bread on our way, but I can't eat. Running away has failed and I'm about to turn myself in with no sure-fire way of saving Amelia, let alone proving my own innocence. Am I being stupid to surrender like this?

As I lead the way across the concrete yard in front of the police station, the door ahead opens. I look up. Amelia's brother George is striding out, his mum close behind. George is scowling, muttering something. His mother, pale-faced and dressed in a blue raincoat, looks up and spots me.

'*Carey*?' she gasps.

My heart races. I stop walking. Beside me, Blue looks up.

'Mrs Wilson,' I stammer. I back away, but George storms over.

'What have you done with my sister?' He grabs my arm.

'Nothing. I swear.' I twist away from him. Several passers-by have stopped to watch the scene unfolding in front of them. Blue puts his arm around me and glares at George.

'Where's Amelia?' George demands.

'What are you doing here, Carey?' Mrs Wilson asks. 'Do you know where Amelia is?'

'No . . . no . . .' I take a deep breath. 'But I think I know who might.' I fish in my pocket, fingers trembling, and draw out Amelia's necklace. The little silver heart dangles from the end. 'I found this in Taylor's bedroom yesterday. It was Amelia's.'

Mrs Wilson peers at the necklace. 'Taylor Lockwood? Who Amelia went out with months ago?' She frowns.

'Yes,' I say. 'But Amelia wore it all the time so how did *Taylor* get it? I think maybe *he's* the person who's been targeting Amelia. He's been trying to make it look like me all along to avoid suspicion. I'm worried that he's done something to hurt her and no one is trying to find him!'

Mrs Wilson takes the necklace. 'Amelia did wear this all the time.' Her voice is suddenly uncertain.

George glances at the slender chain. 'She hadn't for weeks,' he says with a sniff. 'Taylor already told me: Amelia sent this back to him on Valentine's Day.'

Is that true? I'm aware of Blue beside me, but I keep my focus on George. 'You've *talked* to Taylor?'

'Of course,' George says. 'Two or three times.'

I frown. Taylor never mentioned any conversations. 'When?' I ask. 'Why?'

'Not that it's any of your business, but the last time was just after Amelia sent him the necklace in February. She asked me to get it back for her, that she'd made a mistake, but Taylor hung up on me.' George grimaces. 'Probably because the two times I spoke to him before that I was having a go at him for upsetting Amelia.'

'You did?' Mrs Wilson sounds shocked.

I'm shocked too. Taylor never breathed a word of any of this.

'Anyway, what about you, Carey?' George asks. 'What were you even doing in Taylor's house yesterday?'

Before I can reply, Blue interjects, his eyes glinting hard and bright. 'Carey was looking for proof that Taylor was the one trying to hurt Amelia.'

I nod. George and his mum look at Blue, clearly noticing him for the first time.

Mrs Wilson's eyes flicker back to me. 'The police told us there was a break-in at Taylor's house last night. They asked if we thought Amelia might have gone there.' She narrows her eyes. 'But from what you've just said I think it was you, wasn't it?'

'I didn't take anything,' I say. It sounds like an apology. The plastic bag containing the stolen jewellery feels hot in my hand. I hold it out. 'See, Mrs Wilson? This was ... someone else took it, it wasn't me.' I sound guilty as sin.

'We've come here to hand it in to the police,' Blue says pointedly.

'Exactly.' I glance, grateful, at him.

Mrs Wilson takes the bag. She peers inside then looks at me. Her face is strained and grey, she must be worried sick about Amelia. I know my mum would be.

'Are you *sure* you don't know what's happened to my daughter?' she demands. 'The police think you were there when she disappeared. And you're certainly not behaving like someone with nothing to hide: running away and now turning up with a load of stolen jewellery.'

I stare at her, despair creeping through me. It was a mistake to think anyone would believe me. Mrs Wilson doesn't. Nor does George. And the police definitely won't.

'In fact ...' Mrs Wilson narrows her eyes. 'Wherever I look, there you are, Carey. Right at the centre of *everything*.'

'Because you're *guilty*,' George says with feeling.

'Come on.' He reaches for my arm again but I dart back, Blue quick beside me. George lunges for me.

Blue shoves him back. 'Run!' he shouts.

We tear onto the pavement, across the road, running as hard as we can. George is panting after us. He's fast but we're faster. Blue nips us up and down little roads, one after the other, until my head is spinning and my lungs burning.

At last we stop down a little side street. Blue looks back the way we've come. 'He's gone,' he says, gasping for breath. 'What an idiot. His mother was horrible too.'

I shake my head, panting. 'It's not their fault. They must be desperate about Amelia. I get it.' I sink onto the ground. 'Anyway, I can't go to the police now,' I say miserably. 'Nobody's going to believe me.'

Blue nods. 'We need to get out of town.'

A painful sob twists in my guts. 'The worst thing is that because everyone thinks I had something to do with Amelia going missing, they're looking in the wrong places.'

'I know,' Blue says with real sympathy. 'But there's nothing we can do for Amelia right now. We need to get out of here. Her mum's probably already got the cops looking for us.'

'OK.' I straighten up. 'Where can we go?'

Blue meets my gaze. The memory of our earlier conversation about my dad rears up. At the time I'd thought Blue was wrong about Dad wanting to make contact. But

274

perhaps he was right. Suppose by putting his address in the note Dad was hinting he *did* want to see us. After all, why else would he have told us where he lived?

Anyway, at this point, what have I got to lose?

I take a deep breath. 'Let's go to Broadcombe and find my dad.'

On the way to the bus station Blue buys me a red hat to conceal my hair and a jacket from a charity shop. The jacket smells and the hat makes me look like there's a big blob of jelly on my head. But I know it's important to keep my identity hidden. I mustn't be recognised or the police will find me.

We buy our tickets and get on board the first bus that turns up. The journey takes just over an hour. Neither of us speak much. I'm full of worry for Amelia, mulling over ways in which I can get the police to investigate Taylor. My imagination roams freely, trying to find something I can definitely lay at Taylor's door, but the more I think about it, the further away I am from finding that single, undeniable piece of evidence against him.

'We're here.' Blue's gruff voice rouses me from my thoughts.

I glance out of the window. We're driving through the centre of Broadcombe. I've never been here before but it's similar to Cornmouth: the same squat terraced houses, the same shabby high streets with boarded-up shops and pound stores and off-licences behind fibreglass panels. As the bus pulls to a stop my heart rate quickens and all thoughts of Amelia and Taylor and the police being after me fade to the back of my mind.

I'm now just minutes away from the street where my dad lives and I'm about to see him for the first time in five years.

RISE

29

Blue turns to me and smiles. 'We need to go left, then second right.'

I nod, taut with anticipation, and we walk on. I've never thought of myself as particularly shy but I'm amazed by Blue's confidence. He talked a guy on the bus into letting him check out my dad's address on Google Maps and now he's just asked an elderly lady to make sure we've remembered the way correctly.

'How do you do that?' I ask, as we take the next turning. 'Just chatting out of nowhere to all those complete strangers?'

Blue shrugs. 'The first thing I realised when I landed on the streets was that I needed to get over being shy.'

'I can't believe you've ever been shy.'

'When I started at my last school I was. We moved when I was fourteen, about a year after my dad died. It was a stupid school that I didn't fit into at all. I was so desperate to

279

make friends and I had no idea how to talk to anyone. I . . . I screwed up, ended up in trouble.'

I hesitate. This is by far the most Blue has ever told me about his past and, in spite of all the thoughts whirring around my head, I really want to ask him what kind of trouble he got into – and how that led him to his life on the streets.

'Look,' Blue says before I can ask any more. 'We're here.'

I glance up. Camber Avenue is much like the roads around it – a narrow terrace of pebble-dashed houses. Blue points across the street. 'What number does your dad live at?'

'Seventy-seven.' I want to wait, to psych myself up, but Blue is already halfway across the road. I'm *so* not ready for this. I need more time. What am I going to say when Dad opens the door? Will he even recognise me? I was ten when I last saw him. And what if he's seen the news about the police wanting to question me? My legs feel like jelly as I follow Blue up the front path. He grins at me, then raps on the door.

My heart hammers. I want to run. But it's too late. The door is opening.

A woman stands in front of us: plump in jeans and a sweatshirt with a mane of fine, mousy hair tied in a ponytail down her back.

'Hi.' It comes out as a croak. My throat is dry. Is this Dad's girlfriend? The mother of his new baby? She looks cross. There are lines on her forehead.

'I'm not buying anything,' the woman says with a scowl.

Oh, she's horrible. Surely this can't be Dad's girlfriend. Why didn't I think she might be here and he might be out? What am I doing here?

I take a step away, but Blue grabs my hand and pulls me back.

'That's OK, we're not selling anything,' he says with a smile. 'We're looking for—' He turns to me. 'What's your dad's name?'

'Alan Logan,' I say.

The woman's eyebrows shoot up. 'Oh my goodness.' She peers at me more closely. 'Are you Carey?'

I nod, feeling sick. Has she recognised me from TV?

The woman smiles and her face lightens so she seems almost pretty. I relax a little. There's no way she'd look that welcoming if she knew I was wanted for questioning by the police.

'Alan said Teddy was the spit of you! I'm Sandy, by the way. Come in, come in.'

I glance at Blue, who gives me an encouraging nod, then step inside. The house is cluttered but clean, with the scent of polish and peppermint in the air. We follow Sandy into the cramped living room. There's a big TV and a pair of faded orange sofas and a large box of kids' toys in multicoloured plastic in the middle of the floor.

'Teddy?' says Sandy.

A chubby fist appears from behind the box. And then my littlest brother crawls out from behind the toys, grinning up at us. He's beautiful, with dark curly hair and huge brown eyes.

'Wow, he does look like you, Carey.' Blue tells Sandy his name, and how we're passing through and how much I've been looking forward to meeting Teddy and seeing my dad. I'm so glad he's talking because I'm completely tongue-tied. I crouch down and hold out my hand to Teddy. He crawls determinedly over, then hauls himself unsteadily up beside me. He's dressed in the cutest little red jumper and chinos.

'Hello,' I say. 'I'm Carey. I'm your sister.'

Teddy smiles up at me.

'He likes you,' Sandy says. 'Your dad was always saying how he wanted you two to meet.'

I glance at her, bewildered. 'Dad never said that to me.' I blush at the level of hurt in my voice. It must be obvious to the others too, because Blue looks away and Sandy's face falls.

'I know, pet,' she says with a sigh. 'That's the thing with Alan. He feels a lot for people, but he's not very good at ... he always says he's a great starter and a poor finisher.'

'So where is he?' I ask. Teddy grips my hand and tries to haul himself up.

Sandy chews thoughtfully on her lip. I glance at Blue.

282

He shakes his head very slightly. But it's enough for me to realise what must clear to Blue already.

'He's gone, hasn't he?' All the excitement and hope of the past few hours drain away. 'My dad doesn't live here any more.'

Sandy nods. 'He got restless back in September, said he needed to go to London, the opportunities for work ... that he'd be back every weekend but—'

'But he left and you haven't heard from him since?' Clearly Dad has done to Sandy and little Teddy exactly the same as he did to my family.

'That's right.' Sandy flumps down on one of the sofas. Teddy turns from me, lets go of my hand and crawls over to her. She picks him up, absently, tears in her eyes.

'How old is Teddy?' Blue asks.

'He'll be a year at the end of April,' Sandy says, a shake in her voice. 'I'm so pleased you've come to see him, Carey, I kept telling your dad he should get in touch. I didn't feel like it was my place to reach out to you and your family.'

Teddy is struggling to get down from Sandy's lap. She sets him on the floor and he crawls determinedly towards me. I hold out my hand for him to use as balance while he pulls himself up. He's so gorgeous, all chubby arms and sturdy little legs and that beautiful, big-eyed face.

'How could Dad leave him?' I ask.

'It's just what he does,' Sandy says wearily.

'But Dad wrote. He sent a picture just after Teddy was born. He even put your address.'

'I made him send that picture,' Sandy says with a sigh. 'And I made him put the address on. I told him to invite you all over but he told me to stop nagging. He said he knew what to write, that he'd got the words just right.'

I snort. 'It was literally just the picture and an address and a . . . a few basic sentences. All it said was that the baby was called Teddy. My little brother Jamie was really upset about it. My sister threw the whole thing away, didn't want our mum to find it.'

Sandy nods. She looks stricken. 'I'm so sorry.'

Blue clears his throat. 'Carey?' I look up into his anxious face and the full horror of our situation dawns on me. We have just spent our last money getting here and it's obvious that there was no point trying to find Dad. That there will never be any point.

'I told you this would happen,' I hiss.

Blue looks crestfallen and I immediately feel guilty.

'Sorry,' I whisper. It's not Blue's fault my dad is such a waste of space. And at least I've met my new brother. I wish Jamie and Poppy could see him too. I smile down at him, holding out my hand for him to grip. Teddy burbles happily at me, his plump fist wound around my fingers. I look up at Sandy.

'Can I come again, another time?' I ask. 'Maybe bring my brother and sister?'

Sandy nods. 'Course, whenever you like. Teddy would love to meet them, they're his family. And you must definitely all come to his first birthday party.'

'Thanks, I'd love that.' I look down at the faded carpet, wondering if normal things like kids' parties will actually ever be part of my life again. Sandy might have missed the local news bulletin but the police are still looking for me and poor Amelia is still missing.

'We should go,' Blue says. I can tell he's wondering if the police will find us here. I don't see how they can – Mum has no idea where Dad lives and no idea that I know and I'm certain neither Jamie nor Poppy will have remembered this address.

Still, Blue's probably right to be careful. There's no point taking chances.

'Will you be getting the bus back to ... to Cornmouth? That's where you live, isn't it?' Sandy asks.

I nod. It seems weird to imagine Dad over here, telling Sandy about his old home with us, while we had no idea about her and his life here.

'You should let your mum know you're on your way home,' Sandy goes on, then, catching the look on my face, raises her eyebrows. 'Your mum does know you're here, doesn't she? She'll be worrying if she doesn't hear from you.'

'Sure,' I lie, feeling guilty. 'Don't worry, Mum knows I'm fine. Er, Blue's right, we should go.'

Sandy sees us to the door, little Teddy in her arms.

'Don't be a stranger,' she says. 'Come again and bring Jamie and Poppy too. Teddy would love to meet them.'

'OK.' I smile and give Teddy a little kiss on the cheek. He babbles at me, kicking his legs in delight. 'Bye-bye, Baby Bear.' I'm using the pet phrase we have at home for Jamie. A stab of guilt pierces me as I think again of how upset and worried Mum and the others will be.

Blue and I wander away from the house. We've let Sandy think we're on our way back to Cornmouth but in fact we have no idea where to go next. I check my pockets. Just under thirteen pounds left. That's enough for another pair of bus tickets somewhere local and maybe a couple of sandwiches.

Then what?

'Put your hood up,' Blue warns as we turn onto a busier street.

I do as he says.

'We need to get some food then find somewhere for tonight,' he goes on. 'Seti always used to say finding shelter for the night was the priority, especially when it's cold.'

'Yeah. Sure.'

'I'm sorry I got you thinking maybe your dad would be there.'

I shrug.

'Was it weird seeing your brother like that?' Blue asks.

'Kind of . . .' I glance at him. He has told me so little about his own circumstances. 'Do you have brothers or sisters?'

'No,' he says. He looks away.

'So . . . you've never really explained how you ended up here, living rough . . .'

Blue shrugs. 'I don't really like to talk about it.'

'Come on,' I say. 'You know all about what happened to me.'

There's a long pause.

'Like I said, after my dad died we moved and I went to a new school. I got in with a bad crowd of people, went along with some stuff I shouldn't have, then ended up taking take the blame for . . . for something that happened.'

'But why did that mean you had to leave home?'

'I didn't,' Blue says. 'That is, I didn't leave my home with my mum. She . . . didn't cope well when Dad died. Getting worse and worse until . . . around the time I got into trouble . . .' he lowers his voice, 'Mum had to go into a psychiatric hospital, she's still there actually. I visit her every now and then, but . . .' He trails off.

'Oh, Blue.' I stare at him, horrified. 'I'm so sorry.'

'So I got put into foster care. *That's* what I ran away from.'

'I see,' I say, though I'm aware I don't really understand at all. I can't imagine what it would be like to lose both your parents. 'Wasn't there anywhere else you could go?'

'My dad's parents were dead and my mum's family live in

287

Poland. I only met them a few times, so they're practically strangers. Anyway, I didn't want to go to Poland.' He stands up. 'Look, we've got a bit of cash for tonight, we should get some food. At the squat Seti and a couple of the others used to bring stuff back, but before I met her I got food from the bins behind—'

'Do you think they shoplifted the food?' I ask, wide-eyed. It hadn't occurred to me before, but after Seti's performance at Taylor's house it makes sense.

'Possibly. Probably.' Blue grimaces. 'But when you're starving you don't ask too many questions. And when you can't go home, you have to find a way of fitting in with the home you've got.'

Home. We're passing the entrance to a shopping centre. It's full of people intent on going in and out of the shops. I've only been gone a couple of nights, but it seems like a million years since I was in my own home with Mum nagging and Poppy teasing and Jamie demanding I play with him. I'm being really selfish not calling them.

'I should let my mum know I'm OK,' I say, scanning the passers-by. 'I'm going to ask if I can borrow someone's phone.'

'Of course,' Blue says, a wistful note to his voice. 'They're your family, you shouldn't give up on them.'

I go over to a group of teens hanging round the entrance to a nail bar.

'Excuse me,' I say, smiling at a girl with bright blonde hair hanging on the arm of a tall, handsome boy in a biker jacket. 'I really need to make a call. Could I borrow your phone? I'll give you a pound.'

The biker jacket boy snorts. 'A pound? Make it a tenner and I'll consider it.'

The others laugh.

'A pound's all I've got,' I say, feeling desperate.

'No way.' The blonde girl makes a face. 'Get lost.'

'Please.' The rest of the group are looking at me now. 'I'm not going to run off with it, and I'm not calling abroad or anything. It's really important.'

'Who'd you need to call so bad?' the blonde girl asks.

They're all looking at me now. I can see Blue in the background, arms folded, watching closely.

'My mum,' I say, unable to think of a lie that will sound in any way convincing. 'I need to let her know I'm OK.'

'Ah,' the blonde girl says nastily. 'She wants to call her mummy.'

'Stop it,' says the shortest guy in the group. He has a dark scar on his forehead.

'Come on, she's gonna take it and call America or something,' the girl protests.

'No,' I say. 'I promise. It's just Cornmouth.'

There's a short pause. 'Here.' The boy with the scar holds out his phone. 'You can use mine. And you don't need to pay, so long as you're not too long.'

The other guys prod him and laugh. I take the phone and shuffle sideways so I'm out of earshot. The group watch as I open the keypad. I can't phone Mum directly, because I don't know her work or her mobile number off by heart. But I can call Poppy and she'll be able to let Mum know I'm OK. Besides, it'll be easier to speak to my sister. Mum is going to be furious with me.

I punch in my sister's number.

The phone rings and my heart beats faster.

30

The borrowed phone rings a second time. A third.

Come on, Poppy.

'Yeah?' My sister answers at last.

Tears spring to my eyes at the sound of her voice.

'Poppy?' I say. 'It's me.'

'Jeez, Carey!' Poppy gasps. 'When I told you to run I didn't think you'd take this long to get in touch. It's been two whole days. Where are you? Are you OK? Mum's going mad worrying and the police are—'

'I'm fine.' I sniff back my tears. 'Tell Mum I'm fine and ... and I didn't do anything ...' I hesitate. 'She does believe that, doesn't she?'

'Honestly, Carey, she's in such a state she doesn't know what she's doing half the time.' Poppy sucks in her breath, her voice shaking. I glance up. The guy whose phone I'm using is watching me. He raises his eyebrows as if to ask how much longer I'm going to be. 'Listen,' Poppy goes on. 'I was wrong to encourage you to run off before. You should come home. We'll go to the police together. You didn't do this. We'll make them realise and—'

'How will we make them realise?' I demand. 'I told them before I didn't do anything and they didn't believe me. And they refuse to investigate Taylor, so—'

'Taylor?' Poppy says. 'You still think it was him? The police say he has an alibi.'

'That alibi is a friend of his – he could have got her to lie for him. I even went to his house to look for some sort of proof against him but . . .' I trail off, too embarrassed to tell my sister how Seti conned me into breaking in and stole Taylor's mother's jewellery.

'I was in his house too, earlier today in fact,' Poppy says grimly. 'But none of that matters now. You *have* to come h—'

'You were at Taylor's? *Why*?' I glance over at Blue. He's standing a few metres away, glaring at the guy whose phone I've borrowed. With his shaggy hair and furrowed brow, he looks for all the world like a guard dog, standing over me. I'm suddenly aware of how much I like him, how it feels like I've known him for ever.

'I took Jamie over to play with Blake, Mum thought it might take his mind off worrying about you,' Poppy explains. I instantly feel awful for upsetting Jamie. 'Blake and his mum had just got back from holiday. Taylor was there too with some blonde girl. Snooty cow. Abi, I think her name was.'

'Yeah,' I say, 'I've met her. She's the one he claims he was with when Amelia went missing.'

'His mum was in a bit of a state because the house had been broken into and they had some things stolen.'

Shame fills me. At least by now Taylor's mum should know all that jewellery has been handed over to the police.

'Anyway, Jamie wanted to show me something up in Blake's room so I went up and Taylor's room is opposite. That's where I saw Abi.'

'In Taylor's bedroom?' A few days ago this news would have filled me with jealousy. But now I find that I don't care. I glance over at Blue again. He smiles at me and his face lights up. My stomach gives a funny little skip.

'Yeah, silly cow was simpering all over him, like all flirty but teasing. I hate the way girls do that,' Poppy complains with a sigh. 'This Abi was going, "Ooh Taylor, I found this weird key in your pocket, what's it for? Ooh, is it the way to your heart?" *Ugh!*' She pauses. 'So where are you, Carey? I'll come and get you, just—'

'Tell me about the weird key,' I ask, a thought shifting inside me. 'Did you see it?'

'Yeah. Abi kept whining about it. She was all . . .' Poppy puts on a thin, high voice, '"What's this for? Your secret

293

love nest? It's not very romantic, Taylor, it's got a skull on the end." Blah, blah, puke.'

'A skull on the end?' My blood runs cold. 'Oh, my God, that's the key to the Haunted Hut.'

'The haunted *what*?' Poppy asks.

'It's a place just past the industrial estate, down a dirt track. I've never been there but ... but Taylor was supposed to take me. And he definitely took Amelia there before he dumped her. The last time I saw that key it was buried in Taylor's desk drawer.' I hesitate, searching my memory of last night's rummage through the same drawer.

The key definitely hadn't been in there.

'So why would he be carrying around a key to some weird hut?' Poppy asks. 'Because he was well irritated with Abi for pestering him about it.'

'He didn't say he wanted to go there with her?'

'Definitely not,' Poppy says. 'In fact he got seriously annoyed with her, accused her of sneaking around in his stuff. But Carey ...' Her voice cracks. 'I've answered your questions. *Please* come home.'

I bite my lip. The guy whose phone I'm using is walking towards me, an expectant look on his face.

'I think I know what's happened to Amelia,' I say quickly.

'Never mind Amelia, just—'

'I think Taylor met her in Bow Wood and argued with

her ... maybe hurt her, I don't know. He certainly dumped her mobile there. Then he took her to the Haunted Hut.'

Poppy sucks in her breath. 'You mean he's keeping her prisoner there?' She sounds confused. 'Why on earth would he do that?'

'I don't know ...' I can't bring myself to express what I'm really afraid of: that Taylor lured Amelia to the hut then attacked her, leaving her stranded there hurt and afraid, or worse ...

'Anyway, the industrial estate is miles from Bow Wood,' Poppy persists. 'Surely someone would have seen them if they'd gone all that way?'

'Not necessarily.' The past few days have taught me how easy it is to keep a low profile.

The guy is right in front of me now. He holds out his hand for the phone. My time's up. Out of the corner of my eye I can see Blue hurrying over.

'I have to go, Poppy.'

'No, wait. Carey, you need to come home. Let the police—'

'Tell Mum I'm safe.' I ring off and hand the guy his phone. He takes it without a word and turns away.

'Is everything OK?' Blue asks.

I nod, though in reality nothing is OK. Blue frowns, then takes my hand.

'Tell me the truth,' he says.

'I'm even more convinced Taylor's behind it all,' I say as

we walk towards the shopping mall exit. 'He set me up from the start. He hacked into my computer and sent Amelia all the SweetFreak messages and then got someone at our school to put that dead pigeon in her locker and now I think he's attacked her and . . . and she's in the Haunted Hut.' I feel sick at the thought. Is Amelia still alive?

'The haunted *what*?'

'It's an abandoned hut just past the industrial estate.'

'Why would Taylor do any of that?' Blue asks, clearly perplexed.

'Because he *likes* manipulating people and he doesn't care who gets hurt. There are just too many coincidences. He has Amelia's necklace which she *never* takes off and the key to the hut was in his pocket.'

'OK.' Blue frowns. 'Even if he does have her necklace and has recently used the key, it doesn't prove they're connected *or* that he took the necklace from Amelia *or* that he's locked her up in the hut.' He pauses. 'Like I said, even if Taylor did the hacking and hid the dead pigeon like you're saying, which seems unlikely, as in *really* not his style, I don't see why he would kidnap Am—'

'Amelia must have found out Taylor was SweetFreak.' I take my hand away from Blue's. My heart bumps against my ribs. 'Somehow she found out the truth so she called him and demanded they met. *That's* who she was going to see when she disappeared.'

Blue stops walking. We're on the street now, outside a betting shop with a picture of a footballer in the window. The sun beats down on our heads and yet I shiver. Why is Blue refusing to accept what seems obvious to me?

'Carey, please,' he says, his eyes dark and intense. 'I really don't think Taylor would kill or kidnap—'

'How do you know? You don't even know Taylor.'

There's a long pause.

'Actually I do,' Blue says.

I stare at him. 'What?'

'You remember telling me about the boy Taylor set up to take the blame for the school fire?'

'Yes, of course.'

'Well . . . That was me.'

'You're kidding.' I can't believe it. 'No, that boy's name was Mooney, I remember them all saying at the party.'

'Yeah, that's my name. My surname, anyway. That's why I got the nickname Blue in the first place. Blue Moon, like in the Man City song. I liked Blue better than my real name but at stupid Bamford House lots of people just get called by their surnames.'

'You were at school with Taylor?' My mouth gapes. 'Why didn't you say when I told you the story?'

There's a long pause. A chill wind whips across our faces, sending a plastic bag scudding across the pavement ahead.

Blue shrugs. 'I kept meaning to tell you, but I was embarrassed. Ashamed.' He pauses.

'Go on.'

'After my dad died, we came into a big lump sum of money and my mum decided to send me to Bamford House. She thought she was doing the right thing, that going private would mean smaller classes and opportunities she never had. Whatever, I didn't want to leave my old school and I hated it at Bamford. I never fitted in.' He pauses. 'I didn't want you to know how weak I was but the truth is that when Taylor invited me to join his gang I was pleased, even though I didn't really like him or his friends. I thought it meant I was being accepted, but Taylor just wanted somebody he could boss about. I shouldn't have gone along with the fire, but I didn't know how to say no. I swear I didn't light it, but I did stand by while Taylor did. I made it easy for him to pin it on me. Which is exactly the sort of thing he does. You're right that he's manipulative. A total chancer. But that's the thing: Taylor is impulsive. Spontaneous. Reckless. All this SweetFreak stuff was planned, premeditated. That's not him.'

'You're wrong,' I insist. 'You don't know what he's capable of.'

'Or maybe you're just trying to make Taylor guilty because it's what you want to believe.' Blue frowns. 'If the police thought he might be responsible they'd already be investigating him.'

298

'You've got a lot of faith in the police for someone who took the blame for a fire because they failed to investigate it properly.'

'Actually, I think the police knew I was innocent. They certainly suspected other people were involved. But the school needed a scapegoat and I was an easier one than Taylor.'

A feeling of utter desolation sweeps over me. It's not just that Blue doesn't believe Taylor's guilty. Far, far worse than that is the fact that he didn't tell me the truth about knowing him in the first place. I turn away, tears pricking at my eyes.

'You lied to me,' I say.

'I didn't, I just didn't tell you the whole truth,' Blue insists. 'Which you didn't either, when I met you. Remember? I only found out why you were on the run because the news was on in the squat.'

'That was different.' I force my tears back. I don't want Blue to see me cry. I don't want anyone to see me being vulnerable about anything, ever again.

'Thanks for nothing.' I walk away, my fists crammed deep into my pockets.

Blue hurries after me. 'Stop, Carey. Wait.'

I spin around. 'Get away from me.'

Blue's eyes flash for a second. Then he stops walking.

I start running: along that street then down the next. At first all I want to do is get away from Blue, but as I stop at a sign for the bus station to catch my breath I have a new purpose, a new direction. Never mind horrible Blue. And never mind the stupid police.

If they won't believe Taylor is guilty, I'm going to have to prove it myself. I'm going to the Haunted Hut to look for Amelia.

31

Two hours later, the light is fading from the afternoon and I'm back in my home town at the top of the high street. I am literally at a crossroads. In front of me lie the shops and CCTV cameras and, beyond them, Taylor's place and the police station. To my left is Lower Cornmouth and the squat. My own house is to the right.

Keeping my hat pulled low while I'm in the ticket office, I spend the last of my cash on a bus to the big Sainsbury's on the edge of Cornmouth and the industrial estate which lies just beyond it. I get off with a bunch of women whose empty shopping bags flap in the wind. It's almost five in the afternoon now and the clear skies are darkening. It's cold with a chill breeze, but at least there's no sign of rain. I shiver as I hurry through the industrial estate and out to the wasteland beyond.

I haven't been here before so I'm relying on what Taylor

301

told me: up the unmade road and along the mud track. It's almost completely dark now. The only light I can see is coming from the small white-painted house at the end of the mud track. That must be the hut. As far as I can make out there are two floors, with boards over all the windows. How on earth am I going to get inside? I haven't brought any tools with me. I stare up at the light that shines through the cracks in the boards over one of the first-floor windows. Is Amelia in there? Is Taylor with her?

I hesitate for a second. Maybe I should go back after all. Call the police. But I'm here now, I need to look for myself. I draw closer. The front door swings off its hinges. My heart thumps. That doesn't make sense: why would Taylor need to break in? He already has a key.

The door creaks as I push it open. I'm in a living room – or a space that was once a living room. There's a stained carpet and marks on the walls where pictures once hung. Cables and broken pipes extend from the skirting board, which is cracked in several places. There's no light in the ceiling, just a piece of dangling wire. I can see a kitchen off to the left and a set of stairs leading to the first floor where the light is shining.

A floorboard above my head creaks. My heart is in my mouth as I creep towards the foot of the stairs.

The stupidity of what I'm doing hits me. I shouldn't have come, and definitely not alone. I want to turn back, to run away as fast as I can, but my feet keep moving me towards the stairs. I have to see Taylor. I have to know for sure Amelia is being kept here.

Shadows and slivers of light through the cracks in the boards over the window fall across my path as I reach the stairs. The footsteps are directly above, on the landing. My stomach twists into a tight knot as I peer up to the darkness of the first floor. A figure appears at the top of the stairs. I'm so expecting it to be Taylor that my mouth gapes in shock as I realise who is standing there, eyes glinting as she looks down at me.

It's my sister. It's Poppy.

32

Poppy and I stare at each other. It may be my imagination, but my sister looks a hell of a lot less surprised to see me than I am to see her.

'What are you doing here?' I blurt out.

Poppy beckons me up the stairs. 'After you told me about the hut I ... I guessed you might come here looking for Amelia.'

I hurry up the steep uneven stairs, gripping the narrow bannister for support. 'So is she here?' I hiss.

'No, the place is empty. But I think she *has been* here.'

'What about Taylor?'

'No.' Poppy hesitates as I reach the top of the stairs. There are only two rooms, one on either side of the landing 'Actually, I'm sure Taylor doesn't have anything to do with this.'

'What?'

'Look.' Poppy disappears into the room on the left.

Bewildered, I follow her. A small lamp stands on a rickety table next to a pack of AA batteries. There's a blow-up mattress on the floor covered by a sleeping bag with a pink teddy bear peeking out of the top. A bin bag and various shopping bags are scattered across the room. A red jumper spills out from the top of one; an empty sandwich wrapper from another. A row of water bottles are lined up under the window and shoved in the corner I can just make out a scattering of Superdrug and Bourgeois make-up on the threadbare carpet.

'Does this look like a prison?' Poppy asks.

'No.' The truth lands, punching like a fist: Amelia wasn't kidnapped by Taylor. Or anyone else.

She ran away on purpose.

'I'd say she's settled herself in nicely,' Poppy says, gazing around the room with arched eyebrows. 'Unbelievable.'

My mind reels. 'But if Amelia pretended to be kidnapped,' I gasp, 'that means . . . *she's* the one who framed me.'

'You deserved it,' Amelia snaps.

I spin around.

Amelia is standing in the doorway, glaring at me. Several long, slow seconds pass as the words I need to say roil up inside me.

'You're admitting it,' I say, numb with shock. 'It was *you*.'

She nods. The enormity of the revelation weighs down on

305

me like a rock, weakening my legs, tensing my entire body. I lean against the wall for support as Poppy takes a protective step towards me. I instinctively move closer to her, grateful beyond words that she's here.

'Why?' I gasp.

'You betrayed our friendship,' Amelia spits at me. 'You *devastated* me.'

'How?' I ask, tears springing to my eyes. 'That doesn't make sense. You *know* I didn't do anything to hurt you, you did it to yourself. *You're* SweetFreak.'

'Lying bitch,' Amelia snarls.

'Carey's not lying,' Poppy says quietly.

I shake my head, now completely confused. 'Amelia, you've just admitted that you've been *pretending* I was the one trying to hurt you; that you went missing all by yourself. Which means *you* put the dead bird in your own locker and before that you sent *yourself* the SweetFreak messages and the death threat.'

'No,' Amelia insists. 'I did the pigeon and set up the phone call about our "argument" in the woods, but only because you started it. *You* sent *me* messages as SweetFreak first. This is all because of *you*.'

'But—'

'Amelia's not lying, Carey,' Poppy interrupts. 'Neither of you is lying.'

Her face is riddled with guilt and shame.

'What are you saying?' I ask, my throat hoarse.

'Neither of you sent the SweetFreak messages,' she says, her face flushing a deep red. 'It was me. *I* started it.'

My mouth gapes. The many conversations my sister and I have had over the past few months flash through my head, how before the messages Poppy was angry with me for exposing her fling in Spain, how afterwards she took my side and supported me.

'*You* sent them, Poppy?' I gasp.

Amelia frowns.

My sister takes a deep breath. She faces Amelia head on. 'I was mad at you for deliberately showing your brother that video of me kissing someone else,' she says. 'George said you taunted him about it.'

'Is that true, Amelia?' I demand. 'Because you told me George *stole* your phone to snoop on it.'

Amelia shrugs. 'I don't see why that matters now.'

'Of course it matters—' I start.

'Wait, Carey, let me explain.' Poppy swings around to face me. 'I sent Amelia the first few SweetFreak messages and was going to send some to you too, for being so stupid and mean as to send the video to her in the first place. But then I started thinking how much more satisfying it would be if I could break up your friendship, if I could get Amelia to think that *you* were SweetFreak. Then I would get back at you both and nobody would ever know it was me.'

307

I stare at her, my head spinning.

'*You* sent me those horrible messages?' Amelia's voice shakes. 'You threatened to *kill* me?'

'I never, ever meant that as a serious threat,' Poppy pleads. 'I nearly didn't send it at all.' She turns to me again. 'I put the NatterSnap graphics together, then it took a couple of days to catch you inputting your password. Even then I had second thoughts. In fact I'd almost decided not to go through with it, when I heard you go out through the bathroom window to meet up with Amelia and I thought how I was never going to see George that way again . . .' She grimaces. 'It's hard to explain but this rage came over me . . . anger that you and Amelia were going on like nothing had happened when my life was ruined. So I went into your room, put on gloves so there'd be no fingerprints and sent the death threat from your laptop. I used the delay function to try and disguise the time it was sent and also so it would arrive when you were both at school the next morning. Maximum impact. I know it sounds really calculated but . . . but I swear I wasn't thinking straight. I was just so angry.'

There's a long pause.

I draw myself up, my fury building. 'And you being angry justifies devastating Amelia and making me look like a total cow in front of Mum and all my friends?'

'No of course it doesn't.' Poppy's eyes fill with tears. 'I never dreamed it would go this far. I was just so furious.

I thought you'd been deliberately cruel, both of you. I didn't realise that you were just thoughtless. And I *definitely* didn't realise how much the SweetFreak stuff would upset you . . .'

'I thought I'd been betrayed by the one person I relied on, my one true friend,' Amelia says, her voice shaking. 'My mum and dad didn't understand me and Taylor wasn't interested. Carey was literally all I had.'

Poppy nods. 'I'm so sorry.' She meets my shocked gaze. 'I'm so sorry I did that to both of you.'

'I went through hell thinking Carey had sent those messages,' Amelia says, voice rising. 'I thought she didn't care about me at all.'

I can't take it in. My sister was SweetFreak. She lied to my face, covered up what she'd done.

'You let me take all the blame,' I whisper. 'Why didn't you say something when you saw how bad it was for me?'

Poppy gives an uneasy shrug. 'When the police got involved I was scared and . . . and I thought things would blow over if the messages stopped. Which after a month or so they did sort of start to. Amelia was coming back to school; I thought you'd make up and it would all get better.'

'But instead it got worse.' I look at Amelia. 'Because you decided to keep the whole thing going by putting that stupid bird in your locker?'

Amelia stares at me, her jaw clenched defiantly.

'Why did you do that?' I demand. 'What was the point?'

'That wasn't my fault,' Amelia insists. 'I swear I didn't have a choice.'

'How d'you figure that?' I ask.

'After the SweetFreak thing it . . . everything changed at home,' Amelia stammers. 'Mum took time off work so I didn't have to go to school and it was nice, you know. She was suddenly interested in me again – paying attention for once. But then her work got busy, so she said it was time for me to go back to school.' She pauses again. 'I tried to contact Taylor but he had blocked me which made me feel worse than ever. When I saw Poppy say how you'd got rid of the pigeon on NatterSnap I crept over to your house and took it out of your bin and took it into school the next morning . . .'

'So that everyone would think it was me and you'd get your mum's attention back and not have to come to school,' I breathe.

Amelia acknowledges this with a tiny nod. 'Things got better again after the pigeon. Mum was home mostly and people started being nice to me, like Rose and her friends coming round.' She pauses. 'But then it started to wear off and I realised Rose was only my friend for show. I didn't want to go back to school after Christmas and Mum said it was OK for me to take a few weeks and got me some tutors. But by February she was on my case

310

again, moaning about the cost, and I kept hoping I'd hear from Taylor but I didn't. On Valentine's I even sent him the necklace he'd given me.'

I exchange a look with Poppy. So Taylor had told George the truth about that.

'But he still didn't get back in touch and . . . and soon after that I found out you'd been seeing him.' She glares at me and the venom in her eyes is hard to bear. 'It was the last straw. Even after everything I thought you'd done to me, I couldn't believe you'd do *that*.'

I open my mouth to protest, but close it again. After all, I did start dating Taylor even though I knew it would upset her if she found out.

'Who told you I was seeing Taylor?' I ask.

'Rose,' Amelia says.

Of course.

'I could see Rose was loving breaking the bad news,' Amelia explains. 'It was so humiliating. I hated you so much and felt alone all over again. Mum kept going on about the cost of my tutors and how I needed to get back to school . . .' Amelia goes on. Her voice shrinks as she speaks. She sounds unbearably miserable. 'I had to do something to make a difference again.'

'So you decided to pretend to go missing?' I ask, hardly able to believe it.

Amelia nods.

'You *wanted* everyone to worry about you?' Poppy asks, clearly horrified.

'I left a message for Mum, then I went to Taylor's house hoping to see him, face to face, but when I saw Carey and Jamie leaving his house … well, that's when it all fell into place, like it was meant to be.' She sighs. 'I followed them to Bow Wood, then paid a random boy to call the police and describe Carey and me arguing there. I left my mobile behind too, like a false clue for the police, to stop them looking anywhere near here for me.'

Poppy rolls her eyes.

'I can't believe it,' I say. 'You deliberately set me up.'

'So what?' Amelia's voice hardens. 'I thought you'd betrayed our friendship and sent me a death threat. It didn't seem like that big a deal to—'

'Not that big a deal?' I echo, a fresh anger swamping me. 'I was nearly arrested!'

'So what! Even if you weren't behind SweetFreak, you still *stole* Taylor from me!' Amelia snaps, her voice rising.

'You need to get real about Taylor: he's an idiot,' I snap back. 'I'm sorry you were upset when I dated him but I didn't *steal* him from you.'

'Oh, really? That's so typical of you, Carey,' Amelia snarls, her sad fragility vanishing entirely. 'You *always* think you're in the right. Can't you see how easy it was for me to believe you did the SweetFreak stuff?'

'What?'

'You were always insensitive to how I was feeling. You didn't understand me at all though you thought you did. You were so ... so self-absorbed and impatient. That night we met at the rec when you were late, the evening before the death threat ... I could tell you thought I was stupid to get so upset over Taylor. And later I realised why – you wanted him for yourself.'

Is any of that true? My head is whirling too fast for me to work it out, but something tells me that although she has gone far too far, Amelia does have a point about how I acted when Taylor dumped her. I remember feeling irritated with her and, though I know I tried not to show it, maybe my lack of sympathy was more obvious than I realised. Which wasn't very supportive of me. And when I think about how insecure I started getting over Taylor myself, I can kind of see how it happened to Amelia too.

Thud! Downstairs the hut door slams open. Footsteps echo up from the ground floor. I start. Amelia gasps. 'Who—?'

'Ssh.' Poppy puts her finger to her lips as the footsteps grow louder.

33

Footsteps patter across the concrete floor downstairs, right below us. I hold my breath as a girl giggles.

A familiar voice cuts though the cool air: 'Maybe the lock broke, this place is ancient.'

It's Taylor.

Amelia stumbles back dramatically. Poppy shakes her head.

I just feel numb.

The three of us stand in silence as the two sets of footsteps reach the bottom of the stairs.

'Ooh, Taylor, this is sooo scary.' The girl gives a high-pitched, nervous giggle. I don't recognise her voice, but I know one thing for sure: it's not Abi.

'Just hold on to my arm.' Taylor sounds ridiculous, all puffed up and phoney. 'I'll protect you from the ghosts.'

'OK,' the girl simpers. How come she doesn't hear how pathetic he is?

'I've never been here with a girl before,' Taylor goes on. 'It can be our special place.'

My jaw drops. He said exactly those words to me, less than a week ago. Amelia lets out a low sob. I glance at Poppy. She shakes her head.

'What a douche,' she mutters.

I glance at Amelia, her face creased with misery, and suddenly all our anxieties about Taylor seem silly. He wasn't worth the amount of time I spent worrying about how he felt. He was never really interested in me or Amelia or, probably, the girl he's got downstairs right now.

'What's upstairs?' The girl giggles again.

'Let's explore. Come on, Estelle.' The sound of Taylor striding across the ground floor turns into the creaking of the stairs as the two of them climb up. The girl, Estelle, lets out a constant series of shrieks and stage whispers.

'Ooh, something touched me! It's so dark ... this is the scariest thing—' Then a gasp. 'What's that light?'

'Probably just an old hurricane lamp some tramp left behind,' Taylor says. 'Nothing to worry about.'

'But suppose the tramp is still here?'

'Let's take a look. I'll protect you. Come on.'

Their footsteps turn slowly in our direction. Poppy folds her arms and Amelia shrinks back into the shadowy corner.

'I'm scared,' we can hear Estelle whimpering.

'There's nothing to be—' Taylor walks into the room. His jaw drops.

I brace myself as he looks at me, his face contorted with confusion.

Estelle appears behind him. 'Aagh!' she yelps.

Taylor's eyes widen as he turns from me to my sister, and practically pop out of his head as he spots Amelia. 'What are you doing h—?'

'You *pig*!' In a single, swift lunge, Amelia is across the room, shoving him backwards. Taken off guard, Taylor staggers backwards.

Estelle shrieks yet again. She looks about the same age as me, petite with short red hair and a snub nose. I glance at her neatly pressed jeans and shiny lipgloss and wonder how much time *she* spent getting ready to come out with Taylor.

'How many girls have you brought here?' Amelia demands.

Estelle watches, wide-eyed.

'I don't know what you're ...' Taylor trails off as he catches sight of the sleeping bag on the floor and the various scattered clothes and plastic bags. 'I thought you were missing. Are you *staying* here?'

'This is *your* fault,' Amelia says. She's crying now, shrinking back away from him. 'You started *all* of this.'

Taylor stares at her blankly.

He clearly has no idea what he's done. Before I know

316

what I'm doing I've marched over, hands on my hips. But it's Estelle I'm addressing, not Taylor.

'You're worth better than this,' I say, looking her in the eye. 'Taylor doesn't treat girls very well.' I turn to him at last. 'Do you, Taylor?'

'It's not my fault if you got the wrong end of the stick, Carey,' he protests.

'For Pete's sake,' Poppy snaps.

'I haven't got the wrong end of anything,' I say. 'And while I'm not saying this is *all* your fault, you certainly haven't helped.' I take a deep breath. 'You were nice to me when nobody else was, but I think that was because you *knew* I was vulnerable. You sucked me in and then you lied to me.'

'I didn't lie.' Now Taylor sounds injured.

'Yes you did,' I counter. 'You were flaky about turning up for things, you pretended you'd never been to this hut before when I knew full well you'd already been here with Amelia.'

'Is that true?' Estelle asks.

'Yes,' Amelia says sulkily.

'Plus you'd talked to Amelia's brother several times when we were going out and you never mentioned it to me, just like you never mentioned Amelia had sent you back the necklace you gave her. I bet you even knew exactly what I'd been accused of when we met up but pretended you didn't. You seem to like messing with people's heads, having power over them.'

317

'Quite,' Poppy adds with feeling.

There's a long pause. Taylor looks at each of us in turn. He opens his mouth as if he's about to say something.

Then he shuts it, his eyes registering defeat. A moment later he turns and hurries away. His footsteps echo up the stairs as he tramps down to the ground floor. Estelle gives us a final frightened glance, then hurries after him. Amelia sinks down to the floor. She looks upset.

Which is when I realise that I'm not.

I feel free, for the first time in months. Poppy sent the SweetFreak messages and the death threat. Amelia put the dead bird in her own locker, then later, when the attention was dying down, decided to run away.

It wasn't George or Rose or even Taylor. They – in their different ways – just picked on me when I was at my lowest ebb.

But I'm free of them now. And I'm free of SweetFreak.

All I need is for Poppy and Amelia to admit what they've done to the police, and my name will be cleared.

'I can't believe Taylor brought *other* girls here,' Amelia says with a groan.

'Yeah, well he did,' Poppy says tersely. 'So what's the plan, Amelia?' she asks, gazing around at the messy room. 'Now you've worried your family to death and sent the police chasing after Carey?'

Amelia shrugs. She still looks shell shocked.

Despite all that's happened, I feel sorry for her. I know how frightened and unhappy I was two days ago when I ran away from home – and I reckon Amelia's been feeling just as lonely and miserable – for months.

'How long were you planning to stay here?' I ask, more gently.

Amelia wrinkles her brow. 'Not long, just a few days. One of my tutors gave me this book about ancient cultures sending young people into the wilderness as a rite of . . . rite of passage I think it's called, a way of facing their fears and finding themselves.'

Poppy raises an eyebrow. 'So you thought you'd hang out in an empty hut on the edge of a Cornmouth industrial estate?'

'It was the only place I could think of,' Amelia says simply. 'I just wanted to be away from home long enough for everyone to notice I'd gone.'

'That's sad,' Poppy says sarcastically.

But it is sad. It's *seriously* sad. I can't imagine a life in which I wasn't right in the centre of my family, part of everything. Even though Mum thought I was guilty she carried on supporting me, all through the past few months when absolutely everyone else turned their backs. And Mum, Poppy, Jamie and I were always a unit.

'What a mess, Amelia,' I say with a sigh.

'I know,' she says. Misunderstanding my meaning, she's looking around at the clothes scattered over the floor.

'To be honest I haven't spent much time inside the hut. I've been out walking, doing some shopping, trying not to show my face. The nights are a bit creepy but . . .' She trails off. 'I just wanted people to miss me. I wanted to matter . . . I even imagined Taylor might come looking for me.'

'Which was never going to happen,' Poppy says with feeling.

'I guess it wasn't,' Amelia says softly, her eyes filling with tears.

I lean against the wall behind me, feeling light-headed. Nothing is as I saw it: Amelia was more insecure than I realised and Poppy was more upset with me than I could have imagined. Nothing justifies what they've both done – but now I can see that maybe there were things I shouldn't have done either. I could have listened and sympathised more back in September when they were both so upset about George and Taylor.

I could have been a better friend and a kinder sister.

And I realise something else too: that all three of us gave stupid boys we couldn't trust far too much control over our feelings.

'You both need to be honest now,' I say. 'You both need to start telling the truth. To everyone, including the police.'

'Yes,' says Poppy.

'I can't,' says Amelia.

'Of course you can,' Poppy says. 'I'll tell everyone

I sent you the first SweetFreak messages and that I'm very sorry. But you have to own up to the pigeon and to running away.'

'But the pigeon is my *reason* for running away.' Amelia's eyes widen with fright. 'I can't tell my parents I put it in my own locker, they'll kill me.'

'Well you aren't pinning it on me,' Poppy says. 'Or my sister.'

A light flashes outside. The sound of a slamming door echoes up to us.

Amelia rushes to the window.

'It's the police,' she shrieks. She turns to Poppy. 'Did you call them?'

'Nope,' Poppy says, walking to the door. 'But I'm going straight down to tell them everything.'

'Did you call them?' Amelia asks as Poppy disappears. '*Carey?*'

'It wasn't me.' I peer out of the window. Blue is standing beside the police van, shuffling from side to side. He looks desperately uncomfortable and then he glances up and spots me and smiles.

My insides cartwheel as I smile back. Blue must have brought the police here. Which means he cares about me, was worried about me.

Amelia grips my arm. 'I can't tell them I lied about the dead bird. You have to back me up on that. Tell them it was

Poppy. She did the SweetFreak stuff, she might as well have done the bird too.'

Her eyes are wide with fear, her mouth trembling with anxiety. For a moment I'm torn. Poppy was a mean cow to send horrible messages to Amelia and a cowardly one to fail to own up to doing so. But what's done is done. Poppy says she regrets what she did and all the hurt that's been caused, and that she's willing to take responsibility now. Amelia, on the other hand, still wants to lie her way out of this situation, not caring about who she upsets.

Outside, my sister appears. I watch her talking to two of the police officers, who look up at the window where Amelia and I are standing. Blue waits at the edge of the group. I don't think Poppy has even noticed him.

Amelia darts back out of sight. 'Please, Carey, you have to back me up, you *owe* me.'

I stare at her. 'Owe you for what? I get what you're saying about me maybe not being very supportive, but we were still best friends. Which should have meant you trusted me when I said I wasn't SweetFreak. And you certainly shouldn't have made up more stuff to blame on me. On top of which I've been worried sick about you. Everyone has. I know I ran away too, but you let everyone think something terrible had happened to you.'

'You've always been a rubbish friend,' Amelia spits. 'Always putting me down or making snide remarks, thinking you're so much better than me.'

Silence falls. A few weeks ago I'd have leapt to my own defence at this point, arguing with her, desperate to show that I was a great friend. But now . . .

'I'm sorry if I wasn't always there for you,' I say. 'I never meant to make you feel bad. But, Amelia, there have been enough lies. It's time to tell the truth.'

She stares sullenly at me.

There's nothing more I can say to her. I hurry down the stairs and out into the chill evening air. There are five or six police officers milling around. They're all focused on Poppy, not noticing as I scurry over to Blue.

'Thanks for coming,' I say.

He gestures to the police van. 'I thought you'd be angry about me calling them but I was worried. In case it *was* Taylor.'

'I know,' I say. 'And I'm not mad at all.' I take a deep breath. 'Taylor was here, but he didn't have anything to do with it, you were right about that. It was Amelia herself. And my sister. My sister started the whole thing.'

Loud voices rise into the air. Lights flash around us. Somebody calls my name. I think it's DS Carter, though I can't see him.

I ignore it all. Blue moves closer. His eyes are dark in the night air, his face just centimetres from mine.

'So . . .' He takes a deep breath. 'So did you see Taylor?'

'Yeah,' I said. 'He's an idiot.'

Blue smiles. Hesitates. 'Carey?' he says, his voice low and husky. 'I need to ask you some—'

'Carey.' DS Carter strides over. 'We need to talk. Please come with me.'

'Wait here,' I say to Blue.

'It's OK,' he says. 'You have a life to get back to.'

'But—'

'Carey!' DS Carter snaps. 'Now.'

'Please wait,' I urge Blue.

But somehow I know that he won't, that he won't want to have to talk to the police officers himself and that as soon as no one is looking he will slip away quietly. Reluctantly I let DS Carter lead me over to the police van. Poppy is standing there, still talking to one of the other officers. Amelia appears from the shack, flanked on either side by two female police officers.

'You've got a lot of questions to answer,' DS Carter begins.

I'm barely listening. I'm turning around, searching for Blue in the small crowd around the van. But it's obvious immediately.

Blue has already gone.

34

I stare at the place where Blue stood.

'Carey?' It's Poppy. She turns to DS Carter. 'Please can I talk to my sister, just for a second?'

DS Carter nods and Poppy turns back to me. We face each other in silence for a few moments. Poppy's hair blows in front of her face and she forces it angrily back. It's such a familiar gesture and it brings with it a pang of grief that my sister has been prepared to put me through such a terrible few months.

'I've told the police I sent all the SweetFreak messages, including the death threat.' Poppy glances at the police officer, then moves closer to me. 'I'm so sorry I tried to put the blame on you.' She pauses. 'And even more sorry that I didn't own up to it sooner. Will you forgive me? Are we OK?'

I look deep into her eyes and see genuine shame and

heartfelt misery. I'm still devastated, but I can see now that Poppy only acted as she did because *I'd* devastated *her*. And I'm still furious, But somewhere deep inside I know that I won't stay that way, that Poppy and I are sisters. Family.

And, like Blue said, you shouldn't give up on your family.

'No, I don't forgive you,' I say, letting just the faintest shadow of a smile creep around my lips. 'But one day maybe … OK?'

Poppy flushes, nodding. And then DS Carter signals for one of the other officers to take her away and I'm bundled into the police van and driven away.

The next few hours are a blur. I'm taken to the station, where Mum turns up and bursts into tears as she hugs me and berates me simultaneously. Poppy is given a warning for the original death threat and for failing to own up to it – then the three of us go home.

It's bizarre to be back here, everything so familiar and yet changed utterly in the two days I've been away.

I'm allowed to stay off school the next day. So is Poppy. Mum takes Jamie to school then comes home instead of going to work and we talk and talk for hours, each of us explaining how we have felt about what has happened over the past few months. I'm not wild about doing this, but Mum insists, and once we've started I find it a huge relief to be able to tell her and Poppy just how awful my life has been since

September and that the death threat exploded my known world into terrifying and unrecoverable fragments.

There is shouting (mostly from me), plenty of self-loathing (mostly from Poppy) and tears and hugs shared between us all.

If that sounds cheesy then it isn't. It certainly doesn't end with all of us skipping off into the sunshine without a care or with all our bad feelings soothed away entirely. But after a few hours Mum takes us into the kitchen and makes us help her prepare some soup for lunch. There's something about the effort of chopping and blending and fetching bowls and slicing bread that binds us together. In some ways it makes me feel better than all the talking. Whatever, by the time Mum leaves to pick up Jamie I know for sure that in time we'll be a proper family again, maybe even stronger than before.

That night I hug my sister before I go to bed and she cries on my shoulder. I lie awake, wondering what it will be like at school tomorrow. I haven't heard a word from Amelia, though I know (because DS Carter calls Mum and tells her) that she's now denying she put the dead pigeon in her own locker. At least the police don't believe her, not after discovering that she wasted their time by faking her own disappearance.

In spite of my anger, I actually feel sorry for her. She must be really messed up not to be able to admit the truth even now. Once I'd have been desperate to talk to her, to try and make things right between us. But not any more.

I toss and turn, unable to sleep, while the house darkens and settles around me. I wonder where Blue is. Has he crept back to Seti and the squat? Or has he gone off somewhere on his own? Why didn't he stay to say goodbye?

Well, I know the answer to that: he wouldn't have wanted to be around all those police officers, especially after being framed by Taylor for that fire at his school. Poor Blue. I know how awful that is. Though, now I think about it, Blue's situation was worse than mine. His mum wasn't well enough to help him whereas mine stuck by me, even when she thought I was guilty. And for all that Poppy did a terrible thing, I couldn't have got through the past few months without her support. Blue had no one in his corner.

But why didn't he ask for my number before he slunk off? Or some other way of staying in touch with me?

Has he had enough of me?

I don't really believe this, but the thought leaves a hollow feeling in my stomach that stays with me when I wake up the next day. I get dressed and force down the cereal Mum places in front of me. Jamie chatters on, super-excited to have me home and planning our next excursion to Bow Wood to play *Warriors* at the weekend. But all the time I can only think about Blue.

Mum, who is taking another day off work, drops Poppy

and me at school. We walk across the car park in silence as the hubbub of arrival time surrounds us. As we reach the front door Poppy turns to me.

'Your form teacher's going to tell the class you're innocent, that you were set up,' she says. 'Mum asked that my name wasn't mentioned, that the whole thing will die down more quickly if there's no one to pin the blame on, but I totally understand if you need to tell people it was me.'

I consider this. There is, undeniably, something appealingly vengeful about the prospect of Poppy being pointed and sneered at as I have been for the past few months.

But even as I relish this thought, another rides beside it – that leading a hate campaign against my sister will just keep the whole issue going. Not to mention make her life as big a misery as mine has been. And Poppy doesn't deserve that, not after sticking by me for so many months.

'Nah,' I say. 'I'm not gonna say anything. Don't want my friends thinking my sister's a freaking nut job ... Even though she is.' I grin.

Poppy grins back. 'See you later.' She squeezes my arm and runs off to her class.

I trudge towards my form room. I don't expect Amelia to be there today, but surely she will be back soon and when she is, what's to stop her carrying on lying about everything?

I hang back for ten minutes or so, watching everyone chattering and laughing as they head into the form room.

There's Rose and her Clones, huddled in a tight knot. Heath hurries past, clearly heading for his own room. Rose looks up hopefully as he walks by but he doesn't notice her. I can't stop the small smile that curls around my mouth as I catch the sullen look this brings to Rose's face.

Everyone is inside and the bell has just rung. I wait another minute until I see Mrs Marchington striding along the corridor. Then I scurry inside and over to my desk, keeping my head down to avoid catching anyone's eye. I sense Rose looking at me, nudging one of her friends. And then the teacher is here, taking the register. She doesn't call out Amelia's name, presumably because I'm right and Amelia isn't coming in today. I'm dreading seeing her when she does turn up. Our friendship is over. Not because I'm still angry with her – though I am – but because she's still denying she did anything wrong. She isn't who I thought she was.

And maybe I'm not the same person any more either.

'I have two important announcements,' Mrs Marchington says in her crisp, no-nonsense voice. 'Firstly to tell you that Amelia Wilson will not be returning to school.'

My head jerks up.

'As many of you know she has not been well for some time so she, er, is moving on.'

A low whispering begins across the room.

'Silence,' Mrs Marchington snaps.

I sit back, realising I'm not that shocked. Of course

Amelia wouldn't want to come back to school and face everyone. That would be too hard, too upsetting for her.

For a moment I feel a terrible desolation that I probably won't see her again and that – one way or another – Amelia is still trying to run away. And then the piercing misery ebbs away, leaving just a dull ache. I'm sad, yes, and angry that Poppy's SweetFreak death threat sparked off this whole business.

But more than anything, I just want to get on with my life,

'Secondly,' Mrs Marchington carries on, 'I realise that rumours have circulated that a member of this class has been involved in a cyber bullying campaign. I can confirm that these rumours are completely unfounded, that the guilty parties have now been identified and are not, repeat not, members of this class or indeed year group.'

More whispering. I sense faces turned to look at me and keep my head down, not wanting anyone to see how I'm burning with embarrassment. Mrs Marchington hushes us again, gives a few more minor notices which I don't take in at all, then sweeps out, urging us not to be late for our first class.

I'm due in Science just along the corridor. I get up and gather my books. A small crowd huddles around my desk.

'Carey?' It's Rose.

I force myself to look up. She's standing there with the Rose Clones and half the class watching.

'How're you doing?' Rose asks with a smile.

I gaze at her suspiciously. Is she trying to trick me by pretending to be friends again? 'I'm fine,' I mumble.

'I was wondering if we could have a chat later, about *The Sound of Music*?' Rose carries on, clearly unperturbed. 'Maria's such a massive part and the show is coming up in just a few weeks. I'd like to get your opinion on a couple of the scenes. If you're free?'

It's an olive branch. More, it's a public offer to rehabilitate me in the eyes of my classmates. If Rose is friends with me, then all the girls will be. And if the girls say I'm OK, the boys will follow.

I hesitate. I don't want to be friends with Rose. She's manipulative and mean. And yet it would be stupid to push her away too publicly.

'Sure, I'd be happy to talk about the part.'

'Great.' Rose nods and I can see that she's relieved.

The rest of the class turn away. The sound of their chatter rises up around us. I lean forward. What I have to say next is for Rose's ears only.

'I'm sorry you were bullied at primary school,' I whisper. 'But if you ever try taking it out on people again, I swear I will show you up for the nasty piece of work that you are.'

I draw back. Rose's jaw drops. She stares at me for a second. 'Fine.' She forces a smile on to her face. 'Laters.' She strides away, followed by her little group.

A couple of the boys start joshing by the desk, teasing me.

'So you're not the Cyber Bully?'

'Oooh, Scary Carey!'

I tell them to get lost, but I grin as I do it. They're taunting me because it's safe. If they really thought I was the kind of person who would send my best friend a serious death threat they'd be keeping their distance. And, anyway, after everything I've been through, I don't care what they think.

The boys clearly sense that they're not going to get a rise out of me. Their teasing soon stops and the rest of the day passes without anyone else mentioning SweetFreak at all. Poppy comes to find me at lunch break to make sure I'm OK. She seems lighter than she did yesterday or this morning. I feel the same way. It's like a load has lifted, the past is behind us and something today has turned us in a new direction. The only thing I'm sad about is that Blue has gone. I get Mum to call the police and ask if they can track him down so I can pass on a message – just to say hello and that I'm fine – but the police have no idea where he is.

35

Another month passes. I have a final session with Sonia – she insists this is good practice, even though the basis on which I was sent to her has dissolved away to nothing. I am grumpy about going, but in the end it's the best session we've had – a chance for me to rant and rage about Poppy betraying me and Mum not completely supporting me and Dad letting all of us down. I end up shouting, in floods of tears, with Sonia simply sitting and listening for once – and afterwards it does feel that something has shifted, that I have properly started to let go of the whole horrible business.

A few days later *The Sound of Music* is performed to great acclaim. I watch the dress rehearsal with the rest of the school and have to concede that Rose makes an excellent Maria: she's sassy but vulnerable and sings and dances really well. It's hard not to feel resentful, though it helps when several people in my class come up and whisper in my ear that Rose

is good, but I'd have been better. News trickles through about Amelia. Apparently she's just started at Bamford House for Girls, the sister to Taylor's private boys' school. I can just imagine how delighted she would have been to get her parents to cough up for that and wonder if it means she's seeing Taylor again. It soon turns out, however, that Taylor is dating yet another girl. It's Poppy who tells me this, as she returns from picking up Jamie from a playdate with Blake.

'So Taylor's totally moved on from that whiny Abi and silly Estelle from the hut. His latest victim is some posh girl with long dark hair down to her bum. I heard him telling her how he "hadn't expected to feel this way about her".' Poppy rolls her eyes. 'What a jerk!' Then her face falls. 'Oh, sorry, I didn't mean to upset you by telling you that, I just—'

'It's fine,' I reassure her. And it is.

I don't miss Taylor. Or Amelia. I'm not even angry with her any more.

I'm still wary of Rose and those girls in my class who took against me so easily, but I'm on a friendly basis with everyone again, back working hard for my end-of-term tests and spending lots of time playing with Jamie.

One Saturday Mum takes me and Jamie and Poppy to visit Sandy and Teddy. It's a bit awkward at first, but soon everyone's chatting and laughing, and Mum and Sandy really get on. Sandy invites us all to Teddy's first birthday party which is coming up soon. It's a great day, with all of us together, and the very best part of it is seeing how much Jamie adores both Teddy and his new role as a big brother.

Feeling more positive than I have for ages, as soon as we get home I go online and join a drama group that meets near the town hall on Saturday mornings. A couple of sessions in and I love it. It's so much fun: we do acting exercises and improvisation and the people are nice. It's like I'm starting to move on, to feel more like myself again.

It's almost the end of term and there's a warmth in the air as I leave school. I'm thinking about the *Guys and Dolls* auditions coming up for the summer show in my drama group and wondering what song to sing when a familiar voice calls my name.

'Carey?'

I spin around. Blue is hurrying over the road towards me. He's dressed in different clothes – dark blue jeans and matching trainers with a cool grey jacket. His hair is shorter and cleaner than before but it's the same warmth sparkling from his bright eyes, making my pulse race.

'Hi,' I say, the swarms of students pouring past us forgotten as I stand on the pavement.

We look at each other. 'It's good to see you,' Blue says.

My heart sinks a little. Whatever Blue is here for, it can't mean much for him to see me if he's waited a whole six weeks to do it.

'I wanted to wait until I was placed before I came ...
before I saw you ...' He stutters to a halt.

'Placed?' I ask, wrinkling my nose.

'With a foster family, in Lower Cornmouth,' Blue
explains. 'I was dying to see you again that night, at the
shack, but there were so many police and your sister ...' He
tails off again.

'You're with a foster family?'

'Yeah, like, I didn't want to see you until I was sorted,
until I knew it was going to work out with the family. But
it has ... it is ... I mean, they're great. Anyway, I waited
because I couldn't do what I want to do ... if I'm ... if I'm
living on the streets.'

I frown. 'What do you want to do?' I ask, feeling confused.

A big grin flashes across Blue's face.

'Ask you out,' he says. 'Obviously.'

'Oh,' I say, a delicious glow creeping through my
entire body.

'So?' Blue asks, arching an eyebrow. 'What do you say?
Are you going to make me wait any longer? Or should I just
take the hint and leave?'

'No.' I laugh. 'That is, yes.'

And with the traffic fumes swirling around us and the
sunshine beating down on our heads and the pavement firm
beneath our feet, we kiss.

337

Carey's story might be fictional, but some of the issues that she and Amelia deal with could be familiar to you or your friends. There are lots of places you can go for advice or help if you're worried about cyber bullying, a few of which are listed below along with tips to stay safe online and advice on how to cope with online bullying.

Staying Safe Online

1. Don't post personal information online – like your address, email or phone number.

2. Think carefully before posting any pictures or videos of yourself. Once they are online, they are no longer private and you can't be sure who might see them.

3. Never share your passwords, and choose strong passwords that are hard to guess. Update your privacy settings regularly.

4. Not everyone is who they say they are online. Don't accept friend requests from people you don't know and don't meet up with people you've met online. Speak to your parent or carer about people suggesting you do.

5. If you see something online that makes you feel upset or uncomfortable, leave the website, turn off your computer and tell an adult straightaway.

Dealing with Bullying Online

1. Tell an adult you trust if you are being bullied on the internet or by phone.
2. Don't respond to bullying messages – it could make things worse.
3. Block users who send you horrible messages.
4. Save any horrible messages, emails or texts you receive, and make a note of the times and dates you receive them, as well as the user's ID.
5. Don't pass on any cyberbullying videos or messages.

For more advice

https://www.childline.org.uk/info-advice/bullying-abuse-safety/
http://www.bullying.co.uk/cyberbullying/
https://www.thinkuknow.co.uk/
http://www.safetynetkids.org.uk/

ABOUT THE AUTHOR

SOPHIE MCKENZIE was born and brought up in London, where she still lives with her teenage son. She has worked as a journalist and a magazine editor, and now writes full time. Her debut was the multi-award winning *Girl, Missing* (2006), which won the Red House Book Award and the Richard and Judy Best Children's Book for 12+, amongst others. She is also the author of *Blood Ties* and its sequel, *Blood Ransom*, *The Medusa Project* series, and the *Luke and Eve* trilogy. She has tallied up numerous award wins and has twice been longlisted for the Carnegie Medal.

@ **sophiemckenzie_**
www.facebook.com/sophiemckenzieauthor
www.sophiemckenziebooks.com